SO-ABS-765

SISTERS UNDER THE SKIN . . .

"Daddy, who's this?"

Longarm turned to face the open doorway. Two young ladies were standing in it, each one dressed in a long white frilly nightgown, their luxurious, straw-colored hair falling far beyond their shoulders, all the way to their narrow waists. They looked at least eighteen.

"Mr. Long, may I present Marilyn and Audrey, Emilie's sisters. The shy one is Audrey. The outspoken nymph is Marilyn."

Marilyn reached out at once and took Longarm's hand boldly. "Oh, Mr. Long, please do bring Emilie back to us!"

"Yes!" cried the other, rushing up and taking his other hand in hers. He felt her warm eagerness as she pressed it in her excitement. "Please do! We have all been wretched at the thought of Emilie in the hands of those terrible people!"

"Emilie is a match for any man!" Marilyn explained proudly, with an angry toss of her head. "But that's just it. She won't submit easily."

"Let's hope she won't have to," said their father . . .

*Also in the LONGARM series
from Jove*

LONGARM
LONGARM ON THE BORDER
LONGARM AND THE WENDIGO
LONGARM IN THE INDIAN NATION
LONGARM AND THE LOGGERS
LONGARM AND THE HIGHGRADERS
LONGARM AND THE NESTERS
LONGARM AND THE HATCHET MEN
LONGARM AND THE MOLLY MAGUIRES
LONGARM AND THE TEXAS RANGERS
LONGARM IN LINCOLN COUNTY
LONGARM IN THE SAND HILLS
LONGARM IN LEADVILLE
LONGARM ON THE DEVIL'S TRAIL
LONGARM AND THE MOUNTIES
LONGARM AND THE BANDIT QUEEN
LONGARM ON THE YELLOWSTONE
LONGARM IN THE FOUR CORNERS
LONGARM AT ROBBER'S ROOST
LONGARM AND THE SHEEPHERDERS
LONGARM AND THE GHOST DANCERS
LONGARM AND THE TOWN TAMER
LONGARM AND THE RAILROADERS
LONGARM ON THE OLD MISSION TRAIL
LONGARM AND THE DRAGON HUNTERS
LONGARM AND THE RURALES
LONGARM ON THE HUMBOLDT
LONGARM ON THE BIG MUDDY
LONGARM SOUTH OF THE GILA
LONGARM IN NORTHFIELD
LONGARM AND THE GOLDEN LADY
LONGARM AND THE LAREDO LOOP
LONGARM AND THE BOOT HILLERS

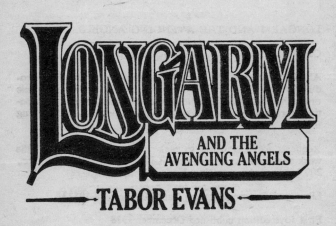

LONGARM

AND THE
AVENGING ANGELS

TABOR EVANS

A JOVE BOOK

Chapter 1

It was a Monday morning and it wasn't raining. The high, clear air of the capital of Colorado seemed reasonably fresh and invigorating as Longarm stood by the open window. Of course it was early in the morning, before the horse manure of a new day was pounded into its golden essence by countless hoofs, sending its pungent fragrance into the heavens to mingle with the coal smoke and soot that was already blackening every new building in Denver. But that was Denver after twenty-odd years—horse shit and coal smoke. And always from some place—he wished to hell he knew where for sure—came the smell of burning leaves.

As he peered down at the narrow streets, Longarm heard the bed springs squeak behind him and knew the girl was waking up. He was naked and did not want at this moment to turn and face his guest. After all, he had to report to the chief in less than an hour.

He sneaked a quick look over his shoulder and saw that she had just turned over, drawing the sheets up around her naked shoulders, the luxurious spill of her auburn hair tumbling down over the coverlet. She was breathing steadily, which meant she might well be asleep still. But then you could never tell.

Longarm left the window, padded across the threadbare carpet to the dressing table, and peered at his reflection in the mirror. He was a big man, lean and muscular, with the body of a young athlete. But there was nothing young about his face. It was seamed and

5

cured to a saddle-leather brown by a raw sun and cutting winds, both of which he had experienced in abundance since lighting out from his native West-By-God-Virginia. His eyes were a gunmetal blue, his close-cropped hair was the color of aged tobacco leaf, and he wore proudly and kept well-trimmed a drooping longhorn mustache that added much to the ferocity of his appearance on those few occasions when ferocity as well as firepower might be decisive.

As he loomed above the dressing table in the early morning dimness, he heard another squeak of the bed springs behind him—and this time he knew it was for real. He turned easily, catlike, aware as always that his movements had an almost hypnotic effect on others.

The girl—her name, she had told him the night before, was Rosalie—had a foolish little Allen pepperbox in her hand. It was a relic, at least twenty years old and of such an ancient and uncertain design that it would often fire all six barrels at once. As Longarm loomed closer, she raised the pepperbox and aimed it at his naked chest.

"I'll fire!" she cried in a frightened voice. "I warn you!"

Longarm smiled and sat his naked rump down on the edge of the bed. "Ain't it a little late for you to be protecting your honor, miss?"

"But I didn't *mean* that last night! I didn't mean that to happen!"

"Didn't appear to me like you was acting, ma'am. Leastways, you sure put your whole heart and soul into it." He grinned at her past the wavering pepperbox. "Fact is, what happened between us was mighty nice."

She scooted up angrily in the bed and propped her back against the brass bedstead, the little gun still trained on Longarm's chest. "It was my body that betrayed me, Mr. Longarm, I assure you! My heart and soul had nothing to do with it!"

"Why don't you put that little toy down now, Rosalie? You got my attention, all right."

6

"No!" she cried firmly, steadying the weapon. "I am going to shoot you, Mr. Longarm! I am going to send you to your Maker!"

"Mind if I ask why? I didn't think I was *that* bad last night. And by way of apology, I might remind you of the number of drinks you insisted on buying for me."

"That's not the reason!" she fumed. "What I mean is, you were—fine." She became intolerably flustered at this point and her face went dark with embarrassment. "*That's* not the reason!"

"And what is the reason?"

"My brother! Merle Bond! You're the one that sent him to prison! You testified against him. I heard your testimony. I was in court. When you stepped off that stand, the judge had no choice but to sentence Merle to all those years! You did it with your testimony!"

"Why, thank you, Miss Bond. I'm glad you think so."

Her eyes widened in fury. She brought up a small, pink hand to steady the weapon and seemed intent on pulling the trigger. "How dare you say that!"

"That's easy, Rosalie. I believe in using the most direct route to wherever I'm going. Sometimes I might seem uncommonly blunt, but I don't mean any harm by it. I'm glad my testimony gave that jury the backbone to convict your brother. He is one mean son of a bitch, if you'll pardon the liberty."

"Oh!"

"I can't help it." He smiled sadly at her. "It's the truth and that's the long and the short of it. Wish it weren't, I surely do."

Tears welled into her dark blue eyes and began to roll down her fresh, round cheeks. There was nothing hard about her, he remembered from the night before. She was as soft and cuddly as a kitten—until she caught fire. And then it was all hands to battle stations and hang on for this one! The pepperbox trembled. She seemed determined to pull the trigger.

Longarm got up casually and looked down at her.

7

Convulsively, she brought the weapon up again so that it was still trained on his chest. "I *am* going to shoot you!" she cried between clenched teeth.

"Then do it, Rosalie, and get it over with."

She closed her eyes and squeezed the trigger. As the tiny hammer came down on an empty chamber, Longarm reached down and gently but firmly took the weapon out of the girl's hand. She collapsed onto a pillow, her head buried in it, sobbing.

He watched her for a moment, then turned and walked over to the dresser and dropped the Allen beside the pile of tiny rounds he had taken from it the night before. He poked through the rest of the clutter atop the dresser, found his bar of soap, and brought it over to the washstand. Pouring water from the pitcher into the china basin, he dipped a wash rag into it, soaped it, and began washing himself about the face, neck, and shoulders. He was in the midst of rinsing off his face and neck when he heard the sobbing subside rather abruptly, and heard the bed springs jounce.

Reaching for a towel to dry himself, he looked back at the bed. Rosalie was sitting bolt upright, staring at him. She was still paying no attention to her nakedness, and this time he found it difficult not to notice her breasts. What was it that fellow Solomon called them—*like two young roes that are twins?* Well, maybe. And then he saw that she was looking at him.

"Longarm?"

"Yes?" He finished with the towel and tossed it onto the foot of the bed.

"Would you come over here?"

With a sigh, Longarm crossed to the bed and sat down, facing her.

"You knew—about that gun, I mean."

"I found it last night while you were sleeping."

"You were just toying with me."

"I wasn't sure what you wanted."

"You weren't sure? You mean you suspected who I was?"

8

"I knew I'd seen you before somewhere and that it would be a good idea for me to remember. But like I said, I wasn't sure."

She closed her eyes, as if determined to keep her temper and remain composed. Opening them again, she said, "Those were terrible things for you to say about my brother."

"I just said he was a mean son of a bitch. And he was."

"He was just a high-spirited boy!"

Longarm nodded. "That's right. A high-spirited boy who robbed three stages, killed a driver and a shotgun on his third attempt, and later shot up a saloon, killing one of the bar girls. He resisted arrest and the posse that chased him to his hideout lost three good men. When they sent me after him, Rosalie, the price on his head was fifteen thousand—dead or alive. I brought him in alive. I didn't have to, but I did."

"And I should thank you for that, I suppose!"

"You can if you want. But maybe you already thanked me. Last night."

She tried to generate a head of steam over that comment, but couldn't quite manage it. And then her eyes dropped to that portion of Longarm's anatomy that made the most sense at times like this.

She looked back at him, her eyes softening. The memory of last night clouded her eyes, softening the anger she had tried so hard to retain. "Oh, Longarm," she whispered. "I'm so confused."

Longarm stood up. "Let's put it this way, Rosalie. You're a woman—one hell of a woman and that's nothing to be ashamed of. I can see what you planned, all right. You'd ply me with drinks, get me to take you up to my room, and then you would avenge your brother's life sentence. You've been reading too much of that Ned Buntline crap, if you'll pardon my bluntness."

She closed her eyes and shook her head. "Don't keep asking me to pardon your language, Longarm.

9

I'm used to it by now. But of course you're right. I guess I was being overly romantic."

"And foolish. But I guess you loved your brother. And I guess that excuses it some."

"I tried so hard to raise him properly, Longarm. But when mother died, he just went wild. I followed him out here, but he was determined to go his own way. And that meant guns. And robbing. And killing." She bowed her head and began to weep softly.

Longarm stood where he was, watching her, waiting. After a little bit, her crying abated and she glanced up at him. "Aren't you going to . . . comfort me?" She managed what she thought was a seductive smile, but it just didn't make the grade.

"Is that what you want, Rosalie? Comfort?"

She wiped her eyes. "I don't know. Last night, we—"

"Forget last night. You had a reason for coming up here and trying to tire me out." He grinned quickly at the thought. "How did you know I'd be the one to tire *you* out?"

She blushed and wiped tears from her eyes hopefully. "I tired you out *some*," she insisted. "But you were so—nice."

"You had a reason last night, Rosalie. What would your reason be now? I think you just better get dressed and go home and start thinking like a good girl again, and stop reading that Ned Buntline crap."

"You mean you don't—!"

"I mean I got a job to go to and you don't know me well enough to start bedding down with me on a regular basis. Not unless you're trying to gain instruction in a new line of work—where the only rest you get is standing up."

"Oh! You're so cruel!" She snatched up the bedclothes and covered her lovely breasts. "If you wouldn't just stand in front of a girl like that with nothing at all in front of you . . . !"

"Beg pardon, Rosalie. Guess that *did* sort of cloud the issue some at that." Longarm reached for his knit

10

cotton longjohns. He pulled them on while standing up and then reached for his brown tweed pants. They were a size too small and he had his usual struggle getting them on. At last he cursed his fly shut and straightened, the pants as snug as a second skin.

"That's much better," Rosalie said. "I don't feel so threatened now." There was a hint of deviltry in her voice. Glancing quickly over, he saw the gleam in her eye.

"As soon as I leave here," he said, "I'll expect you to dress and go back home, wherever that is. Understood?"

"You're not married, are you, Longarm?"

"No."

"Engaged?"

"No."

"Well then, why do you want to get rid of me?"

"How old are you, Rosalie?"

She hesitated. "Twenty!"

"Closer to eighteen, I'd say."

"I'll be nineteen next March!"

"I'm close to forty," he lied. "You're old enough to be my daughter. Come to think of it, I must have some daughters around your age at that."

"What's age got to do with it? It didn't seem to be such a terrible nuisance last night."

Longarm sighed, bent over, and fished under the bed for his boots, then sat on the edge of the bed and tugged them on. They were low-heeled cavalry stovepipes more suited for running than riding, which was just what Longarm wanted. He spent as much time afoot as he did in the saddle, and with these boots he could outrun almost anyone.

But how was he going to outrun this girl? He stood up and turned to look down at her. She was still sitting up and holding the sheet over her breasts, but her shoulders were bare and her face was flushed. Her eyes . . .

"Damn it, girl! I don't want any! You got that?"

11

"You don't have to shout!"

"Yes I do, it seems like. Now listen here to me. I'm a lawman. That means I go most anywhere they send me. I'm here today, gone tomorrow. I find my loving where I can, and I don't look back. I'm not interested in paying for it, which means I can go without if I have to. What I don't want and what I will never want, as far as I can see, is a wife on my neck—or a girl sitting in some hotel room waiting on me! Now if you don't make tracks, girl, back to wherever you came from, I'll haul you in for attempting to shoot a peace officer. I've got your weapon here as evidence, and my testimony will be accurate. That means, Miss Rosalie, that I won't leave out a thing!"

"You wouldn't!"

"If it would knock some sense into that pea brain of yours, I would do it. Yes I would."

"Oh!" She glared at him. "Oh!"

He turned his back to her and put on his gray flannel shirt. He fumbled with the string tie, fastening it into a tolerable knot, then tucked the shirt into his pants. His gunbelt he had stashed under some clothes in the second drawer of the dresser. He pulled the gunbelt out and strapped it around his waist, adjusting it to ride just above his hips. The rig holding his double-action Colt Model T .44-40 was a cross-draw, and he wore it high. He drew the revolver smoothly, effortlessly, then turned about and leaned back against the dresser, his gun held out carefully in front of him.

Aware of Rosalie's eyes on him, he proceeded to inspect this most important tool of his trade. The barrel was cut to five inches and the front sight had been filed off. He didn't want the revolver's barrel to catch in the open-toed holster made of waxed and heat-hardened leather. Moving then to the bed and still apparently ignoring the girl, Longarm emptied the cylinder on the bedsheet at the foot of the bed. He dry-fired a few times to test the action, easing the hammer down with his thumb, as always, then reloaded.

12

Before thumbing each cartridge home, he held it up to the window for a quick, minute inspection. He loaded only five cartridges into the cylinder. He didn't want to lose a foot jumping down off a train or a bronc, so he kept the firing pin riding safely on the empty chamber.

He holstered the Colt, and finished dressing swiftly. He took the change and his wallet off the top of the dresser and pocketed them, ducked into his vest and frock coat, dropped the pepperbox and its cartridges into the coat's right side pocket, then inspected critically his Ingersoll pocket watch. It was on a long gold-washed chain with a clip at the other end. He placed the watch in the left breast pocket of the vest, leaving the chain dangling. Then he reached in under the mattress at the foot of the bed and pulled out a stubby, double-barreled .44 caliber derringer with a small brass ring soldered to its butt. This he clipped to the loose end of his watch chain and dropped the pistol into his right breast pocket, allowing the chain to drape innocently across the vest front.

"You . . . had a gun there?" Rosalie asked.

"That's right. I would have had it under my pillow, but I wanted to leave you room for that pepperbox. I stashed my gunbelt and Colt in the drawer in case you proved more anxious to kill me than I figured."

Rosalie took a deep breath. "I've been very foolish, haven't I?"

"Yes."

"And this . . . isn't the beginning of anything, is it?"

Longarm shook his head. "Nothing personal, Rosalie. It's just the way I'm built. Some men are for marrying, some men are for . . . " He shrugged and smiled at her. "No hard feelings?"

She considered the question seriously for a moment or two, then looked him squarely in the eyes and shook her head. "I guess not. Just tell me one thing, Mr. Longarm."

"What's that?"

13

"Why is it that the ones who want to settle down are so much less fun than the others?"

Longarm laughed. "Maybe it just seems that way now. Just give yourself time. You'll find a man who's fun and who also wants to settle down. Just keep looking."

"That's what I've been doing."

"You've got some time left, you know."

"I suppose."

Positioning his snuff-brown Stetson carefully on his head—dead center, tilted slightly forward, cavalry style—he smiled at the girl.

"You need a shave," she said.

"I plan to get one from the barber," he told her.

"And you want me to dress and leave as soon as you are gone."

"My landlady—an understanding soul—will be up here in less than thirty minutes to make sure. She knows I'm a lawman working for the government and she is a great help." Something occurred to him. "Do you . . . need any money?"

"No. Didn't you say you never had to pay for it?"

"That's not why I asked," he said, with a gentleness that surprised even him.

She ducked her head. "I'm sorry. A train ticket back to St. Louis would cost me more than I have left right now."

He nodded, took out his wallet, and dropped a twenty-dollar certificate on the bedspread. "I know the train schedule," he told her. "I'll have someone at the depot watching to make sure you're on that train for St. Louis this afternoon."

She swallowed, eagerly. "Is there one then?"

"There is."

"Thank you," she said, reaching for the certificate. "This is more than generous of you." She turned her face up to his, fully expecting a goodbye kiss, he realized.

He bent swiftly and kissed her lightly on the fore-

14

head, then swept past her and to the door. Pulling it open, he turned to look back at her.

"Remember. I'll have someone watching that train. Be on it, young lady!"

There were fresh tears running down her cheeks as she nodded. Longarm pulled shut the door and hurried down the stairs to find the landlady. It was curious. He should have felt twenty dollars poorer and more than little irritated. But he didn't. He felt good, in fact.

Longarm's shave took longer than he had expected it would. Glancing at his watch as he passed the U.S. Mint at Cherokee and Colfax, he turned the corner and started for the Federal Building. Once inside, he strode through the lobby as swarms of officious lawyers hustled their legal briefs in one door and out another, talked excitedly in groups, or hurried upstairs and downstairs, sweating themselves into such a fine frenzy that their oil-plastered hair was already coming unstuck. At the top of a marble staircase, Longarm came upon a large oak door. The gilt lettering on it read: *UNITED STATES MARSHAL, FIRST DISTRICT COURT OF COLORADO.*

Longarm pushed the door open and strode into the outer office. The pink-cheeked clerk was playing with his typewriter. The newfangled piece of machinery raised a fearsome clatter.

"The Chief in?" Longarm asked the clerk above the clatter.

The fellow turned. "Oh, it's you, Mr. Long!"

"That's right. Custis Long." Longarm grinned at the clerk. "You don't have to announce me. You just go ahead and play that thing. You sound great." Longarm started for the inner office.

"Just a moment, Mr. Long," the clerk said. "I believe Marshal Vail—"

Vail appeared in the doorway. There was a harassed look on his face. He growled, "Can't you ever make it in here on time?"

15

"It's this damn clerk," Longarm said. "He makes me wait out here."

Vail glared at the clerk, who began to sputter indignantly. When Vail saw Longarm's sudden grin, his shoulders slumped and he waved Longarm past him. "Get in there, Longarm," he said, "and stop upsetting the clerical staff." As Longarm moved past him into his office, Marshal Vail closed the door and smiled sardonically at him. "You're not going to like this."

Longarm slumped into the red morocco leather armchair across the desk from his superior and tipped his head slightly as he regarded the marshal. "They want me to rescue Sitting Bull from the Wild West Show?"

Vail's eyebrows shot up a notch. "That wouldn't be such a bad idea, at that." Then the man moved behind his desk and began pawing through a pile of paper. "That might be a lot easier than this little job." He found what he was looking for and squinted at Longarm. "Ever been to Utah?"

"Sure. Remember that jasper I caught up with in Provo? Tried to get lost in a band of them Mormon night riders. What the hell did they call themselves?"

"Avenging Angels."

"That's right. Sounds like a Ned Buntline joke."

"They are no joke, Longarm." He looked down at the dispatch he had retrieved as Longarm took out a cheroot and stuck it into his mouth. He didn't light it, just began chewing on it. "Seems a bunch of Mormon fanatics somewhere in Utah have kidnapped a Mormon girl from Salt Lake City. The Mormon authorities have requested federal help in getting her back." Vail leaned back and looked at Longarm, just the trace of a smile on his pasty, indoors face. "I'm sending you. Washington wants the best man for the job." Vail shrugged. "What choice did I have?"

Longarm shrugged. "Who do I contact in Salt Lake City?"

"Wells Daniel. You won't contact him. He'll contact

16

you. Stay at the Wayfarers. It's a new hotel. I understand it's reasonable."

"Who is this Daniel?"

"A high muckymuck in the Mormon Church. That's all I can tell you. But you work through him."

"I've got the feeling you know a lot more you ain't telling."

"And if you notice, none of it's written down. This is a political hot potato, Longarm. As I understand it, there are members high up in the Mormon church who are sympathetic to this kidnapping—or at least to the fanatics behind it."

"I see," said Longarm dryly, working the cheroot about in his mouth. "So the federal government is called in to do the dirty work. I don't know if I like this so awful much. What can you tell me about the kidnapping?"

Vail shrugged. "I don't even know the girl's name. She was taken from her home at night and hasn't been heard from since. A note was left by the fanatics, but nothing's been heard from them either. She's supposed to be a very pretty young thing who'd make a fine addition to some Mormon's harem."

Longarm frowned. "From what I hear, those women are supposed to make a choice about joining one of those households."

"They are. This one, it seems, wasn't given that choice."

Longarm nodded and got to his feet. The thought of a young girl hauled off like that didn't set right with him. "You got my expense vouchers? I'll need a railroad pass, too."

Vail nodded. "See my secretary." He looked up abruptly at Longarm. "Oh. I almost forgot. You remember that punk desperado—Bond, Merle Bond—the jasper you caught up with last spring?"

Longarm grew suddenly alert, his teeth chomping down hard on his unlit cheroot. "I remember."

"Did you know he had a sister?"

17

"Not until recently."

"Well, according to Deputy Wilson, she's in town looking for you."

"That so?"

"Well, she's armed, according to Wilson. Armed and dangerous."

Longarm interrupted Vail with a wave of his hand. Then he took out the old Allen pepperbox and the cartridges and dropped them on Vail's desk. "Miss Bond is no longer armed. And tell Wilson to check the train depot tonight. I've already seen the young lady and told her to be on tonight's train for St. Louis."

Vail got to his feet. "You mean you've already tangled with that girl?"

"I guess that's what you'd call it."

Vail's face went pale. "And you let her go?"

"She's just a kid, Chief. A foolish young thing with romantic notions about paying back those that testified against her brother. I disarmed her and got her promise. She'll be on her way back to St. Louis tonight. Relax."

"For God's sake, Longarm! Before that foolish kid landed on your doorstep, she killed the poor son of a bitch in Cedar Creek who testified at her brother's trial—Amos Beedle, the stagecoach driver. He was number one on her list. *You* were number two!"

Longarm took a deep breath, his teeth clamping down hard, cutting through the cheroot. He spit the end into the wastebasket, then looked at Vail.

"I guess she won't be on that train to St. Louis, then," he said. "Just the same, it might be a good idea for Wilson to check it out."

Without a word, Vail nodded. He was still standing, thunderstruck.

"By the way," Longarm asked, "what did she use to kill the stage driver?"

Vail slumped back down into his chair and nodded at the pepperbox. "She used all six barrels." He sighed. "At least you didn't give it back to her."

18

Longarm stuck what was left of his cheroot back into his mouth. "I'll go see about them travel vouchers and the railroad pass."

He turned then and made for the door. As he pulled it open, Vail cleared his throat. Longarm turned. Vail leaned forward onto his forearms.

"You take care of this business in Salt Lake City with a minimum of fuss, Longarm, and I just might forget to include this business with Miss Bond in my report to Washington."

"Chief?"

"Yes?"

"Have I ever asked you to wipe my ass before this?"

"Hell, Longarm, I was just—"

"Well, I ain't asking you to do that for me now. You hear? You want to include that there business with that little tramp, you go right ahead."

Longarm left then, slamming the door firmly behind him.

Longarm sat morosely on a faded red plush seat at the rear of the passenger car of the Union Pacific's *Hotel Express*. There was nothing luxurious about his accommodations, and Longarm's large frame was more than a little weary of the tedious ride. The coach was noisy, filled with smoke and with the stench of unwashed humanity. Looking about him, Longarm found it difficult to keep his temper at times. What he saw and what he heard made him stir restlessly in his seat.

His fellow travelers were not elegant, not by a long shot. They were dressed carelessly, sloppily, many times in ragged garments and more often than not clutching dirty bundles. Most of the men had revolvers stuck carelessly in their belts, a piratical gleam in their eyes. They were unshaven usually, some were bearded. Their talk was loud and filled with profanity that took no note of the women and children forced to endure their company. Those men with wives tried not to notice the language and the single men's insolent stares, lest

19

they be forced to stand up to them and lose their lives in the bargain.

Salt Lake City was the next stop. They were only a few hours away, having passed through Provo less than an hour ago. It was close to three in the afternoon and the heat inside the coach made Longarm's skin crawl. Babies were bawling and the voices of mothers scolding their restless children were a constant irritant to all those in the coach without offspring.

The door to the coach opened and Longarm saw a bearded desperado step inside, pulling the door shut behind him. There was something particularly offensive about the man, something that sounded a deep warning bell within Longarm. Had he seen this man before? Did he know him?

The fellow lurched down the aisle, found an empty seat next to a drummer, and squeezed in beside him. The drummer had been dozing. He awoke with a start, began to protest the abrupt manner in which he had been joined, then immediately thought better of it as he took in his new companion. No longer casting about in his memory for some clue as to where he might have met the fellow before, Longarm smiled at the drummer's reaction.

He took out a cheroot, lit it with a sulphur match that he ignited with a single flick of his thumbnail, and turned his attention to the landscape stroking by the train window. They had left the Utah Lake behind and Longarm could see the towering, snow-clad peaks of the Uinta Mountains to the east. The grade was now steadily downhill, and he realized the heat would get progressively worse as they neared the Great Salt Desert. Pine-covered ridges swept up to and fell away from the train as it racketed along. Great stretches of barren, uninhabited land met his gaze. Used to the long, arid stretches of the West, Longarm was nevertheless mildly depressed by this glimpse of Mormon country. Only a band of religious fanatics, he supposed, could make a land like this bloom. Or would want to.

20

A woman entered the coach. She seemed very tired and a bit desperate for a place to sit. She was a gaunt but attractive young woman; her head was enclosed in a severe, dark blue bonnet, her dress was heavy and extended down to her feet, which were encased in heavy black shoes, laced high and tight. She appeared to lose her balance for a moment, then began to move hopefully down the aisle toward Longarm.

She must have gotten on at Provo, Longarm realized, and had not yet been lucky enough to find a seat. He moved closer to the window, touched the brim of his hat as she met his gaze, and smiled. With enormous relief, she hurried toward him and the seat he offered her beside him.

As she passed the jasper who had entered the coach just before her, however, she let out a tiny cry. Longarm craned his neck to look and saw that the man had reached out and grabbed the woman by the wrist. She tried to pull away but the fellow just increased his pressure on the girl's wrist and pulled her back toward him. The man got to his feet as he pulled the girl to him and smiled. It was not a pleasant smile.

"Well, if it ain't Annie Dawkins!" the fellow exclaimed, his leering smile freezing the girl's feet to the floor, it seemed.

"Jason Kimball!" the girl managed. "You leave me be! I ain't a Mormon no more and you can't collect no more tithe from us!"

The fellow's leer deepened. "Why, sure I can, Annie. You is in arrears, you is! We'll just collect you and even up the books! How's that?"

The girl Annie tried to pull away, but the fellow had a firm grip on her arm and wasn't about to let go. Still holding onto her, he looked down at the drummer, who all through this had been trying to ignore the ruckus completely, his head turned resolutely while he contemplated the grim Utah landscape.

"Get up, drummer," the fellow ordered him in a harsh, grating voice that brooked no argument. "Me

21

and my friend here wish to sit down in the same damn seat. Git!"

Longarm would never go looking for a fight; he would, in fact, leave an unfriendly bar rather than provoke a confrontation. A peaceable man who liked his solitude, he preferred always to mind his own business. But he was sorely tried at this juncture. The sight of this walking carrion manhandling the terrified girl caused his stomach to rumble dangerously. The fellow was nothing but a murderous, loud, profane old blackguard in an unclean shirt. His laugh was a demented horselaugh, and his walk was a buccaneer's swagger.

Glancing quickly about, Longarm noticed that there was not a single male in the coach who did not have his eyes averted. The children were all being forcibly made to look elsewhere and they were all uncommonly hushed. The sight of this universal cowardice caused Longarm to grind the end of his unlit cheroot, and at last, when he saw the quivering drummer sidling out of his seat to make room for the blackguard, he got reluctantly to his feet and started down the aisle.

The drummer was in the aisle when Longarm reached them. When he saw Longarm's empty seat, his eyes lit and he tried to move past Longarm to get to it. Longarm restrained him with a hand on his left shoulder and gently pushed him back and out of the way. Then he turned to the girl. Tears of anger and frustration were rolling down her youthful cheeks. She looked at him with wide, hopeful eyes.

"May I be of assistance, Ma'am?" he asked her, lifting his Stetson slightly. "I saw you were looking for a seat."

Before she could answer, the fellow who had been bullying her spoke up roughly. "Here now, what the hell are you about, mister? You leave Annie be. She's with me now!"

"Why don't we leave that to her?" Longarm inquired, his voice gently conciliatory.

22

Longarm turned his eyes to the girl. "Would you care to join me, Miss—?"

"Dawkins," the girl said eagerly, wiping away her tears quickly with the back of her hand. "Annie Dawkins."

"Hey, now!" protested the bully. "You just stand back there, mister! Who says you can interfere, you dirty gentile!"

Longarm smiled at the man. "That's right. I'm a gentile. And what are you—a Mormon?"

The girl pressed anxiously toward Longarm. "He's—he's an Avenging Angel! Maybe you better not get mixed up in this." Longarm's quiet, almost gentle aspect had about convinced her that he was no match for this Avenging Angel.

"You heard her!" blustered the man, pulling himself up to his full five-feet-ten or so. "That's what I am, all right. So you better mind your own business."

Longarm smiled at the man. "You don't smell like an angel."

The fellow's eyes went hard. He reached his right hand up and began to tug on the handle of a big Colt he had stuck in his belt. Longarm slapped the fellow in the face with his left hand, drew his Colt with his right, and brought the gun's barrel up swiftly, catching the fellow across the side of his head. The Avenging Angel slumped back into his seat, glassy-eyed, his jaw slack, a broad red welt rising swiftly across his cheek bone.

Holstering his weapon, Longarm swiftly disarmed the man, then frisked him expertly for any hidden weapons. Finding none, he looked up and nodded to the drummer.

"You can have your seat back now. When this fellow wakes up, keep him amused with dirty jokes." Longarm grinned at the look of pure terror on the man's face.

Straightening, Longarm turned to the girl and tipped his hat. "My seat is this way, Annie."

23

Her eyes still wide—and a look of pure, undiluted gratitude filling them—she nodded, did a quick curtsy of a sort, then preceded him down the aisle to his seat. Longarm allowed her to get in first so that her seat would be next to the window. Longarm took from her the little carpetbag she had clung to all through this unpleasantness, and placed it in the rack over their seat. Then he sat down beside her and smiled at her kindly in an effort to quiet the young girl's thudding heart. Her face was flushed and it was obvious that she did not really know how to account for her good fortune.

For his part, Longarm did not know how to explain his own lack of good sense. Twice now within two days he had allowed a pretty face to obscure his role as a law officer. He should have brought in that sweet little murderess when she pulled that weapon on him, ridiculous as it appeared to him at the time. And this most recent bit of gallantry did nothing at all to insure his quiet entry into the case of the missing Mormon girl. Every Mormon and gentile in this coach—and soon, he had no doubt, throughout the train—would be discussing in hushed tones the way he had rescued the Fair Young Maid from the Avenging Angel. Longarm might as well have entered Salt Lake City wearing a sign announcing his profession and his intent.

He sighed, stretched his legs as much as was possible, and took from his inside breast pocket a fresh cheroot. This one he was tempted to smoke, despite his vow to quit the filthy habit.

He spat out the stub of his previous cheroot and poked the fresh one into his mouth, then turned his head to nod at the girl. He didn't want his preoccupied silence to make the woman feel unwelcome.

"You can light that, if you want," she suggested. "I won't mind."

He smiled his appreciation, took out a match, and lit it with his thumbnail. As he sucked the pungent

24

tobacco smoke into his lungs, he leaned back, placated somewhat.

"Perhaps I should explain," the girl said softly.

"That ain't necessary, ma'am," Longarm said.

"Call me Annie," she insisted quietly.

He smiled at her and took a deep drag on his smoke. "Annie, then."

Frowning, he leaned back in his seat. What was the matter with him? He could use any information he could get on the Avenging Angels, and this girl beside him might very well be a gold mine of such lore. Maybe he was getting old. He had never heard of senility setting in at his age, but he sure as hell wasn't acting very bright lately.

"Of course," he said, turning to look at her, "it did seem strange for a man to do something like that in front of so many people. Did he know you from somewhere?"

She nodded quickly. "My father drew a terrible farm in the lottery years ago. It was in southern Utah. Brigham Young told my father and the others to grow cotton there. But we couldn't. No matter how hard we worked. The soil was alkaline, and the grasshoppers and crickets were everywhere. We were lucky if we could grow enough food for our table."

She sighed and looked away from Longarm, her gaze following the shifting contours of the semi-arid landscape. She was seeing it all again, Longarm realized, in her mind's eye. Talking about it had upset her.

"You don't have to tell me about it if you don't want to," Longarm suggested gently.

She looked back up at his face. "But I do. I owe you an explanation. You see, we did so poorly that we couldn't pay our tithes. So Brigham Young sent the Avenging Angels after us. And even then we couldn't hardly gather enough to satisfy them. So my father left the church."

"Did that help?"

She shook her head sadly. "They said he couldn't

25

leave the church. They said they were excommunicating *him*. And so we lost everything."

"I'm sorry, Annie. What happened to your family?"

"I don't know what happened to my father. He rode out one night—to talk sense to those Avenging Angels, he said. He never came back. My mother just gave up after that and died soon after. My sisters—like me— have become fallen women." She bowed her head in her hands and wept softly.

Longarm said nothing and did not try to comfort her. Instead he quietly, patiently puffed on his cheroot, being careful not to blow any smoke toward her. At last she recovered her composure and looked at him.

"So you see, Mr. . . ?"

"Long," he told her, smiling. "Custis Long."

"So you see, Mr. Long, you seem to have saved from that terrible man only a piece of soiled goods."

"Guess you've got a right to be ashamed if it makes you feel any better, Annie. But I always thought soiling came from inside."

She raised her eyebrows in surprise at Longarm's comment. Surprise and appreciation. "Yes, of course, Mr. Long. You're right. But there aren't many people in the Mormon community—or anywhere else, for that matter—who would agree with you. You have no idea how difficult they make it for a woman without a family or a husband. I tried to get a job as a seamstress in Provo and Salt Lake City, but since the Saints own all the establishments that use seamstresses and since my family and I were excommunicated . . . " She shrugged. "So I went to work for Ma Randle at the Utah House."

"A saloon?"

"Yes—among other things."

"I thought Mormons didn't drink."

"There are many gentiles living in Salt Lake City, Mr. Long. And many Mormons *do* drink. Have you ever tasted Valley Tan?"

Longarm shook his head.

26

"Wait until you do." Her eyes danced mischievously. "It is a kind of whiskey. Only the Mormons make it and we're the only ones who can drink it, seems to me."

"Annie," Longarm said, noting that the girl had recovered her composure well enough to handle tough questions, "what was that fellow going to do with you? He said something about collecting you and evening up the books. I assume he had some plan—some way of using you."

She shuddered involuntarily and nodded. "Yes, he did, Mr. Long. He would take me as his wife—or as one of his wives."

"I thought the Mormons could only do that if the girl was willing." He watched her narrowly.

"That's the way it *should* be, and that's the way it is, usually. But not for them—not for the Avenging Angels." She looked out the window of the coach. "They're out there. Everywhere. Waiting. Small colonies of squatters." She shuddered. "One of my sisters is with them. I haven't heard from her in a year." Then she uttered a bitter laugh. "Celestial marriage, Joseph Smith called it."

Longarm leaned back in the chair. He had almost finished his cheroot and he had just glimpsed a portion of the Great Salt Desert through the coach window. He was almost to Salt Lake City, and Annie to the Utah House.

Not long after, the train creaked to a stop. As Longarm got to his feet and lifted down Annie's carpetbag, he saw the Avenging Angel she had addressed as Jason Kimball getting to his feet as well. Once in the aisle, he glanced in Longarm's direction. The look on his face would have curdled the heart of an Apache. Longarm just smiled at the man and nodded briskly.

Jason strode angrily down the aisle to the door of the coach, not at all gentle with those he brushed aside.

"You have made an enemy there, I'm afraid," said Annie, watching the man go. "But I thank you from the bottom of my heart."

27

"I wouldn't say any day of mine was entirely wasted, ma'am, when I gained an enemy of that stamp. When carrion like that starts thinking of you with any kind of charity, you ought to wonder what you're doing wrong."

The train jolted to a stop. He stepped back and let the girl precede him down the aisle while he followed, carrying her carpetbag and his own canvas gladstone. He could not help noticing her trim figure and the thick curls that coiled on her slim shoulders. Despite her severe dress, there was no doubt in his mind that Annie was all woman and he did not wonder at Jason Kimball's eagerness to take her into his harem to settle past debts.

Hell, Longarm told himself, he wouldn't even need that much of an excuse.

Now hold it right there, old son, he told himself somewhat sheepishly. *Just you back off. You've already muddied the waters enough. The Chief told you to keep low—not to spend the taxpayers' money sparking a fallen woman with pretty ankles!*

With a sigh directed at the unsought-for complexities of a lawman's life, Longarm followed the girl from the train and was immediately engulfed in a tide of gushing femininity.

Three shrieking, delighted young ladies had darted across the platform to welcome Annie, and she was reciprocating their greeting most heartily. His face reddening to find himself in the midst of all this feminine clatter, Longarm put down Annie's carpetbag and tried to sidle out of the crush. But Annie reached out before he could get away and caught his arm.

Squeezing it fondly, she called out above the happy babble, "Thank you so much, Mr. Long. You are very kind!"

Longarm nodded his goodbye to her, aware suddenly of the curious, approving appraisal of the three young women, and pulled away. A tall, imposing woman close to her mid-thirties, with a handsome face and magnifi-

28

cent dark eyes, stopped before him. She didn't seem to have the bust her size would have deserved. Indeed, she was almost as straight as a razor. But her waist was slim, her hips ample. This was obviously Ma Randle, the owner of the Utah House.

As the girls moved off across the platform, chatting gaily, the madam's dark eyes regarded Longarm coolly. "Thank you, sir, for escorting Annie from the train. I trust you are under no misapprehension concerning Miss Dawkins?"

"You mean do I know where she works?"

"Yes, that's precisely what I mean. I own the Utah House and the adjoining facilities, and Annie is one of my nicest girls. I am very fond of her."

"Yes, I can see that," Longarm remarked. "She must be great for business."

"That is not my only concern."

"If you'll excuse me, ma'am." Longarm started to move past the woman.

"Just a moment. You don't understand. I simply wanted you to realize that if you do come to visit Annie at the Utah House, you are most welcome. Only I would hope you won't make a fuss if you find she is occupied with other . . . customers." She sighed. "Annie is very popular, and sometimes men who are taken by her make a fuss when they find her already with someone."

Longarm smiled in spite of himself. "No chance of that, ma'am. My expense voucher don't cover that expense, and besides, my interest in Miss Dawkins has just about evaporated." Longarm caught sight then of Jason Kimball standing with four other cutthroats on the far edge of the platform. They were dressed in the same nondescript fashion, falling somewhere between that of a pirate and that of a highwayman. They were all uncommonly interested in Longarm. "But you better keep those sharp eyes of yours peeled. One of them Avenging Angels over there—the good-looking one with all the hair—put in a claim for Miss Annie on the train. But I lost my head completely and went to her

29

aid and assistance. Shoulda known better. Now if you don't mind, ma'am, I've got business."

Frowning, Ma Randle turned quickly to face Kimball and the men with him. Then she turned back to Longarm, restraining him with a gloved hand on his arm. "You mean that man was on the train? The one in the middle? And you tangled with *him?*"

"I just told you, ma'am," Longarm said patiently. "Now would you please unhand me? I really do have work to do—and you have four young ladies to escort back to your place of business." The five men, he saw, were walking toward them.

She let go his arm, as if she had touched a hot stove. "Of course," she said, stepping back. "Please forgive me for detaining you."

Longarm smiled, touched the brim of his hat to the madam, then crossed the platform to the few remaining hacks waiting and climbed into one rather beat-up old carriage. He gave the name of the Wayfarers—the hotel the chief had mentioned—to the driver. As the man cracked his whip over the backs of his horses, Longarm leaned out the side window to look back.

He was in time to see the five Angels piling into another carriage. In a moment it had started up and was following Longarm's. Longarm leaned back in the seat and frowned thoughtfully. He was sorry he had been so short with that madam, but he had seen at once what was happening. As the crowd thinned out after the train's arrival, the five men were encouraged to make a move. Kimball, it seemed, was not a man to let a grudge simmer for too long. With a small army at his back, he liked to take immediate action.

Longarm took a silver dollar out of his pocket and handed it out to the driver. "Take this. There's a carriage following me. Go down the next side street you come to and keep a steady pace. I'll be getting out first chance I get. Don't slow down. Keep right on going, back to the station. Do you understand?"

The man shouted back that he did.

30

Longarm hung on as his carriage wheeled suddenly down a side street a few moments later. Looking out the window, he saw that the carriage was still following. Then Longarm's carriage turned on to another street. The pursuing hack was out of sight around the corner. Longarm opened the carriage door and jumped out. The canvas gladstone was so heavy he almost lost his balance, but he kept on his feet and darted into a tobacco shop, almost tipping over the massive wooden Indian standing in the doorway.

Looking out around the Indian, he saw the hack racing after his carriage, the horses straining mightily to keep up with five men to haul. As soon as the hack had left the side street, Longarm walked back to the main thoroughfare and hailed another hack.

As he climbed wearily into the carriage, he had an ominous feeling in the pit of his stomach. And his stomach, over the years, had never been wrong.

Chapter 2

As Longarm rode down Salt Lake City's Main Street, he was impressed, in spite of himself. The street was a broad one, as were all the streets, it seemed. They were all squared nicely and construction was going on at a brisk pace. Through the open window of his carriage he could see the arched Tabernacle roof, looming impressively above the other buildings. Beside it, he caught a glimpse of another building under construction. It was of a much more massive design and was obviously the beginning of a great cathedral or temple. About the building site he saw massive blocks of granite and atop the slowly rising structure he glimpsed the gaunt outlines of four giant cranes, their taut guy wires gleaming in the late afternoon sun.

Everywhere he looked Longarm noted a grim, purposeful activity with little or none of the careless buffoonery encountered in the usual, swiftly growing settlements of the West. Nevertheless, the clean lines of the buildings and residences with their invariable white picket fences and neat gates, the spacious avenues, the somber but well-tailored dress of the men and women, had a curiously unsettling effect on Longarm. He became slightly depressed and lost some of the enthusiasm he usually carried with him into a new assignment. It was almost as if he had stumbled east by mistake. The impressive orderliness of the city fell over him like a pall and he reminded himself that Mormons did not use alcohol, coffee, tea, or any other stimulants. No wonder

32

so many of them were hung up on multiple wives. What else was there to do? As his carriage pulled up in front of the hotel, Longarm got out with a grim resolve. He would accomplish this business as swiftly and as adroitly as he possibly could, then retreat to wilder, more congenial lands.

He paid the driver, entered the Wayfarer and approached the desk, a massive affair standing along the far wall of the impressive, thickly carpeted lobby. Potted plants were everywhere and the cuspidors gleamed like loot from some pharaoh's tomb. Nicely dressed men and women promenaded about the lobby casually. Under the pillars and along the walls, the richly upholstered chairs and couches held many portly gentlemen reading newspapers and illustrated weeklies. Longarm winced when he saw the liveried bell boys. His allowance for tipping was miniscule and these fancy young lads were used to exorbitant sums simply for giving an old boy the right time. Longarm decided he would carry his gladstone himself and find his way up the stairs to his room without any help.

"Yes, sir?" the desk clerk inquired, his large, disdainful eyes noting Longarm's rough attire. "What can I do for you?"

"A room."

"Single occupancy, sir?"

"If you see anyone else with me, don't believe it."

The fellow sniffed with his long, bony nose at Longarm's flippancy and handed him a pen with which to sign the register. Longarm signed it, the clerk read it and at once lost his air of superiority.

"Ah, Mr. Long. I have a communication for you."

The clerk reached back to a letter file, flipped through the envelopes, and handed a letter to Longarm addressed simply, *Custis Long, U.S. Marshal.* Tearing it open, Longarm was reminded once more that his coming to this city was getting to be a very poorly kept secret. The short note read:

33

Mr. Long:
At seven this evening you will find in the lobby of your hotel a gentleman in a dark bowler hat, wearing a red carnation in his lapel. When he sees you, he will leave. Follow him. He will take you to us.

Daniel

Longarm grinned slyly at the cloak-and-dagger effect of the note—and he sincerely hoped that the fellow sent to meet him would be wearing considerably more than a dark bowler hat and a red carnation. He slid the note back into the envelope and looked at the clerk.

"You have a room for me?"

The clerk dropped his key onto the desk. "Number thirty-four, sir. Third floor." His palm slapped down on the bell and two bellboys started for him, hungrily.

Longarm lifted his bag and waved them off, ignoring the sudden disdain that leaped into their eyes. *Cheapskate* was what they were calling him, he knew, but in such a grand and fancy establishment, a full-course meal could run as much as a dollar, and he shuddered to think what his room was going to cost. Already he could see himself arguing with a clerk over every single item on his expense voucher when he got back to Denver. He shook his head at the indignity of it and exploded inside. He told himself with a quick, iron resolve that he would have himself a hot bath and the best meal the hotel could put before him, and to hell with those prissy little pencil pushers!

Fired with this burst of independence, Longarm turned at the foot of the broad, carpeted stairs and beckoned to one of the bellboys. Taking out a cheroot, he lit it and followed the uniformed minion up the grand stairway.

At seven that evening the lobby was filled to over-

34

flowing with gentlemen in dark bowler hats. Fortunately, only one had a red carnation in his lapel. Longarm followed the man out of the lobby and into a carriage that took Longarm to a broad avenue to the east of Main Street, and slowed up at last in front of a substantial residence set back behind a high stone wall, faced with stucco. Through the gate they rode, and when the carriage pulled up, Longarm's silent companion with the red carnation hopped out and helped Longarm down.

When he rang the bell and was ushered in ahead of Longarm, it soon became apparent that the man with the carnation was Wells Daniel's butler. A tall, well-tanned, and healthy-looking man in his fifties met him with his right hand outstretched.

"Mr. Long, is it?" the fellow asked, shaking Longarm's hand firmly.

Longarm nodded.

"I'm Wells Daniel. Come in here, Mr. Long. We're all anxiously waiting for you. We've heard much about your abilities and we are sure you're just the man for this unfortunate business."

As he talked, Daniel escorted Longarm into a large, high-ceilinged room with shelves of books lining the walls. High, many-paned windows faced out into the night. Much of the furniture was of leather and highly polished. The carpeting was so thick that neither man made a sound as they walked in. Sitting around a long mahogany table were three men. They rose as Longarm entered, and as Daniel introduced each man, he smiled courteously and shook Longarm's hand. Each handclasp was strong, and Longarm got the immediate impression that he was in the presence of men accustomed to giving orders in this highly organized, impressively efficient community of Saints.

Indicating a chair to his right, Wells Daniel said, "Sit down, Mr. Long. I trust your journey was an uneventful one."

"Call me Longarm, if you want," he told the man.

35

Then he took out a cheroot and lit it. No one raised an eyebrow. "I did happen to meet one of your Avenging Angels on the train. Seems he wanted to collect a long-standing tithe."

The man introduced to Longarm as Burns Meeker leaned forward. He was a fat fellow with small eyes and a very red, beefy face. "Go on, Longarm. I think this might be important."

"He was eager to collect the tithe in the form of a young lady riding on the train."

"And you," Burns Meeker said, smiling slightly, "talked him out of it."

Longarm nodded.

"Do you know who this man might be?" another of the men asked. This was Job Welling, a tough-looking, broad-shouldered gent who looked like he belonged at the head of a gang of roustabouts, not in this gentleman's castle. "This might be one of the fellows we're after."

"His name was Jason Kimball."

Job's eyebrows arched up a notch, then he leaned back in his seat and looked at Burns Meeker. With a slight smile he addressed Wells Daniel. "Looks like your man might have found the scent already." He seemed pleased.

"I need more to go on," said Longarm. "I am hoping you fellows can give me some much-needed information. First of all, why haven't you sent your own law officers after the people who kidnapped this girl?"

"That's simple," said Wells Daniel. "Our sheriff, Amos Barker, is the brother of a man we feel is a member of this group of fanatics who have taken the girl. His name is Karl Barker."

Burns Meeker smiled at Longarm. "He's a good friend of Jason Kimball, I hear."

"What's the girl's name?" Longarm asked.

"Emilie Boggs," said the other man, the only one who had not yet spoken. "My daughter, and I want her back, Longarm. Untouched."

36

This was Quincy Boggs, a lean, angular fellow with mild blue eyes that seemed perpetually wide open since his brows were practically invisible, so light was his hair.

"I'll do what I can," said Longarm. "How long has she been gone now?"

"At ten tonight," Boggs said, "it will be three days."

The man's voice quavered, but did not break or crack. Boggs was evidently under great stress and Longarm could feel the iron control the man was exercising over his emotions. As a result, Longarm felt their intensity with even greater clarity. He would like very much to bring this man's daughter back to him. Untouched, as he said. But it was a long shot at best.

"The other reason we cannot rely on our own authorities, Longarm," continued Wells Daniel, "is that these fanatics are sincere. Lorenzo Wolverton, their leader, has had a revelation, it seems. He feels that Emilie Boggs was revealed to him in a vision, that she is destined to be his Celestial Bride—come hell or high water."

"What he means," interrupted Job Welling, "is that we dare not move on these men openly. All we need to do to make their cause respectable is to turn them into martyrs."

"What is their cause?" Longarm asked.

"Polygamy," snorted Boggs. "Celestial wives. A return to the old ways of Joseph Smith—and Brigham Young."

"Brigham Young hasn't been dead that long," Longarm reminded them.

"No," snapped Boggs. "And more's the pity."

"That remark is uncalled for," snapped Burns Meeker, turning to Boggs, his tiny eyes narrowed. "But I can certainly understand your distress. Unfortunately, it is this kind of talk—this attitude of yours that you have made no effort to conceal over the years—that might well have brought on your present troubles."

37

"I am quite well aware of that," said Boggs. Boggs glanced across the table at Longarm. "The leader of these . . . fanatics is an ally of Mordecai Lee, one of Young's relatives and reportedly a leader of that rabble who perpetrated the Mountain Meadows Massacre. I have made no secret of my contempt for those men and their actions."

"There you go," said Meeker, thrusting his massive head toward Boggs, "admitting to a gentile that there was such a thing!"

"Easy, gents," Longarm said. "Let's just simmer down and eat this apple one bite at a time. I ain't interested in that massacre, or any hurt feelings in discussing what might have happened. All I want to know is where is this feller, Lorenzo Wolverton. Seems to me that's the long and the short of it. Once I know that, I can simply go there and get that girl back for Mr. Boggs, here." He glanced at the man. "Though I sure ain't going to guarantee she'll be untouched."

"Mr. Longarm," said Job Welling, his wide blue eyes regarding Longarm coldly, "these men might be fanatics in a sense, but they will not force Miss Boggs to their will."

"I see. They'll convince her. Is that it?"

"Precisely," said Welling, glancing over at Boggs, as if daring him to contradict him. The man had failed completely to catch the irony in Longarm's statement.

Boggs, however, just shook his head at the man's lack of understanding and looked over at Longarm. "We don't *know* where their settlement is, Mr. Long. We know only that they are in the area somewhere. One of their number you met earlier today on the train—Jason Kimball. We've called on you to find them and bring back my daughter, with a minimum of fuss and without creating any martyrs to their cause."

"In addition, Longarm," said Wells Daniel, smiling slightly, "we cannot—after this meeting—offer you any public support. Too many of our conservative col-

38

leagues would be infuriated to learn that we had gone to the federal government for aid in this matter."

"In other words, after this meeting you are cutting me loose. I'm on my own."

"Yes," said Meeker, his small eyes fixed almost malevolently on Longarm. "I for one will deny that I ever saw you."

Longarm nodded wearily. "By the way," he said, "who the hell are you, anyway? What's your position in this town?"

"A fair question," said Wells Daniel. "I am a member of the Council of Twelve Apostles; the rest of the gentlemen here are members of the First Council of Seventy."

Longarm smiled. "That don't mean a whole hell of a lot to me. What I meant was, have any of you jaspers got any political heft I could count on in a pinch?"

"Longarm," Wells Daniel said, a slight, amused smile on his face, "political power and the power of the Mormon church are well nigh inseparable in Salt Lake City. But as we said before, you cannot look to us in the future. We cannot allow ourselves to become involved openly in dealing with Wolverton and the rest of his Avenging Angels."

"You have daughters of your own. Is that it?"

Job Welling spoke up. "Daughters and wives and sons, not to mention our own lives."

Longarm stood up and looked around the table at the four men. "You ain't told me a hell of a lot, that's for sure. Somewhere out there is a band of Avenging Angels with a young girl. You want her back with as little fuss as possible." He glanced at Boggs. "Untouched."

"I want her back," said Boggs, "and I'm not so allfired particular how much fur flies or how many petty factions are disturbed by it."

"We all know how you feel, Quincy," said Wells Daniel, "and Mr. Long knows how we feel."

39

"Then let me out of here and I'll get to work," Longarm said.

"Of course," said Wells Daniel, as he got up from his chair. With a gracious smile, he escorted Longarm from the room.

At the door, as they waited for his carriage to be brought around, Wells Daniel said, "I more or less side with Boggs in this matter. Get the girl. If heads must roll, so be it. But get the girl. This outrage must not go unpunished, no matter how sincere the perpetrators."

"But I'm not to count on any of you fine fellows if I get myself caught between a rock and a hard place."

The carriage drew up in front of the steps.

"That's right, Longarm. That's the way it has to be."

Longarm nodded. "And if I do manage to bring the girl back, what do I do with her?"

"Bring her here. I'll contact Boggs."

Longarm touched the brim of his hat and left Wells Daniel standing in the open doorway. As the carriage drove off, Longarm did not look back.

"Ah, Mr. Long," caroled the desk clerk, "your sister arrived an hour ago and I sent her up to your room. I hope you don't mind. She was so . . . distraught when she discovered she had missed your train this afternoon."

Longarm swallowed the surprise he felt at this announcement, nodded to the clerk as he took his key from him, then hurried across the lobby and up the stairs. As he started down the hallway to his room, a piratical character who smelled faintly of sheep dip and whom he recognized at once as Jason Kimball, stepped out of a doorway and thrust the barrel of a revolver into the small of Longarm's back.

"Keep right on going to your room, Mr. Custis Long, U.S. Deputy Marshal."

"No need to be formal," Longarm drawled. "You can call me Longarm."

40

Jason responded by thrusting the barrel of his revolver still deeper into Longarm's back. When Longarm got to his door, he paused and reached into his jacket pocket for his key.

Mistaking the reason for this move, Jason Kimball swore savagely and brought the barrel of his sixgun down on the top of Longarm's head. As Longarm fell, barely conscious, to the floor of the narrow hallway, his key dropped out of his hand. Realizing his mistake, Kimball picked up the key, unlocked the door and pushed it open. Sitting up groggily on the floor, Longarm at first did not know what to make of the sudden explosion that erupted from his room.

He saw Kimball stagger back and then fire twice into the room. Another shot from inside the room caught the man in the face, pieces of which went slamming into the wall behind him. The gunfire had thundered monstrously in the hallway, and as Longarm pulled himself to his feet, doors were being flung open on both sides of his room. He ignored the astonished faces that peered out at him and reached out to catch the falling Jason Kimball. The man turned dumbly to him, then collapsed forward onto his knees, his bloody face burying itself in Longarm's pants. Longarm stepped back, allowing the fellow to collapse forward onto the carpet, ignored the two men hurrying down the hall toward him, and looked into his room.

The light that filtered in through the open doorway was little help, beyond revealing the dim form lying on his bed. Fumbling for a match, he entered and lit the lantern on his dresser. Turning to the bed, he saw the body of Rosalie Bond. A pearl-handled over-and-under Remington .41 was still clutched in her lifeless hand. Where her slim waist should have been, there was only a bloody tangle of dress and shattered flesh. A rapidly spreading stain was growing under her body.

A florid-faced man, his eyes wide with excitement, was standing in the doorway. "What have you done, you fiend!" he demanded.

41

Another one crowded into the doorway beside him, this one taller and seemingly just as belligerent. When he saw Rosalie Bond, he swore and looked at the other fellow. "You saw this?"

The redfaced fellow nodded enthusiastically. With an indignant stab of his forefinger, he indicated Longarm. "That man there! He caught these two together!"

The other's eyes lit up. "Aha!" He turned to someone in the hall behind him. "Get the hotel manager! Get the sheriff! We'll hold this fellow here! Hurry!"

As footsteps pounded down the hall toward the stairs, Longarm reached over and took the Remington from Rosalie's hand. He hadn't realized how dedicated she had been to the task of paying back those who had worked so effectively to bring her brother to justice. A consummate actress, she had convinced him that she was only a frightened little girl on her way home to St. Louis when he left her. *Such a foolish girl,* he thought. *Such a waste. But thank you, Rosalie. You just might have saved my life.*

He got up from the bed and looked down at the girl for a moment, then examined the Remington. It was a definite improvement over the pepperbox. With a single shake of his head, he dropped the weapon onto the coverlet and turned to face the two men still trembling with indignation in the doorway.

"Get out of my way," he told them quietly, aware of a splitting headache all of a sudden.

"Sir!" cried the florid one, "you must stay right there until the sheriff comes. You will have to answer to him for this night's dastardly work!"

If Longarm had been in the proper frame of mind, he would have smiled. The fellow sounded like a character in a Ned Buntline story. He reached under the bed for his gladstone, lifted it, and pressed it gently but firmly against the two men. When he felt them begin to ease back, he heaved. They were sent flying out of the doorway and went down on their backs in a tangle of arms and legs.

42

He stepped over them, shouldered his way through the crush of spectators, and hurried down the hallway. He used the main stairway to the second floor, then took the back stairs to the street level. He came out in an alley behind the hotel. Moving off in the darkness, he headed west. This would take him to the other side of the railroad tracks. The driver of the carriage that had brought him back from Wells Daniel's place had told him that this was where the Utah House and a few other such establishments were allowed to flourish.

Ma Randle hurried to greet him. "Mr. Long!" she cried. "How nice to see you again so soon." She caught sight of the large stain on his pants—and then noted the gladstone in his hand. "Are you—are you planning on moving in?"

Longarm looked quickly around. He was standing in the lobby of a very elegant house. Gas light cast a soft, pulsing glow that was reflected in the many gold-framed mirrors that covered the walls. The bar was farther in, and the dark green of gaming tables glowed in the soft light. The click of rolling dice came to him clearly. Liquor, gambling, and sex in the land of the Mormons. Who would have believed it? Longarm looked at Ma Randle.

"I'd like to talk to Annie," he told her.

"Annie?" She smiled in sympathy. "She's occupied, I'm afraid. The gentleman has requested her for the entire evening." She indicated the gaming tables. "She's in there now with her escort. Gambling excites him, it seems."

Longarm nodded. "I'll wait, then."

She frowned. "Will none of my other girls do?"

Longarm felt unduly conspicuous standing there. "Could we go someplace private?" he suggested to the madam. "Someplace where we could palaver without me looking like some country bumpkin inquiring about the price of a girl?"

She laughed, her dark eyes gleaming with pleasure

43

at the way he put it. "Of course, Mr. Long. Step into my office."

She led him into a suite of rooms off the lobby. The first room he entered was obviously her office. The furniture was almost stark in its simplicity, leather for the most part, curtains without frills at the windows and a large desk dominating one wall. As he entered, he glimpsed through an open doorway a bedroom containing what appeared to be a very large canopied bed, its coverlet fashioned of gleaming red silk. Garish but exciting.

Ma Randle turned in front of her desk and leaned back against it to face him. Longarm put down his gladstone, took off his Stetson, and sank wearily into a comfortable arm chair. "I'll be honest with you, Miss Randle," he said. "I'm riding the owlhoot trail. There's a good chance the sheriff is looking for me right now. But that's a long story. What I need from Annie is information concerning that jasper who tried to take her away with him on the train."

"Jason Kimball?"

"That's right. He seemed to know her and she appeared to know quite a bit about him."

"Why are you interested in him, Mr. Long?"

"Call me Longarm," he said, smiling. "It's not him I'm interested in now. It's his friends."

"But you want his whereabouts for a start?"

"Well, I'm afraid I already know where he is now."

"Oh?"

"He's on his way to the city morgue. Either that or he's still lying on the carpet outside my hotel room."

"You . . . shot him?"

As she asked this, she pushed herself away from the desk, her dark eyes widening in alarm.

"No, I didn't. But like I said, that's a long story. Right now I'd just like to talk to Annie for a few minutes. I need to know where Kimball and his friends would be hanging out."

"Why do you need to know this? They are very

44

dangerous people. No one dares get mixed up with the Avenging Angels—and that's who you are talking about. And you have *killed* one of them?" Her voice was hushed with the enormity of what she was asking.

"I told you. I didn't kill him."

"Just because he was interested in taking Annie away! How gallant, but how foolish!"

Longarm looked at her for a moment, wondering if she was perhaps playing with him. When he realized she was serious, he was impressed. These Avenging Angels had everyone buffaloed, it seemed.

"If you want," she said, "I'll help you get out of Salt Lake City. But it will cost you."

He looked at her. She was wearing her hair up in a fashionable pile on her head and her slender body was sheathed in a dark maroon, low-cut satin gown. A single pearl glowed softly as it hung from its pendant just above the slight cleft of her small breasts. That was all the jewelry she wore, but her eyes, again, seemed more than a match for any jewelry fashioned by man.

"Thank you for offering to help me, Miss Randle. But I'm not leaving until I speak with Annie."

"What makes you think Annie is the only one who can tell you about these people?"

"You know someone else who can?"

"How do you think it is possible for me to operate this . . . establishment in Salt Lake City, Longarm?"

He shrugged. "I imagine the usual methods, Miss Randle. A payoff here, a favor there."

She smiled coldly. "You may call me Felicia. I hate 'Ma Randle' almost as much as *Miss* Randle." Her smile faded away entirely. "At sixteen I was invited by my sister to join in a Celestial Marriage with her husband. She was working very hard, you see, and not only that, she was lonely. The Sealing Ceremony was very impressive. And then . . . " She shrugged and looked away. "As soon as I could, I fled that man—and all his chattering, imbecile wives. Of course I was excommunicated and warned never to go to the gentiles with

45

my story. And the Avenging Angels left me one alternative—this place. They were the ones who gave me the money to open the Utah House."

"You're in their pay, then."

"I hate them. Also, Longarm, I fear them. No one can escape their fury. They ride with God on their right hand and the devil on their left. They are blackhearted fiends who show no mercy and kill with impunity." She shuddered. "What poor little Annie could tell you about them would barely fill a thimble, I'm afraid."

"But you are working for them."

"I am one of their soundest investments. It is as simple as that. But I hate them, Longarm. If I could, I would stop them. But nothing can stop them. Nothing."

"You said you thought you could help me."

"If I knew what you were after, I might be able to help you."

"Why would you want to?"

She smiled. "I hate them—and I like you. The men who come here—the men who must pay for the company of a woman—are not appealing to me. Men of your caliber, it seems, do not often frequent the Utah House. It is one of the unfortunate aspects of my profession that few would imagine. I daresay you are surprised."

Longarm shrugged. "It makes a kind of sense, at that."

"Then, if you'll help me, I'll help you."

"You know where the Avenging Angels might have their settlement?"

"There are many such settlements throughout the territory, Longarm," she replied, "but I assume it is the one headed by Lorenzo Wolverton, the one to which Jason Kimball belonged, that you are interested in."

He was impressed with what she must know as soon as she mentioned Wolverton. He nodded. "That's right."

46

"Of course I can only make a shrewd guess as to where it is. But it seems to me a most likely location. And it is near here."

"Where?"

She smiled, took his hand, and led him gently toward her bedroom. "You must earn what help I can give you," she told him, her eyes lighting mischievously. "And I warn you, if you are not all that my fevered imagination tells me you are, I will most probably not be able to remember a thing about Lorenzo Wolverton and his loyal followers." She smiled disarmingly at him. "Not a single blessed thing."

She paused in the doorway to her bedroom and let him go in ahead of her.

"Make yourself comfortable," she told him. "There's a pitcher of water on the commode next to the bowl and a bottle of whiskey on the dresser. I'll be right back. I must leave someone in charge, you see."

She turned and disappeared quickly through the door of her office.

It was a shame, but he did not trust her. Which meant he would simply have to play this one by ear— or some other portion of his anatomy. Longarm knew that the usual practice in sporting houses was to keep your boots on. He felt, however, that something other than the usual was called for under these circumstances. He tugged off his boots, stepped out of his pants, and pulled off his longjohns and vest and jacket. He hung his gunbelt on the bedpost at the foot of the bed where Felicia would be sure to see it.

Placing a chair at the head of the bed, he carefully folded his vest over the back of it, allowing the watch chain to hang in full view. If Felicia had a question about it, he was certain he would be able to come up with something light and humorous. Then he pulled his Colt from his rig and proceeded to empty its chambers into the side pocket of his coat.

Certain he had taken care of any surprises from that quarter, Longarm padded over to the wash bowl on

47

the commode, poured water into it, and added a healthy measure of whiskey. He cleaned himself thoroughly —a whorehouse ritual he considered perfectly civilized. Then with only his shirt on to cover his lean nakedness, he sat on the edge of the bed to wait, a bemused smile on his face.

He wished the Chief could see what he was willing to go through for the government.

Felicia returned, flushed and eager. She moved swiftly through her office, turning down lamps as she went. Closing the bedroom door, she turned down the single lantern on her dresser and faced him, an appreciative smile on her face as Longarm stood up. She undid her hair and let it cascade down over her shoulders. Then she reached back and unclasped her gown. It shimmered in the soft glow of the lamp and fell to her feet. In a twinkling, her petticoat followed. Then she turned her back to Longarm. He stepped close, aware of the intoxicating perfume of her long, dark tresses, and with fumbling fingers managed to help her unlace her French corset. By the time he had finished with it, he was aware that she had already stepped gracefully out of her lace-trimmed drawers and added them to the growing pile at her feet. At last came her chemise, and she stood naked before him. Only her stockings remained, but she left these on, and Longarm was not about to bring the matter up.

"I warn you," she said softly, stepping toward him, "you had better be good."

She reached out and unbuttoned his shirt. As she pulled it off to reveal his complete nakedness, she started to say something.

Longarm placed a finger over her mouth. "Talk with your body, Felicia," he said.

She smiled, touched his face lightly, then traced a soft line down his cheeks, down his heavily corded, deeply tanned neck to the tightly coiled hair of his chest. She kissed his shoulder and he felt the moist heat of her tongue sliding along the slope of his shoulders to

48

the strong cords of his neck. And then she began nibbling delightfully on his ear lobes. All the while her fingers had been working their magic on his back and thighs. Now they began to caress him, gently at first, then more vigorously. She pulled her lips from his ears then and kissed him hard, her tongue darting, her rich dark hair spilling over his shoulders.

A flame of hot desire lanced upward from his groin and he felt his pulse quickening. He pulled away from her teasing tongue and laughed aloud. Reaching down, he took her by her slim waist, lifted her off the floor, and heaved her gently backward onto the bed. She uttered a tiny cry of surprise at the ease with which he had lifted her. And then he dropped beside her on the bed, his powerful fingers thrusting between her thighs, finding her moistness.

It was her turn to laugh now, a deep, husky sound that sent shivers down his back. She moved to him hungrily, eagerly. He shifted and was on her. Her hand reached down and guided him home. He began thrusting while she started rotating her hips with a frantic, delicious abandon. Yet as he drove into her, her violent writhing almost dislodged him.

He grabbed her hips firmly, slowing slightly the wild movements of the woman under him until at last she flung her head back and raked her nails down his back. In that instant they came as one, Longarm still driving, feeling himself explode within her, her entire body shuddering, wrenching in ecstatic reaction. Once more, and then again, she climaxed until at last she went limp beneath him.

But she kept her arms about him. "You kept it in!" she cried, her eyes filled with the sweet pleasure of it. "How ever did you manage?"

"You do go on some at that, Felicia. I've heard of some women a mite too quiet under a man. I reckon you've got the opposite problem."

"Again!" she breathed. "Please, again!"

He tried to protest. This, after all, had been a very

49

long day. But her foreplay was inspired and soon he found himself more than ready.

"Let me get on top," she requested eagerly. "It will be easier for you!"

Without waiting for his response, she climbed on top of him and soon Longarm found himself hard put to keep up with her; but she kept driving down upon him until at last she uttered a long, low moan and began to shudder. He climaxed then as well, and suddenly she leaned forward, her mouth found his shoulder, and her teeth dug into his flesh. He felt for a moment as if he'd been flung into a gunnysack with a wildcat, but at last—after a final orgasm—she collapsed, exhausted, onto him.

She laughed huskily, her face resting on his hard chest, her hair spilling over his face and neck. "How was that?" she whispered, her voice low, warm.

"That was fine, Felicia."

She lifted her head abruptly from his chest. He saw sudden concern in her eyes. "Longarm, there's something I must tell you—"

Before she could say anything further, Longarm saw the dark shape looming over them and the gleam of a sixgun.

"Get off him, Felicia!" The voice was harsh, masculine.

Longarm grabbed both of Felicia's arms above the elbows and flung her upward toward the shadowy figure. Her tumbling body caught the man in the chest, and as the fellow stumbled backward, Longarm reached for his vest. His fingers caught at the gold chain. He pulled the derringer from the pocket, then rolled back across the bed.

By this time the intruder was back on his feet, a tall man with his hat still on, a badge pinned to his vest gleaming in the lamp's glow. Felicia had sent for the sheriff, it seemed.

"Get out, Longarm!" she called to him. "Save yourself!"

50

This was Amos Barker, the man he had been told was a brother to one of the Avenging Angels he was after. Barker turned as Felicia called out, gun in hand, tracking Longarm's rolling, twisting progress across the silken coverlet of the huge bed. He fired quickly and the round buried itself in a pillow. The air was suddenly alive with tiny feathers. As Barker brought his revolver around for a second shot, Longarm dropped to his knees on the floor, steadied his right hand, aimed, and fired. The slug planted a neat black hole in the center of the sheriff's forehead.

The man looked startled as he backed slowly toward the dresser, his gun hand swinging down. He began to slide down the front of the dresser, twitching convulsively. Once, twice, three times the gun in his hand discharged, filling the bedroom with its thick, acrid smoke.

Barker's first shot caused a low cry from Felicia. The second shot silenced her. By the time the third round had been pumped into the woman's body, Longarm was at her side. He pulled her to one side as the sheriff slipped sideways and crashed heavily to the floor. Longarm cradled Felicia's head in his arms. In the dim, smoky light, he saw her dark eyes flicker open.

"I'm hit, Longarm. Am I going to die?"

A quick examination of her wounds did not encourage Longarm. He said, "You'll be all right. But you promised to help me. Remember?"

She smiled dreamily. "It was so nice, Longarm. I never should have sent for Barker. I tried . . . to warn you."

He nodded. "Never mind that, Felicia. You had to keep on the right side of them, so you sent for Barker. I understand that. It's all right. But now tell me. Where is that settlement?"

Someone began pounding on the door to Felicia's office and Longarm heard voices shouting through the door.

"You're not angry with me, Longarm?" Felicia asked with genuine concern.

51

"Of course not," Longarm reassured her. "Just tell me. Please, Felicia."

"They're living in the badlands . . . west of the Salt Desert. Follow the tracks after you leave the last water tower." She closed her eyes and leaned back. "Hills, badlands," she murmured. "Beautiful valley. In the middle of the badlands . . . Little Zion . . . "

A boot began kicking against the door. Longarm started to get up, but Felicia's hand reached up and grabbed his arm.

"Stay!" she cried. "I'm cold . . . so cold!"

Taking a deep breath, he went down on one knee beside her again and continued to cradle her head. Suddenly her grip on him relaxed and her arm dropped lifelessly to the floor. He lowered her head gently to the carpet.

He got quickly to his feet and yelled into the office, "Hold your horses! I'm coming!"

The pounding on the door ceased abruptly.

"This is Sheriff Barker!" Longarm yelled. "You damage that door and I'll have you pay for it! Get back away from there!"

An immediate argument started up on the other side of the door, but it seemed to him that the voices quieted as the crowd moved back from the door.

Longarm dressed quickly as the tumult on the other side of the door slowly built to its former intensity. At last, snatching up his gladstone, he strode quickly through the office to the door and flung it open. At sight of him, they recoiled. He moved swiftly into their midst, using his gladstone as a buffer.

"Damn it!" he cried. "Can't a man get any peace and quiet anywhere in this town? You woke up Ma!"

This astonished most of them, confused the rest. They stood back and watched his tall form stride angrily to the door before one of the girls broke from the crowd and darted into the office. Pulling open the door and stepping out into the night, Longarm hurried down

52

the steps of the Utah House, disappearing into the darkness, heading for the railroad tracks.

He was leaving a trail of dead bodies in his wake, and he could not count on help from the men who were behind his mission to this place—except for one of them. Quincy Boggs. It was his daughter Longarm was after, and there was no doubt in his mind that Boggs would give him all the assistance he needed, especially now that Longarm had a line on where the settlement was.

The tracks, gleaming in the moonlight, appeared just ahead of him. Hurrying across them in the darkness, he glanced to the west, his eyes following the gleaming rails of the Central Pacific. Somewhere out there in the darkness lay the vast salt wasteland known as the Great Salt Desert—and just beyond that, in a desolate place of rocky hills and cliffs Felicia had called the badlands, a bunch of Mormon fanatics had built themselves a community.

He shook his head as he headed for the hack stand on the other side of the train station. Those Avenging Angels were sure as hell going to make it tough for a lone Deputy U.S. Marshal to take back one of their women. And this night's frustrations were liable to make them plumb out of sorts. They were probably getting their welcome mat all brushed and ready for him right now.

Chapter 3

"My God, Mr. Long!" Quincy Boggs exclaimed. He pulled Longarm quickly inside and closed the door.

Turning to the buxom housekeeper who had refused to let Longarm cross the threshold at that time of night, he comforted her with a generous pat on the shoulder. "That's all right, Molly. I know this gentleman."

Molly had crossed her fleshy arms over her wide bosom in obvious disapproval. Now her gimlet eyes noted the front of Longarm's jacket and pants, as if to say that until such a mess was explained to her satisfaction she would remain opposed to Longarm's presence in the house. Longarm saw the glance and smiled at the woman.

"May as well come out and say it, ma'am. I had a terrible accident. I was hoping some kind lady like yourself could maybe clean my jacket and pants."

The woman unfolded her arms and looked with sudden uncertainty at Boggs. He smiled at her.

"Yes, Molly," he said, "perhaps tomorrow you could see to that for Mr. Long. I am sure he would appreciate it."

"I sure would, ma'am," said Longarm.

"Is this man staying, Mr. Boggs?"

Boggs glanced at Longarm. Longarm nodded.

"Yes he is, Molly. Make ready the third floor guest room, the one facing front."

She pulled herself up to her full five-feet-five, took

54

one last look at the disreputable outcast she had met at the door, then lumbered off, shaking the floor slightly with each footfall.

Boggs looked at Longarm, his lean face creased in a smile. "She's very protective," he explained. "We have three daughters, and with my wife gone she has become as wary as a mother grizzly—for all of us."

Longarm took off his hat and lifted his gladstone. "Where can I stow this for now? I'm getting tired of lugging it around."

"Leave it right there and come with me into the library. You have no idea how glad I am to see you! In heaven's name, man, what have you been up to since last we met?"

Longarm glanced at him. "You mean that business at the hotel?"

"Precisely!" Boggs pushed open the double door leading to the library and stepped aside to let Longarm move past him. "A woman and one of the Avenging Angels were found dead in your hotel room—and you were reported to have fled the scene."

"That about covers it, for now," Longarm agreed, starting for one of the upholstered chairs. "I'll fill you in about the rest of it later."

"The *rest* of it?"

"Daddy! Who's this?"

Both men turned to face the open doorway. Two young ladies were standing in it; each one was dressed in a long, white, frilly nightgown, their luxurious, straw-colored hair combed out so that it fell beyond their shoulders, all the way to their narrow waists. They were at least eighteen; one of them was closer to twenty. It was this one who was the more forward of the two, her eyes staring boldly and appreciatively at Longarm as she pressed into the library with her sister at her heels.

Boggs laughed. "I might have known. Nothing goes on in this house without these two on hand to approve—or disapprove!" The man was obviously de-

55

lighted with his daughters. Longarm got the impression that this had once been a happy house, filled with the laughter of young girls. It was no wonder Boggs was so upset at losing one of them in such a cruel fashion, and so outspoken in his condemnation of the Avenging Angels.

Boggs looked back at Longarm with a smile. "Mr. Long, may I present Marilyn and Audrey, Emilie's sisters. The shy one in back is Audrey. This outspoken nymph is Marilyn." Boggs turned to his daughters. "Girls, this is Deputy U.S. Marshal Custis Long. He has come to bring your sister back to us."

Marilyn—who had wide blue eyes and a sprinkling of freckles on her milk-white cheeks—reached out at once and took Longarm's hand boldly. "Oh, Mr. Long. Please do bring Emilie back to us!"

"Yes!" cried the other, rushing up and taking Longarm's other hand in hers. He felt her warm eagerness as she pressed his hand in her excitement. "Please, do! We have all been perfectly wretched at the thought of Emilie in the hands of those terrible people!"

"Emilie is a match for any man!" Marilyn explained proudly, with an angry toss of her head. "But that's just it. She won't submit easily."

"Let's hope she won't have to," said their father, taking both of their hands and leading them from the room. "Now you must leave us alone. Mr. Long and I have much to discuss. You'll be able to see him again at breakfast. Now scoot upstairs to your bedroom!"

"Oh, is he staying?" Audrey cried, delighted.

"Just for the night. Now, scoot along, or I'll sic Molly on you."

Laughing, the two girls bolted through the doorway and Longarm could hear them talking excitedly and giggling irrepressibly all the way up the stairs.

Boggs closed the library door and turned to Longarm, an indulgent smile on his face. "You see why we want Emilie back, Mr. Long? You see how close we all are—how much we . . . love each other."

56

"You can call me Longarm," Longarm said, dropping back into the upholstered chair. "And yes, I reckon I do understand. You've got quite a handsome flock there."

"There's much of their mother in all of them," Boggs said musingly, as he sat down across from Longarm. "It is as if in losing Helen, my wife, I had been given a little bit of her in each one."

Longarm recognized real emotion when he rode onto it and he had learned a long time ago not to try to tie those kinds of feelings down with words, but this man Boggs seemed to handle the problem without any difficulty—and he left Longarm with a deep sense of what he was feeling. Longarm hadn't been very certain until now—but he guessed he could trust this man for sure. Hell, he didn't really have much choice in the matter.

"Now," said Boggs, "what in tarnation happened at that hotel, anyway?"

Longarm told him as briefly as possible—that a woman out to get him had been waiting in his room for him. When Jason Kimball appeared in the doorway, the fireworks began.

"I knew I couldn't explain it—and from what you gents told me about the local sheriff, I realized I would have quite a time untangling myself. So I took off."

"And?"

Longarm's account of what happened at the Utah House left Boggs shaking his head in disbelief.

"How do you account for the sheriff showing up like that?"

"He's in with the Avenging Angels and the Randle woman sent for him as soon as I entered her place. She knew, I guess, that they were after me and wanted to chalk up some points for her side, looks like."

"How did she know?"

"Jason and his boys saw me talking to her after I got off the train. When they lost me, they went to her.

57

They must have filled her ear some, 'cause just as soon as she could leave me, she sent for Barker."

"Barker dead?" Boggs shook his head in wonder. "For this business, that's no loss, I am afraid, but he was a fine and diligent peace officer."

"You mind my asking something?" Longarm said.

"Go right ahead."

"I can see why you couldn't call on Barker, but what about the Utah Territorial Police?"

Boggs shook his head. "Shot through with Avenging Angels or their sympathizers. Many of them are still wanted for the Mountain Meadow Massacre."

Longarm nodded.

"You must not misunderstand me, Longarm. I am a devout Mormon. Our Prophet, Joseph Smith, was a divinely inspired man. His vision of a modern Zion here in the West has been realized. A new social order is abuilding—and we are in the midst of that great business this very moment! It is God's work we are doing and I, for one, am proud to be a part of this momentous task."

Longarm had heard preachers before, most of them spouting fire and brimstone and tearing at their hair all the while, but Boggs did not strike him as that type. He spoke with feeling and enthusiasm, but kept the fire in his eye banked. Longarm nodded to the man, not so much to encourage him as to let him know he was still in the same room with him.

Boggs smiled. "Sometimes I let my enthusiasm carry me away, I'm afraid. But what I want you to understand, Longarm, is that I hold to the basic tenets of our faith with great firmness and conviction. It is only the foolish notion that a man should have as many wives as he pleases that I find impossible to accept."

"Imagine it could run into quite an expense at that," the deputy observed.

Boggs smiled. "Of course. In more ways than one. Did you know that there are many Mormons, building even now in the West, who do not hold to this nefarious

58

doctrine? Did you know that the Prophet's wife herself, Emma, flew into a rage when her husband showed her the paper enunciating this doctrine? She flung the paper into the fire, as a matter of fact."

"Didn't do her much good, huh?"

Boggs smiled. "No, it didn't." Boggs looked at Longarm with a pleased light in his eye. "It does me good to talk to a gentile like you, Longarm. Gives me needed prespective."

"That so? Glad to hear it."

"At any rate, we must get rid of this doctrine if we are to join the federal government as an equal state. We have lost out already because of this foolish practice. Until we wipe it out entirely, I see no hope of our being accepted into the Union." He shook his head sadly and leaned back in his chair.

Boggs appeared to have run out of steam, but Longarm was not sure and waited in case there was still some in the boiler. He didn't mind sitting in the chair and waiting. He could use a little rest. He had been run ragged this day, and was beginning to feel a mite weary. The room was quiet and comfortable and the many books in the shelves that lined the walls looked as if they had been read. Some books were out on tables and a few were put back onto the shelves upside down. It appeared to him that this room was used quite often—and he could almost imagine the three daughters curled up on chairs and sofas, poring over the books, deep in study one moment, laughingly reading aloud to each other the next.

"Well, Longarm, what are your plans now?"

Longarm looked back to Boggs. "I will need help tomorrow in getting a horse. I intend to ride out to Fort Douglas. I reckon I won't have any trouble requisitioning a couple of army mules. I can load them onto a Central Pacific freight car, then ride as far as that last water stop. From there, I'll be looking for signs, but I'll get Emilie with as little fuss as possible and bring her back on one of the mules. How's that?"

"You make it sound very simple."

"It won't be, and that's a fact. But that's the general plan. You keep repeating that to yourself and you won't get riled up and fidgety waiting for word. 'Course, I know it won't be easy."

"It's dangerous, isn't it?"

"I could get my head blown off. They tried twice already. Leastways, that's what I figure that Kimball fellow had in mind when he escorted me to my room."

"Poor Emilie," the man said, shaking his head. "This whole thing—it's madness."

"You think that fellow Meeker was driving the right spike when he said he blamed your loose talk for what happened to your daughter?"

"I am afraid he was. This is their challenge to all of us who dare to suggest that we call them to account for their barbarities, that we rid ourselves of the doctrine of polygamy. Don't you see? If Emilie submits, if she becomes one of them . . . "

Boggs shook his head in sudden anguish.

Longarm got to his feet. "I reckon I could use some shut-eye along about now, and you appear a bit worn through yourself. If you'll see to a carriage tomorrow that could take me to a livery, I'll be on my way to Fort Douglas first thing in the morning."

"I'll see to that myself. My carriage will take you to a livery on the outskirts of the city." The man got up. "I expect there will be considerable annoyance and perhaps even a little panic at the events of this night, Longarm. You've certainly managed to stir things up." He shook his head. "But maybe that's just what this city needs."

"I wasn't trying to shake up the city," Longarm said, starting for the door. "Just trying to keep my scalp on straight."

Not in a long, long time had a bed felt as good as this

60

one did to Longarm. The city was quiet, the moonlight just beginning to flood in through the large window, the sheets starched and clean. He stretched luxuriously and turned his face away from the moonlit window panes.

He heard a soft giggle, which was immediately stifled.

"Hush!" whispered a voice that Longarm immediately recognized as Marilyn's.

And then two kittenish bodies landed on the bed. Before Longarm could figure out what was happening, the bedclothes were ripped unceremoniously back. In the moonlight, his long flanks and the dark thatch of his pubic hair became startlingly visible.

"Ohhh, look!"

Marilyn and Audrey, both as naked as plucked chickens but considerably more enticing, crowded against him. He turned to face Marilyn, but Audrey was happy to take second best and snuggle up to Longarm's backside, both arms around his chest as she hugged him with all her might.

"He's so big!" Marilyn exclaimed. "Oh, glory! There's so much of him!"

"Keep it quiet!" managed Longarm in a hushed whisper. He didn't know whether to groan in despair or whoop in excitement. He had had busy days before, but this one was getting plain ridiculous. *No fear,* he thought foolishly. *There ain't no way that little fellow is going to get up for* this *one.*

"Poor little thing," Marilyn murmured, as her fingers traced a hot path up his inner thighs.

Longarm tried to pull back, but the sister on his back just squeezed tighter and sank her teeth into the back of his neck. It was amazing, but this seemed to do the trick. He felt himself growing and moved his loins slightly in what should have been an attempt to pull away—but wasn't.

Now, look here, old son, he warned himself, *how*

61

would you explain this if Boggs came in right now— or that old squaw, Molly!

And then it was too late for such worries as Marilyn's mouth found his. She kissed him with delirious abandon and pulled him over onto her. He felt her legs open for him, her fingers guiding him in. In a moment, with Audrey on his back riding him like a bronc, he was probing deep with measured thrusts, thinking, *The hell with it, tomorrow is going to be a long day, the beginning of a long, hot search . . .*

The blazing sun reflected off the hard-packed earth of the parade ground, and Longarm was forced to squint through the glare as he rode up to the headquarters building that served Fort Douglas. It had been a short ride from Salt Lake City, but already Longarm was beginning to feel the oppressive weight of the sun. The headquarters was a long, low barracks that looked to be wilting visibly from the heat. Longarm glanced at the flag on the pole. It hung lifelessly, giving him the distinct impression that if he looked a mite closer, he'd see the flag was singed around the edges.

Dismounting, he dropped his reins over the hitch rail and feeling slightly guilty about leaving the horse standing in that sun, he walked into the building and presented his papers to the sergeant. A moment later he was ushered into the C.O.'s office and introduced to a Captain Meriwether. He was a lean, dusty individual with a clean-shaven face, alert green eyes, and neatly-combed hair the color of bleached mustard. He stood up to shake Longarm's hand, then indicated the chair by his desk with a quick, decisive motion of his hand.

"What can I do for you, Marshal Long?"

"Call me Longarm, Captain."

The man smiled. The smile was properly distant. His head inclined slightly in acknowledgment of Longarm's request. "All right—Longarm. But what is it I can do for you?"

"I need two mules."

62

"Mules?" The captain's eyes narrowed in merriment at the request. "You going prospecting for the government?"

"Not exactly."

"We have fine, blooded stock in our remuda, Longarm. Finest horseflesh I've seen since coming out here."

"Where you from, Captain?"

The man leaned back in his chair, his hands resting lightly on the armrests. He was obviously pleased to contemplate his origins. "Connecticut, Longarm. Lovely, rolling, fertile land."

"Do much riding as a young 'un?"

"Grew up in the saddle, Longarm." He smiled proudly. "It didn't hurt my progress at the Point one bit. That's why I say I know horses. I do. And you're welcome to our best."

"How long have you been out here, Captain?"

He frowned. "A few weeks. A dry, arid, desolate country by my reckoning. And dealing with these Mormons is going to be quite a challenge." He spoke of the Mormons with more than a touch of disdain.

"Not all Mormons are alike," Longarm said softly.

"Perhaps, Marshal," Meriwether said abruptly, "but to the business at hand. We have fine horses if you care to requisition them. Do you still want mules?"

Longarm wasn't anxious to educate this young shavetail from the Point, but what the hell. The man was courteous enough, and meant well, as far as Longarm could see. Maybe it wouldn't do any great harm to try. Longarm cleared his throat carefully.

"Yes, Captain, I do. Like you just said, this here is arid country and right now that sun out there is coming down mighty hard—like a hot fist. And your fine, blooded stock would have one devil of a time standing up to those conditions for any length of time, especially where I'm heading. I reckon it's right the mule was the only animal Noah didn't take into the ark, and like they say, it ain't got any pride of ancestry nor hope of progeny; but a mule is reaching his full get-up-and-go

63

about when a horse is starting to run downhill. Mules can be ornery just like some people we all know, but they can do as much work as a horse on one-third less food, they're subject to fewer diseases, and their tough hide and short hair make them a damn sight more able to shake off saddle sores."

Meriwether smiled. "That's quite a recommendation, Longarm. A very long speech, indeed."

"Sometimes I do run on, and that's a fact," Longarm replied.

Meriwether laughed easily. "No harm done, Longarm. Of course you realize how expensive an army mule is. One hundred and fifty a mule, as a matter of fact."

Longarm winced. "That should tell you something, Captain."

"I must admit I was surprised at how prized this obstinate beast is in this country."

"It's the country that makes the conditions, Captain. It's too big to fight. You got to figure out how to go along, mostly, or it'll just swat you like a fly. The mule helps you to go along."

Meriwether smiled. "I dare say General Crook would agree with you."

"How's that, Captain?"

"The general rides to battle on a mule, Longarm. And I understand he prefers them to horses for packing—can get as much as three hundred and twenty pounds on a single mule." The captain rose to his feet. "Excuse me, Longarm. I'll send an orderly to see to your mules. Meanwhile, I would be honored if you would join me in a small libation. I like a man who talks plain. It's a relief, as a matter of fact."

Longarm thanked the man and leaned back in his chair as the captain left the room. He would have preferred to pick out the mules himself, but he didn't see how he could refuse the captain's hospitality.

And that long speech, along with the ride, *had* left him a mite dry.

64

Longarm ducked his head slightly as the engine's smokestack showered him with soot. Looking up a moment later, he watched the Central Pacific train move off due west. He had had a little difficulty detraining the somewhat skittish mules from the freight car, but they were standing quietly behind him now, ears flicking and like himself, it seemed they were somewhat oppressed by the blistering heat.

It was late in the afternoon and Longarm had no intention of leaving the meager shade provided by the water tower. He had plenty of time. He would move out at night. He looked around at the gleaming white tablecloth that stretched as flat as a rule in all directions. He had availed himself of Captain Meriwether's maps of the Great Salt Desert, as it was called, and what the maps revealed to him had sobered him somewhat.

A desolate expanse of close to four thousand square miles, it was about a hundred miles wide at its narrowest. The north and south edges of the desert were simply too far away to think about. Behind Longarm to the east were the irrigated farms of the Mormons and beyond them, still farther east, the Wasatch Range. Ahead of him, due west, was the Goshute and Toana fault-block complex, a low mass of hills and mountains that loomed ahead of him in the shimmering haze. They looked close enough to reach after a quick gallop, but Longarm knew they were at least thirty miles away. Somewhere among those spurs of rock that thrust out into the desert he would find the settlement. It would need water and that meant a well. The well's windmill would be the finger beckoning him to the settlement. That was the way his hopes were going, anyway.

Longarm let his back slide down the wooden support of the water tower until he was sitting on the ground. He pulled his hat down farther to cut some of the glare and settled down to wait for the blessed, cooling darkness.

65

Longarm had ridden parallel to the tracks for close to twenty miles before he tacked northwest toward a great misshapen shoulder of rock that loomed out of the starlit night. A spur of the fault toward which he was heading, it extended far enough out onto the flats to be the hills Felicia had mentioned.

As the tracks disappeared in the darkness behind him, he noticed the sudden glow in the sky over his right shoulder and glanced back. The edge of something vast and very red loomed above the horizon. Turning back around he saw a long, golden band suddenly appear along the top of the fault. As he watched, the band grew. The flaming globe of the sun was poking its eye out of the east, pouring a rosy brightness over the desert.

At once a cool wind sprang up. Crows, wheeling out of the west, tumbled toward him, cawing frantically. Abruptly they coiled up into the clear air and vanished back the way they had come. Dust devils—only it wasn't dust, it was salt—began dancing toward Longarm from the east. He pulled his bandanna up over his mouth and nostrils and put on the goggles he had purchased for this purpose.

Before the full blast of the sun struck him, Longarm reached the shore of the ancient lake bed and let his mule pick its way across the shale and then into a narrow canyon. The going was rough; the ground was a shattered, broken mess of shale and detritus, but he kept the mule going, the animal behind tugging unhappily on its lead. Slowly they rose into the barren hills, Longarm's optimism fading fast until he found the first faint traces of a wagon's track. Keeping after it, he saw it become a dimly etched roadway that vanished entirely for long stretches.

The immense sun was soon overhead, the wind-whipped sand finding its way into his eyes and nostrils despite his precautions. His tongue reached out to moisten his cracked lips and came away with the tang of salt on it. The sun hung now overhead, the bright

66

white light glancing off the canyon walls and the humped rocks with a withering intensity.

At noon he pulled himself wearily out of his saddle in the shade of a narrow canyon. He had not slept since yesterday. He had ridden through the night and this forenoon. Though he hated to give in to his fatigue, he realized he would have to sleep here in this canyon at least until nightfall, and then keep going somehow through the night. Crows overhead and the snorting anxiety of his two mules as they neared the canyon had alerted him to the presence of water, and as soon as he had unsaddled the mules, they made for the tiny stream, as Longarm followed patiently. He pushed aside the undergrowth, mindful of rattlers, and slaked his thirst, using his hands held together as a cup. The water was ice-cold, almost like a tonic. Sitting down, his back leaning against a portion of the canyon wall, he rubbed his wet hands over his face, washing off some of the grit. His eyes smarted. He took off the goggles and washed them in the cold water.

He turned then to selecting a spot for his dry camp. He was at the moment crouched in a tiny jungle of hard-nosed growth: pepperwood, a scrubby little wavy-leafed oak, Apache plume, blackbrush, and, most spectacular, the coral-colored globe-mallow, its bright presence mottling the canyon floor, with only patches of wild buckwheat to break its dominance. He glanced up at the walls of the canyon looming above him and realized he would not have to endure the direct rays of the sun for the remainder of the day if he stayed right where he was. He decided that his present spot was as good a place as any to camp.

He got up and hobbled the mules, satisfied they would not go far from the stream. They began foraging almost at once. He returned to the stream then and poked through the underbrush with the barrel of his rifle, looking for snakes. He found a nest of gopher snakes, scattered them, and continued his search. His fatigue told him he was silly to continue looking for

67

rattlers, but he persisted doggedly for some time before giving up and starting to go back for his gear.

He froze in his tracks.

Only a couple of inches to the rear of his heels, a small rattler was coiled. There was no mistaking the wedgelike head, the tip of the segmented tail peeping out of the coils. It was, Longarm knew, not a diamondback, but a smaller species Longarm had heard called the horny rattler—a reference to the small, hornlike knobs above each eye. Longarm watched the snake tensely. It was a small, dusty-looking serpent and dangerous enough. Its bite might not kill, but would sure as hell put a damper on Longarm's enthusiasm for this mission.

The heat of midday, Longarm realized, had made the snake sluggish, but not comatose. With one quick stride Longarm left the snake behind, then turned and poked at its head with the tip of his rifle barrel. He could not risk a shot. At this time of day and among these rocks, the report would carry for miles, alerting any settlement in the area. As the muzzle of the rifle neared the serpent, the snake lifted its head from its coils, eyes brightening, narrow black tongue flickering as it tested the air.

Longarm poked at the head. The head wove back, then struck. Longarm heard the click of the rattler's fangs against steel. The wet gleam of its venom was visible suddenly on the barrel. The snake reared, anxious to fight. But Longarm simply poked the rifle at it again, driving it back, herding it away from the stream. Giving up at last, its head aloft—the slit-eyed, weaving head shaped like an infernal ace of spades—tail whirring, the rattler retreated sideways before Longarm's prodding rifle barrel. Across a barren slope of rock it slithered with amazing speed and snapped like a rubber band out of sight under a sandstone slab.

Longarm returned to the stream, redoubled his investigation of the area he had chosen for his camp, found no more snakes, and unrolled his soogan. As the

68

fierce eye of the sun slipped slowly down the western sky, the shadows in the canyon darkened, cooling the place substantially. Longarm, too hot and weary for preparing food, pillowed his head on his arm, enclosed the butt of his Colt in his right hand, and slept.

The sound of low, whispering voices—one of them rising to a querulous whine—and then the sharp report of a slap awakened Longarm. In a split second he was sitting up alert, his Colt in front of him, the barrel pointing into the pitch-darkness from which the sounds had come. Listening, he heard the soft, muffled sound of someone—a girl—crying. A man's hoarse whisper, rough and uncompromising, came to him also. The two of them were with the mules and as Longarm slowly rolled back the soogan and rose to his feet, he heard the soft clop of their hooves as they were being ridden out of the canyon.

He strode from the screen of bushes that flanked the stream and saw the two of them desperately urging on the mules. He ran after them. They heard his footfalls and the one behind—the man—turned in his saddle, then bent low over the mule and began kicking his heels into the animal's flanks. With an unhappy snort the mule quickened his pace, moving alongside the other. The girl was making no effort to hurry, however, and on the narrow trail her mule was able to slow the other one considerably.

"Damn you, girl!" Longarm heard the older man cry.

Ten feet behind them by this time, Longarm told them to hold up or he would shoot. He kept his voice low and as menacing as possible. He had no sense that these two were dangerous, just a mite foolish and maybe a little greedy. More important was where the hell they had popped from. He was evidently nearer the settlement than he had realized.

The fellow twisted around in the darkness to face Longarm, who saw the glint of a rifle barrel. The bar-

69

rel was long, foolishly long, but that did not lessen its power to intimidate and Longarm swung his Colt against the side of the barrel. The clash of steel in the canyon echoed sharply. With an oath the fellow let go the rifle and ducked back around on his saddle. Reaching out, Longarm grabbed hold of his coat and pulled up, digging in his heels. Gasping, the fellow was dragged from the saddle. Stepping back and panting heavily, Longarm let him land on his back. He came down heavily, his vivid cursing silenced immediately. In the dark the man lay still, a large, ungainly package of meat and clothing, his big, floppy hat a black smudge over the spot where his head should be. Searching carefully in the darkness, Longarm retrieved the man's rifle. It looked like an early Hawken.

The girl had pulled up, dragged the mule around, and ridden back to where the man still lay unconscious on the ground. As Longarm returned with the rifle, she said to him, "Did you kill him?"

The cold matter-of-factness of the query chilled Longarm. Without replying, he knelt beside the man and rested the back of his hand against the side of his neck. The blood was still pounding through the carotid artery. He looked up at the mounted girl.

"No," he said, "I didn't."

"Damn," the girl said softly.

"Maybe you'd better get off that mule and give me a picture of all this. And go slow. I just woke up."

"You wake up fast, sure enough."

She dismounted. "It wasn't my idea to steal these mules," she told him. "We seen you climbing up here and waited until dark. The damn fool rode his own horses into the ground a ways back." She paused and looked down at the still figure. "He never could do nothing right."

"That so? Who is he?"

"Ezekiel Bannister. A fool."

"I've been getting the idea pretty strong now—like

70

old meat caught in the sun—that you don't hardly like the man. So what are you doing with him?"

"It ain't none of my doing. He came after me and took me away from Little Zion. Kidnapped me, he did, and when they catch up with him—" He felt her eyes on him in the darkness. "You ain't one of them, are you?" Her voice seemed to catch hopefully.

"An Avenging Angel? Nope. Not hardly. You mentioned Little Zion. Would that be a Mormon settlement hereabouts?"

"It would."

"And Zeke here took you away from there?"

"That's what the damn fool did all right. I was working in the fields this morning and he dragged me away when I went for water. I didn't get no chance to holler out or nothing. I just hope Elder Smithson understands I didn't go willing."

"And who might Elder Smithson be?"

"My husband," she said with unmistakable defiance.

The man on the ground stirred, lifted his shoulders, and groaned softly. His hat tumbled from his head and he turned a pale, bearded face with wide, angry eyes upon Longarm. "Damn you," he managed hoarsely. "I could have killed you and taken the mules. But I let you be."

"Next time, Zeke, you'll know better," Longarm said. He reached out. Zeke took his hand, and Longarm pulled him upright.

The man stood unsteadily, saw his hat on the ground, and reached for it. He was still so groggy that he almost went down again. He struggled upright, however, clapped the sad hat down onto his head, and looked at Longarm.

"I was just aiming to rescue my Sarah from them heathen devils, is all. A man ought to be proud of doing something as needful as that. The Lord ought to look down and bless his progress."

"The Lord looked down," said Sarah contemptu-

71

ously. "and he seen what you was doing and he stopped you. Twice."

Longarm looked at them without comment. The two of them were in the same traces, but they sure as hell weren't pulling in the same direction, and that was a fact. But they had the information he needed, and for that he was grateful.

"You two come on over to my camp here. We'll light a fire to get rid of this desert chill and maybe we can settle things like civilized people."

"Maybe," grumbled Sarah.

"I'm willing," said Zeke, rubbing the back of his shoulder. He was still a bit groggy from the fall and was probably anxious for time to pull himself together before he tried anything.

Longarm led the way back to his camp by the stream, lugging the rifle and noting its heft. The Hawken was a fine firearm and it seemed a shame that this fellow was going to lose it. But Longarm didn't see how he could give it back to the man.

Zeke told Sarah to hunt up some firewood and the girl responded with eagerness. The night chill was causing her to shake miserably, Longarm noted. Zeke stomped his boots unhappily and let Longarm light the campfire. Then they sat crosslegged around it.

"Keep the fire low," Zeke growled unhappily. "Them devils is out there a-hunting me now, I reckon." He grinned wolfishly at Longarm. "I got one of their women, I did. Right out from under their noses."

"We're pretty well hidden in this canyon," replied Longarm. "Now let's have your story. Who are you two, and what might you be doing skulking around stealing mules at this time of night, way the hell out here in the middle of nowhere?"

Zeke cleared his throat and glanced across the fire at Sarah. "Sarah's my bride-to-be and she was forced into one of them Celestial Marriages three weeks ago. They took her from me and I aim to take her back."

72

Sarah spoke up then. "I ain't his intended," she snapped. "That's his idea, not mine."

"But Sarah," Zeke protested, "you laid with me! We done made love three times in the barn and once out back of your pap's house during harvest time. And you told me then how you felt. How warm and good!"

"I always do feel good after," she retorted. "What you want me to say? That I hated it and didn't like it nohow?"

"But I thought—"

"I know what you thought. I shoulda knowed better than to lay with you, but a woman's got her itchin's just like a man and you was always hanging around slobberin' after me like a big, sad puppy dog and I took pity on you. That's the foolish truth of it and now I am getting my punishment for doing you a good turn."

"A good *turn?*"

She sighed, unwilling to continue the idiotic conversation, and Longarm did not blame her. In the flickering campfire her face grew alternately clear and dim, but what he glimpsed of her features was enough to set him to wondering at the lunacy of most adult-appearing men. He thought then of something Mark Twain had written pretty recently about Mormons. Back in Denver, old Wilson had read it aloud to Longarm. Mark Twain had visited Salt Lake City and seen how homely most of the women were. He submitted that anyone marrying one of them was doing an act of Christian charity, while the poor son of a bitch who marries sixty of them has done an act so sublime that the nations of the world should take off their hats to such a man and worship in dumb silence. That was putting it pretty mean, Longarm figured, but it wasn't too far off the mark. There was a cold severity in most of the women he had seen about the city that saddened him without his really knowing why he felt the way he did. And this young woman across from him at the moment seemed just as cold and practical, just as pinched and severe as all the rest of them. The poor fool that had

73

gone after her was a pure and silly romantic for sure, but the woman's cold and humorless way of looking at things seemed almost as bad. There was no softness, no gentleness in her at all.

Zeke looked across the fire at Longarm, his eyes wide and hurt, looking for all the world like a dog that has just been smartly kicked by its master. "I reckon I got Sarah all wrong," he said.

"Yes," Sarah sniffed. "You sure enough did. And now you got me in terrible trouble. I just hope when Elder Smithson catches up with you, he will let me explain that this purely wasn't my idea." She looked at Zeke hard, then. "And don't you dare tell him about us!"

"I'd be ashamed to," said the hushed suitor, pulling away from the mean fury in her gaunt face.

Sarah looked back at Longarm, her face triumphant. "And Elder Smithson *will* catch up to us. He's after me now, I'm sure. He liked me the best of his wives. I could tell that right away." She threw her shoulders back proudly. "Them others was all worn out and always clucking like a yard of hens, scratching and quarreling all the time until it like to made the elder cry. I told him he should take a switch to them."

"You want to go back to Little Zion?" Longarm asked.

She nodded eagerly.

"I'll take you back," he said. "You just show me where it is." He looked at Zeke. "I guess you just might be better off without your intended. You'd make tracks faster, and that's a fact."

Zeke glanced with disillusioned eyes at Sarah. "You just don't love me, do you, Sarah? You don't want to marry me."

"No I don't," the woman snapped.

The man looked back at Longarm. "You let me have my Hawken and I'll be on my way."

"What makes you think I'd trust you with a firearm? You tried to shoot me with it not so long ago."

74

"No I didn't," the man said wearily. "It ain't even loaded."

Longarm reached over and picked up the rifle. Zeke was right. He had gone after his beloved with an unloaded weapon.

"I got the balls and powder in my pouch," Zeke explained. "I just ain't had time to load it."

Longarm considered for a short moment, then hefted the rifle at the man. "Take it and make tracks," he said. "And don't look back."

The man got to his feet and looked unhappily down at Sarah. She did not even bother to return his look. She was, Longarm could see, infinitely weary of the man and his need for her. "So long, Sarah," he said, his voice constricted, as if he still couldn't believe she would prefer living in a harem to living with him. "I hope you'll be real happy at that place."

"I will," she snapped. "I was till you come along. Now git, afore the elder catches up with you and fixes you good. Next time, leave well enough alone." She flung a quick look up at him then. "Just because a woman lays with you, don't think it means anything grand or wonderful. She's more'n likely just scratchin' an itch. Jest like you."

The fellow nodded dumbly, backed out of the circle of firelight, then turned and hurried away through the darkness. As his steps faded, Longarm looked across the fire at Sarah.

"How far is Little Zion?"

"Felt like a hundred miles the way that man was dragging me along after the horses gave out." She shrugged miserably in the night chill and tried to move herself closer to the warmth of the fire. "If we could get to a high place, I could maybe point us in the right direction."

"How long would it take us?"

She shrugged. "The rest of the night and most of the day, I guess."

"We have two mules, don't forget."

75

She brightened. "That's right. We won't be walking."

Longarm looked up at the night sky. The moon was out of sight beyond the canyon wall, but it was full and bright. "We'll start now if you're willing."

She looked at him shrewdly. "What are you up to, mister? You ain't a Mormon, are you."

"No, I'm not."

"You just prospecting out here in all these rocks?"

"Maybe."

"You expecting some reward if you bring me back?"

"Maybe."

She shrugged. Obviously, all she cared about was returning to the settlement. Longarm stood up. With a weary sigh, Sarah stood up also and leaned over the fire for one last taste of its warmth. In the bright light of the campfire, her gaunt appearance and grim lines caused Longarm to wonder again at the devotion the foolish Ezekiel Bannister felt for this woman. That must have been some ride in the hay she had given him.

With Sarah riding beside him, they crested a ridge before noon the next day and caught sight of a dim figure far below struggling closer to the edge of the Great Salt Desert. It was Zeke. From the ridge Longarm could see far beyond Zeke out across the pale expanse of featureless desert to the dim line of the Central Pacific's tracks on the horizon. If Zeke could reach them, he could maybe flag down a train. He would never make it otherwise without a mount and in this heat—already blistering so early in the morning—he would have a difficult enough time just getting to the tracks.

Two lesser ridges loomed between Zeke and Longarm, the terrain formidable, the distance at least four miles. Only because of the shimmering heat that raised such hell with distances could Longarm be sure that the lone figure so far below was Zeke. What clinched it was the long rifle he was carrying.

76

"See him now?" Longarm asked.

"Yes, I see him."

"He's going to have a hard time making it back."

"That ain't my concern."

Longarm looked back at Zeke—and saw at once that he had already lost his chance to make it. A small crowd of riders broke out of a canyon and strung out in a line as they galloped toward him. Longarm saw Zeke pull up and turn. He began to run, then, but it was hopeless. He got just beyond a low finger of a rock and was getting down on one knee, probably to load and prime his Hawken, when Longarm saw him topple forward. He was still on his knees when the other shots caught him in the chest, sending him backward onto the sand.

Only then did the sounds of the shots reach Longarm. The echoes were feeble and lasted only a short while, and then the land was still—as still as the body lying on the sand before the riders. All of them were dressed in black and only one of them dismounted to inspect the dead man. It did not take him long, and he retreated to his horse, carrying Zeke's Hawken. At once the riders wheeled away and galloped back into the canyon and out of sight, leaving Zeke's body for the vultures.

Longarm looked at Sarah. "I guess the Elder Smithson found Zeke."

There was a thin smile on Sarah's face, a grim, cold gleam in her eye. She was satisfied that Zeke had been killed without blabbing anything about her to any of the Avenging Angels. She took pleasure, too, Longarm figured, in the neat, quick way that her people had rid her of a tiresome nuisance. Longarm found himself just a mite uncomfortable with the woman's total lack of feeling or understanding of what Zeke Bannister had felt for her.

"We could fire a shot," she suggested hopefully. "Let them know I'm here, safe with you."

It was pretty clear to Longarm what would happen

77

then. Those riders would make short work of him. They would never let him near Little Zion—not alive, anyway.

"They're well out of sight now," he told her. "And there's no telling how far they might be by this time. I'd just as soon keep going."

"All right," she said, looking at him curiously, "but could we stop in a little while? I need to rest up some. I've been going all night."

"As soon as we find a place with some water," he promised her.

The spot he found was cool enough, tucked well in under an overhanging rock shelf with a small pool fed by trickles of icy water oozing from cracks in the canyon wall. He checked the ground around the water hole for snakes before helping her down from the mule. He wasn't sure, but he had the odd sense that she clung to him a little longer than was necessary.

"I have to tend to some of my needs," she told him, straightening her dress. She looked uncomfortable and Longarm realized how very difficult it must have been for her to ride astride with all the clothes—not to mention the corset—she had on. "You ain't told me your name yet, mister. Don't you think we should be introduced proper?"

"Name's Long, ma'am."

"You can call me Sarah," she told him. She turned then and vanished in among the rocks.

He was about to yell after her to watch out for snakes, but didn't think it proper when she was in that kind of a hurry.

Longarm tended to the mules, lifting off their saddles and watering them. Then he hobbled them and made a dry camp under the rock overhang where it was coolest. He took care of a few things he had to tend to and then filled the canteens. By this time, Sarah was back.

She slumped down close beside him. Quite close.

78

Longarm was not able to move away from her without its seeming obvious, so he stayed put and handed her a canteen. She took it and swallowed the water down greedily, wasting a lot of it out of the sides of her mouth. She handed him back the canteen, then wiped her mouth with the back of her forearm. She looked at him. The water—or something—put a sparkle into her eyes.

"I told you," she said. "I knew Elder Smithson would send riders after me." She looked at Longarm then, her eyes alight with sudden warmth. "You better make sure no harm comes to me. I guess I'm your safe passage through these hills. So you be good to me."

He looked at her, astonished. She was wearing a long gray skirt, a gray bodice with a soiled lace frill on it about the neck and wrists, and a severe black bonnet. Her somewhat scrawny neck was encrusted with week-old dirt, her hair tied into a bun and securely out of sight under the bonnet. There was very little that was attractive about her. And if she meant what he could hardly believe she meant, he did not know whether to jump up and run or just sit there and die.

"You can just rest easy, ma'am," he told her uncertainly. "You're safe with me. I won't hurt you none. You got my word on that."

She caught the uncertainty in his voice and frowned, a little bit like a schoolmarm who just got the wrong answer to a cipher problem. His mistake now, Longarm realized, was in making her spell out what it was she wanted.

Sarah leaned her head on his shoulder. "That's not what I meant," she said, her voice a little breathless—a little desperate, perhaps.

She'd got the itch, Longarm realized in a panic. He decided he would just have to run. He got up quickly, excusing himself clumsily, and hurried over to one of the mules.

Sarah was after him in an instant. "You don't find

79

me attractive. Is that it?" she demanded, her pinched face white, her cold eyes laced with fury.

"Now I wouldn't say that, ma'am," Longarm protested, trying to sound as if he meant it. He turned his full attention to the mule then, patting his neck and pretending to examine one of his eyes.

But Sarah was seething by this time. "Oh, I know you men!" she cried bitterly. "You like only the pretty ones—always the pretty ones. The rest of us ain't supposed to have no feelings. But you try one of us in bed sometime, and you'll see! It don't take a pretty face to pleasure a man—not in the dark, not in a bed!"

"Ma'am, I do think this conversation has gotten a mite out of hand. I wouldn't want to shock you by continuing on with it."

"You're mocking me!"

Longarm sighed. "I suppose what you said is true at that, ma'am. Men do like a woman with pretty ankles and bright eyes. Ain't no harm in that, is there?"

"I suppose not," she snapped, "if *you're* the one with them pretty ankles."

"It's the way of the world, ma'am," he said, trying to mollify her.

"Well, it shouldn't be," she retorted. "And with us Mormons, that ain't the way it is. With us, it ain't how pretty a woman is. It's how good she is in the house and how she fits in with the other wives and how well she pleases her husband after a long day that matters." She paused and shook her head once for emphasis. "And with so many of us to a man, why, there ain't no chance for him to go off looking for a pretty face. He don't have the time. He don't have the energy!" She spoke this last with malicious triumph.

"And I guess maybe," Longarm suggested quietly, "you get some help with all that housework and them farming chores."

"Yes! That's right," she agreed, warming now to her topic. "Oh, I watched how my Ma had to struggle with a patch of nothing under that big Nebraska sky, how

80

it wore her down to a nubbin—and all for nothing. She never even bought a new dress in all the years I knowed her. And she was so lonely!" She shook her head. "At least this way we got help. We ain't lonely at all. And that fool Zeke Bannister wanted to take me away to some miserable shack in the middle of nowhere, so *I* could wear myself to a nubbin for *him!* Just like my poor Ma!"

"He just didn't understand," offered Longarm, careful not to arouse her again. "He loved you and didn't think much beyond that."

"No man does," she snapped. "Fools! Every one of them!" She glanced up at him then. "It ain't nice what happened to Zeke, and I wish it hadn't, I suppose. But I purely didn't need him buttin' in like that and ruining things for me with the Elders. That was a stupid thing he done, coming after me like that."

She frowned thoughtfully and looked away from Longarm. She was run down now, Longarm saw, and maybe letting herself feel at last what had happened to Zeke Bannister. He said nothing further to her and returned to the campsite.

She followed him back, a sullen, unhappy look in her eyes, and sat down opposite him. He handed her the canteen again. She took it and drank deeply. He did not watch her this time. When she handed the canteen back to him, he screwed the cap back on and then waited a decent interval before suggesting it was time for them to get moving again and went to saddle the mules.

When he helped her up onto her saddle this time, he noted that there was a cold, distant look in her eyes. Her hands did not linger on his as she took the reins he passed up to her.

A few hours later they were climbing a ridge she had promised would be a good spot from which to get further bearings. Longarm concentrated on the trail and tried to forget the heat. It had been powerful and

81

unrelenting, yet Sarah had not uttered a word of complaint. She was a formidable woman indeed. It was not a charitable thought, he knew, but he kept wondering if maybe those Avenging Angels hadn't done Zeke Bannister a favor.

"There!" Sarah called out, pointing.

It was close to dusk, and as far as Longarm could tell, the irregular pinnacle of rock Sarah was pointing to was just one more chimneylike projection among the dozens that reached up out of the barren, lifeless wilderness of rock on all sides of them.

"That rock over there," she said firmly. "We're nearly to Little Zion!"

Longarm lagged back as Sarah urged her mule on ahead of him.

Soon she found a trail that took them over a short rise and then along a rocky ledge, beyond which they came to a well-traveled trail that led into a narrow canyon. Longarm followed Sarah into the canyon. After a while he heard the sound of water rushing headlong. Rounding a bend in the canyon, they came upon a prodigious gush of water splashing down out of a great rent in the canyon wall. From a large pool beneath it a steady stream of water poured along the sloping floor of the canyon. So broad was this stream that in spots it filled the canyon completely as it rushed along, at times reaching the bellies of his mules.

At last, as they splashed along through the swift water, the canyon walls parted, the stream was caught in earthen banks, and Longarm found himself riding into a broad and surprisingly fertile valley. Everywhere he looked he saw green, lush fields gleaming in the hot sun and flanked by the inevitable Mormon irrigation ditches. The stream rushing from the canyon was tamed at once by a series of dams, from each of which a complex network of irrigation ditches reached out. It was an impressive accomplishment. Obviously the founders of Little Zion knew what they were doing.

82

In the middle of desolate badlands they had fashioned an Eden.

In the distance, well beyond the fields, Longarm could see a large cluster of weathered buildings with a windmill tower rearing skyward from their midst. In her eagerness, Sarah had ridden ahead. She turned and looked back at him, hauling in her reins.

"Well," she called back to him, "this is Little Zion. You better let me explain how come you're here. We been watched now for some time now, I'm thinking."

Longarm nodded and glanced back at the canyon walls. A lone figure was standing on the rim of the canyon, his body clearly silhouetted against the still-bright evening sky. He was carrying a rifle. Longarm looked farther along the rocky barrier that enclosed the valley and saw another man, this one crouched with binoculars before his eyes. Then from the canyon they had just left came the unmistakable clatter of shod hooves on stone as a company of riders followed after them through the canyon.

Longarm had expected this.

He turned back around in his saddle and urged his mule on toward Sarah. "I would be much obliged," he told her, "if you would impress upon your people how helpful I have been."

As he caught up with her, she surveyed him coldly. "I'll tell them only what I know; that you were in the barrens alone and that when Zeke tried to steal your mules, you stopped him. And that you were curious to learn where Little Zion was, so I brought you here. Why you were so curious, I ain't got no idea. But I figure you'll be telling our people soon enough." She smiled without warmth at him.

"Perhaps I would like to join your thriving community."

"You said you weren't no Mormon."

"Well, just maybe you and your friends might be able to convince me what a fine religion it is, after all." He smiled at her gently. "A poor sinner such as myself

83

could sure use a good set of directions on his way to paradise."

"You're mocking us! I can tell. But we Saints are preparing ourselves for a life everlasting! We'll be like gods in the hereafter. And here we're building for the resurrection and the coming Millennium! So you gentiles go on and mock us! That won't stop us none!" As she spoke her face became lit with a holy zeal; a fire gleamed in her eyes. She pointed suddenly to the fields around them. "See that! Like the prophecies told us—we're making the desert bloom! You just go ahead and laugh at that!"

"All right, Sarah," Longarm said carefully. "Just lead the way."

As they rode along a broad roadway flanking the fields, Longarm noted the number of women laboring diligently in them. The women worked stooped over, cultivating what appeared to be rows of corn with short hoes. The closer he and Sarah rode, the more curious the women became. Soon they halted their labor to peer cautiously out at them from under the beaks of their bonnets.

When Sarah was close enough, a few of the women hailed her in greeting. Sarah smiled and waved back at them, obviously glad to be with her people once again.

After about a mile, Longarm looked behind him. Again he was not surprised. Six riders, grim and unhurried, were pacing them a half-mile to the rear, content to let Sarah lead Longarm into their parlor. They were, Longarm was certain, the same riders Sarah and he had watched cut down without ceremony the luckless Ezekiel Bannister.

84

Chapter 4

Lorenzo Wolverton was the last elder to enter the room.

Longarm, sitting in a wooden chair before the long table with his wrists bound behind him, watched the man enter and then make his way deliberately to the table and sit down facing Longarm. The six other elders had grown absolutely silent the moment Wolverton entered. Now they waited respectfully for him to begin the questioning. But Wolverton was in no great hurry to begin, it seemed.

He was the tallest of the elders, and the oldest, apparently. His full head of hair was a clean, scrubbed white that fairly shone. He had no mustache, but wore a long beard that extended halfway down his chest. It was as immaculately white as his hair. The eyes that studied Longarm from under full, snowy eyebrows were a cold, icy green, the mouth above the patriarchal beard a grim, unforgiving line. His cheeks, however, were pink and unlined, giving his appearance an unsettling combination of purity and wrathfulness.

As Longarm took the measure of Wolverton, the thought occurred to him that for once he might have outsmarted himself. Riding boldly in like this and announcing his purpose in coming to Little Zion might have caught them off-guard for the moment, but Lorenzo Wolverton looked like someone who could eat the apple one bite at a time—and Longarm right along with it.

"I have your credentials here, Mr. Long," Wolverton

85

said, his voice powerful and deep without straining for that effect. "You were not lying. You are a Deputy U.S. Marshal, a minion of the federal government. And you have come here without apology to take from us one of our sisters—a young lady soon to join me in Celestial Marriage."

"That's right."

The man's eyes gleamed now with a powerful ferocity as he contemplated Longarm. "Already you have killed the brother of Elder Barker sitting beside me, and Jason Kimball, one of our people." He paused to let that ominous intelligence sink in. "I do not see how you could have expected to walk in here like this and escape with Emilie Boggs, unscathed." He smiled grimly. "You must have more imagination than that."

"Jason Kimball was killed by a young lady who mistook him for me. The sheriff tried to kill me without waiting for a trial. I shot him in self-defense. Emilie Boggs did not choose to join you in marriage, Wolverton, and my guess is that she has still not volunteered for that honor."

The elders on both sides of Wolverton stirred angrily at this assertion. A few bent their heads in angry conversation. Wolverton quieted them with a single withering glance, then looked back at Longarm, a flinty smile on his face. "Go on, Mr. Long. Speak out. Tell us more."

"I figure you're not butchers and kidnappers here, that you really do want to build a community that will last—and I also figure you're too sensible to think you can do it with stolen women. Now you let me take Emilie Boggs back to her family and it might turn out to be the smartest move the founders of Little Zion ever made."

Wolverton leaned forward, a slight smile on his face. "You do not understand us at all, Mr. Long."

"You can call me Longarm."

"Longarm, then. You are a gentile, an atheist. You believe in nothing except, perhaps, the gun at your

86

side which we took from you so easily. You believe in no miracles, no spiritual gifts. You do not see the Millennium coming, your eyes are blind to revelations."

There was murmured assent to this indictment all down the line as one after another of the elders nodded impassively. Longarm felt like a fish that had been left too long in the sun.

"We, on the other hand," continued Elder Wolverton, "have been blessed. The scales have been removed from our eyes. We await the Resurrection with confidence, the Millennium with certainty!"

Again there was a general murmur of agreement and a nodding of heads. Elder Wolverton had his congregation with him, all right.

"Emilie Boggs was revealed to me in a revelation! Her person appeared before me and in her eyes I read complete acceptance of the truth! It lives within her now, but she does not yet acknowledge it. The false doctrines of her father, of all the other benighted backsliders that surround him and that are poisoning the well of our Prophet's church have temporarily blinded her. But soon she will see as clearly as we do. Soon, of her own free will, she will join us in bringing the Millennium to pass!"

Longarm was surprised the elders didn't leap to their feet shouting hosannas. He had never heard a more eloquent defense of taking a woman against her will. But Longarm was not ready to laugh aloud at the man. He was evidently entirely sincere—as were the rest of the elders. Difficult though it was to believe, they saw nothing wrong in kidnapping Emilie Boggs.

"Think, Longarm," Wolverton intoned, his eyes lit with fervor, "what a salutory experience it will be for that apostate Boggs to learn that his beloved daughter has returned to the teachings of our Prophet—has accepted with glad heart the revelations that sustained us through cruel persecutions and exile—revelations that enabled us to outlast and defeat the despised gentile!"

Longarm leaned back in his chair. This kidnapping of Emilie, then, was as much a political move as it was a desire for the young woman to share his bed. The old fox was going to have it both ways, and Longarm found he had to respect revelations that could work things out as neatly as that.

The elder rose to his feet. The others hastily stood up also.

"Your education is incomplete, Longarm. One might almost believe the angel Moroni has sent you for this purpose." He smiled, enjoying himself hugely. "You will be put to work for Little Zion. You will haul water. You will bend your back under the hot sun. You will see how hard work and devotion to a cause can transform barren earth to fruitfulness. And we will see what you have to say then. Perhaps when Emilie Boggs joins me I will send you back to her father with the joyful news!"

He turned and strode from the room, the others following after. Longarm tried to get a good look at them, but they all looked so much alike with their straggly long gray mustaches he knew he would have difficulty distinguishing one from another if he met them outside.

As soon as the door closed after them, the two Angels standing behind him came forward and hauled Longarm roughly to his feet. Longarm turned on them angrily to protest. He shouldn't have. He was struck viciously on the crown of the head with the barrel of a sixgun and sent plunging into darkness.

Longarm found himself sitting up in a small, lightless room, his hands tied painfully behind him. Someone was poking a spoonful of hot soup at him. He winced painfully. His head was pounding mercilessly. Opening his eyes a painful slit, he tried to focus on the features of the woman who was feeding him. His eyes widened suddenly.

88

"Annie Dawkins! What in tarnation are you doing here?"

"Shh! Eat this and I'll tell you. You've been unconscious for most of the day!"

"What day is this?"

"Wednesday."

The day after his confrontation with the elders. Longarm looked up at the one tiny window. It was not large enough for him to get even one shoulder through, and was barred. Very little light was filtering in through it. "What time is it?"

"Past suppertime. I volunteered to feed you."

"Thanks." He opened his mouth and she shoved a spoonful of food into it. It tasted like a combination of beef and greens. It wasn't seasoned and tasted flat. But he was famished and grateful for the nourishment. His wrists were bound so tightly behind him that he no longer had any feeling in his hands.

"You didn't tell me what you are doing here," he told her when he finished chewing.

"Soon's that devil Jason saw me with Ma Randle, he just came after me that same night. Ma couldn't do a thing to stop him. He told me then that he was going after you later."

"You haven't seen him since, have you?"

"No I haven't." She poked another spoonful at him.

"And you won't. He's dead, Annie."

She nodded. "That's what I heard. Two of his other wives came to visit with me and they told me he wasn't coming back to Little Zion."

"To *visit* with you, Annie?"

"There's a place for them like me that don't really want to marry up with these Angels. They keep us there till we get desperate enough to go through with it. There's been a couple of men in to see me since I heard about Jason. They been sweet-talking me in hopes I'd join up with them. Even their own wives have been in to see me. They need help with the work." She shook her head at the thought as she fed Longarm.

89

"I guess I can sure understand that, Mr. Long. These woman really have to work out here. I never saw the like of it."

Longarm swallowed her last spoonful. Already he felt much stronger. "You're not weakening, are you, Annie?"

"Nope," she said firmly, sitting back and putting the dish and spoon beside her on the beaten-earth floor. He was aware suddenly of a foul-smelling chamber pot waiting for him in the corner and realized just how badly he needed to make use of it.

"Annie, could you please untie my hands?"

"I don't dare to, Mr. Long. They told me if I did, I'd really get it."

"Just loosen the knots, then. I won't make a break or anything for a long time and if anyone comes in after you leave, they'll see I'm still bound. But it'll give me a chance, Annie."

She didn't think about it for long. "All right, Mr. Long."

He turned around so that his back was to her and in a moment she had loosened the rawhide significantly. He turned back around and rested against the wall, letting the blood circulate into his hands. Pins and needles swept into both of them along with the flow of blood. He began to rub them briskly together, as much as their still-bound condition allowed.

"Thank you, Annie. And call me Longarm, if you want."

"All right."

"Annie, I'm looking for Emilie Boggs. Are they holding her nearby?"

Annie nodded. "Only she's not with us and the others. They don't even let her out to work in the fields."

"I've come for her, Annie."

She nodded. "I know. All of us know." She grinned. "You didn't make any secret of it when you rode in with that Sarah Smithson. What'd you think of her,

90

Longarm?" She smiled knowingly. "Ain't she a caution?"

"And a very hard woman, Annie."

Annie nodded in eager agreement. "We call her hatchet-face." She became thoughtful. "Longarm?"

"Yes?"

"Will . . . you take me out of here, too?"

"I'd like to, Annie. But it's Emilie I'm after."

"But I could help."

"You help me get Emilie and I'll come back for you, Annie. That's a promise."

She brightened for a moment, then went gloomy again. "But that'll take so long! I hate it here, Longarm! These men coming to see me are getting to look mighty good."

Longarm smiled at Annie. "Just think of those sunny fields out there, Annie. They stretch quite a ways."

She nodded unhappily. "You'll be working them soon, I hear," she said. "They was talking about that last night. All the women are waiting on you. They want to see how you take it." She smiled. "But I guess you got other plans."

"Will you help me get to Emilie?"

She nodded. "I reckon I will, Longarm. She's in a building like mine, near here. It's the smallest one, and it's fenced in so she can walk outside during the day. I'll tell her you're here and see if I can get you the key to the lock on her door."

"Can you do that?"

She nodded quickly. "I bring her meals most every day, and I know where they keep the keys."

"They've taken my Colt and Winchester," he told her.

"I know where they might be. In the building next door. The arsenal, they call it. But I couldn't get into that room. I just saw the door open yesterday when one of the Avenging Angels was leaving. He just rode in with a bunch of his fellows on some mean

91

errand, from the look of it. There sure were a lot of guns in there, anyway."

"Just get me the keys to Emilie's place, then."

Abruptly the door was flung open and someone was standing in the doorway. Not much light came in past the figure, since it was well into twilight by this time. Longarm looked up at the fellow, but could barely make out any of the features of his face.

"Let's go, whore!" the man replied. "You been in here long enough!"

Annie winced at his greeting, snatched up the spoon and dish, and scrambled to her feet. Without a further word to Longarm, she ducked past the fellow. He watched her go, then looked closely at Longarm, considered a moment, then entered the hut.

"I just better check to see if you're still trussed," he said, grabbing Longarm by the hair and pulling him away from the wall. As Longarm sprawled past him, he was careful to allow him a quick view of his bound wrists before rolling over painfully onto his side.

"Untie me, will you?" he complained. "I can't even use that pot over there, trussed up like this!"

"That's too bad," the fellow said.

In an excess of good feeling, he kicked Longarm in the side and sent him rolling in the general direction of the slops jar. Well-satisfied that Longarm was still securely bound, he turned and left the place. Listening carefully, Longarm heard him lock the beam in place across the door.

He sat up, his side throbbing miserably, worked his wrists loose and then, in a kind of half-stagger, made it to the pot.

It was close to midnight by Longarm's reckoning when he heard the padlock rattle outside his door. He moved back against the wall, stuck his hands behind his back and waited. The door swung wide and a small, chunky figure stole in, closing the door firmly behind him. With the door shut, the inside of the hut was as dark as an

92

Apache's heart; it was only the light from the moon that enabled Longarm to tell that his visitor was a male.

He felt the man looming over him in the darkness and told himself that if this fellow started lashing out with his foot, he'd take him apart right then. He had not yet heard anything from Annie and was unwilling to make a move this early since he was not certain she had yet had time to get to Emilie. So he kept his back against the wall and waited.

The looming shadow stirred, then shifted abruptly and appeared to sit down before Longarm on the dirt floor. "You're awake, ain't you, Longarm?" the fellow said.

"That I am. You know me, do you?"

"I know what you're called. We all do. And I know why you're here. It's Emilie Boggs, isn't it?"

"Yes, it is."

He took a deep breath. "Forget her! Damn it! There's more important business for you to do here! You've got to bring in Mordecai Lee!"

"Who the hell is he?" Longarm asked, but he remembered the name. He was one of the Mormon survivors of the Mountain Meadow Massacre, still at large.

"You know who he is. He was one of the leaders of the Massacre. You're after him, ain't you?"

"I told you. I'm here to return Emilie Boggs to her family."

The man did not reply for a long moment. "You must bring in Lee. He's wanted. That this man should still walk free is an abomination. I saw what he did. I was *there!*"

"Then you're just as guilty as he is."

"But I have repented. Every day since, I have gone down on my knees and begged forgiveness, but I know I am unclean. I know that for me there waits no celestial kingdom. I will go with the unclean liars, the adulterers, the murderers. My deliverance can come only after the Second Resurrection. I accept this will-

93

ingly! But that fool Mordecai Lee denies his guilt. He lives amongst us and is high in our councils! Little Zion cannot prosper under such a curse! Jesus will not listen to our prayers with this man at our side. You must take him from us—rid us of this abomination!"

"How many of you believe this?"

"None. I admit it, I am the only one who sees this. But I have had revelation. I see fire and destruction visited upon us all. And it is this one who brings it upon us."

"You were there, you say—at Mountain Meadow?"

"Yes. Yes, it was terrible. It was worse than that." His voice grew immediately low, somber, as if suddenly he was witnessing the scene once again in all its horror: "The men and the women and the children gathered around me as I entered their fortifications. They believed our promises and hailed me as their deliverer from the Indians. Their guns, I noticed at once, were mostly Kentucky rifles of the muzzle-loading style. Their ammunition was about gone. I do not think there were twenty loads left in their whole camp. If they had had more ammunition, I am sure they would never have surrendered to us, or believed our promises of safe passage . . . I hurried the women and children to the right, on by our troops. When the men left their fortifications, they cheered our soldiers. They believed we were acting honestly." The man stopped talking then, and Longarm was reluctant to start him up again. The picture forming in his mind was not a pleasant one.

"Higbee then gave the orders," the fellow said, his voice barely audible now. "He told his men to form in single file, to take their places, just as they had been instructed earlier—to the right of the settlers. It was my job to kill the sick and the wounded who were in the wagons. McMurdy and Knight were with me in this. We had been told not to shoot until we heard our troops firing on the men who had just marched out. McMurdy had a rifle. I drew my pistol. When we

94

heard the firing ahead of us, we knew it was our turn. McMurdy raised his rifle to his shoulder. He began to pray: *O Lord, my God, receive their spirits, it is for Thy kingdom that I do this."*

Longarm heard what sounded like a sob break from the man before him, but he kept his silence and waited.

"Then," continued the man, his voice now so low that Longarm had to strain to hear him, "McMurdy shot a man who was lying with his head on another man's breast. The ball, I am sure, killed both men. I went to the wagon. I had yet to perform my part in this. I cocked my pistol. Somehow—I can't remember to this day how it happened—the gun went off prematurely. I shot McMurdy across the thigh, my pistol ball cutting his buckskin pants. McMurdy turned to me and said, 'Brother, keep cool. You are excited. You came near killing me. Keep cool, I tell you. There is no reason for being excited.' " Then the man repeated this in a kind of sing-song. "No need to be excited . . . no need to be excited."

He gave a deep, shuddering sigh, seemed to straighten in the darkness, and went on, "Knight shot a man with his rifle, shot him in the head. Then he brained a boy who was about fourteen years old. The boy had come running up to our wagons, and Knight struck him on the head with the butt of his gun and crushed his skull. Soon we were busy. The Indians came up then to help us. One of them from Cedar City—we knew him only as Joe—caught a man by the hair and raised his head up and looked into his face. I saw the man shut his eyes a second before Joe shot him in the head. At last, when it was all over, and I reached where the dead men lay, Major Higbee told me proudly that the boys had acted admirably, that they took good aim and that all the damned gentiles but two or three fell at the first fire . . ."

The fellow stifled a sob. It seemed to Longarm that the man had bowed his face into his hands. When he spoke next, his words were muffled: *"At the first fire!*

95

All but two or three! And then Lee came riding up! He was excited and called it a victory! He cheered us all for a job well done!"

The man was silent for a long while. Longarm sat without moving, astonished and deeply disturbed by this eyewitness account of a tragedy he had heard about only in brief, disjointed accounts. In fact, there were many authorities, Longarm realized, who denied that such a thing had ever happened.

At last Longarm said, "I am not here to bring in Lee—or you, for that matter. I am sorry. Why can't you just walk out of here and tell your story to the federal authorities? Why don't you take Lee with you when you go?"

"I am a coward. I could not leave my family now. I have three wives, eleven children. I am trapped."

"I am sorry for you," Longarm said.

He heard as well as felt the man get slowly to his feet in the darkness. "You have not come for Lee, truly?"

"You heard me right."

"Your proposal that we let you take Emilie back has stirred discussion in our councils. I do not think we can convince Elder Wolverton to relinquish his prize, no matter how politic it might be to do so. He has his revelations. I have mine. But I will speak for your proposal as strongly as I can, though I see no hope for it. I am sorry, Longarm. If the vote goes against you, you will die here."

For a moment Longarm debated the wisdom of leaping upon the fellow and making his break. But he reminded himself that this was not the way he had planned it. He held himself in check and watched as the fellow stepped back out through the door. He heard the man shut the padlock and walk off into the night.

The night air was cold, and Longarm shivered. But it was not the chill from the night breeze that disturbed him; it was the chill that remained in the hut with

96

him as he recalled the Mountain Meadow Massacre and heard once again the words of that tormented elder as he retold his tale of horror.

Longarm was dozing fitfully a few hours later when he heard someone at the window. He scrambled to his feet and went to it. He heard Annie calling to him softly.

"I'm here," he answered through the dirt-encrusted window pane.

"I've unlocked the door. I slipped the key to Emilie's hut under it! Now remember! You said you would come back for me!"

"I will!"

As Annie moved off, Longarm hurried across the dirt floor, picked up the key, and pushed open the door. The moon was not as full as it had been the previous night, but it shone brightly enough in a clear, star-crowded sky. He saw the small, fenced-in house where Annie had told him Emilie was being held.

He reached into his crotch and took from it his derringer. Earlier, during the ride with Sarah while the woman was off among the rocks attending to her needs, he had fastened the small weapon to the inside of his thigh with the gold chain. At the time he had known he must find a better-than-usual hiding place for it. He had realized, once he had made the decision to use the woman as a guide to the settlement, that short of killing Sarah, there was no way he could keep her from informing her people, once she reached Little Zion, that he was skulking about in the area with two army mules. And since that left him no real chance for surprise, he had decided on the brazen approach—and the concealed derringer.

But now Annie's presence in Little Zion gave him a valuable edge. He hoped his breakout could be accomplished without gunplay. So far, it seemed, his gamble had paid off. He had little doubt that his ap-

97

parent stupidity in riding in so openly was the reason they had not guarded him more closely.

That thought cautioned him. Holding his derringer in readiness, he looked quickly around. Not a soul was abroad. The night was as still as death. From what Annie had told him, he guessed the hut next door served as this warlike community's armory. He darted across the narrow yard to the door of the hut and tried it. It was not locked. He pulled it open. Someone was sleeping on a cot next to the far wall. Above him were racks containing rifles of all descriptions. Pegs along another wall held enough gunbelts to outfit a small army. A lantern on a table next to the cot was flickering low, its chimney blackened. Longarm stepped into the small hut and closed the door. In the dim light, he saw the fellow on the cot stir restlessly.

Longarm crossed the room swiftly, and holding his derringer under the man's nose, shook him awake. The fellow came alert the moment he looked into the muzzle of the derringer, all the fight draining out of him.

"Don't shoot," he managed.

"Get up and turn around," Longarm ordered him.

The fellow scrambled to his feet and turned his back to Longarm. Holding the barrel of the derringer between his teeth, Longarm tied the man's wrists behind him with the same rawhide they had used on him. He pulled a heavy Colt from one of the holsters on the wall and rapped the Mormon's head under the base of the skull, not too hard. The man's knees gave out and he collapsed in a heap onto the floor.

Longarm lifted the man and dumped him back onto his cot, his face to the wall. He found a ratty blanket at the foot of the cot and covered the man from his shoulders down. Anyone looking in would think the man was asleep. Longarm searched through the room and found his Colt and rig lying on a table with his hat. It had been knocked off when he had protested their arrest of him.

98

He strapped on his rig and checked out the Colt. They had not bothered to empty it, and he still had on his person the shells he kept in his coat pocket. Next, he lifted down a Winchester like the one that had been in the boot on his mule, clapped his hat on, and slipped out of the building.

The moon was bright enough that the shadows cast by the buildings were quite dark. Longarm darted from one shadow to another until he reached Emilie's prison. He unlocked the door and a slight figure materialized out of the gloom within and flung herself into his arms.

"Are you Mr. Longarm?"

"And you'd be Emilie."

"Yes!"

"Your father sent me—like Annie must have told you. You ready to go?"

"Of course!"

He took her gently by the wrist and pulled her from the one-room hut. "Keep down," he told her as they ran across the moonlit yard toward the shadow of the windmill tower.

Once they had reached it, he pulled her down beside him. The road leading back to the canyon was a broad ribbon of moonlight less than a hundred yards from them. Longarm pointed it out to her.

"Wait for me on the other side of that road," he told her, "behind that clump of rocks. I've got to get the mules and maybe provide a little diversion. That large barn over there—is that the stables?"

She nodded.

"All right. Get going now and keep down behind those rocks. Don't you pay any mind to what happens. You just stay there. I'll come for you."

Holding her skirts well above her ankles, she ran swiftly across the yard toward the road. As soon as she had vanished safely in among the rocks, Longarm headed for the horse barn. Once inside, he began his search for the army mules. When he could not find

99

them, he concluded they had been appropriated by one of the elders, and selected two powerful roans instead.

He saddled them swiftly with saddles he found resting on the partitions between the stalls. Aware of how important a large supply of water would be, he collected a total of six canteens from three other saddles, strung them together with rawhide, and slung three over each of the saddle horns. He had worked as efficiently as he was able in the darkness and was reaching for a lantern hung from a nail when he heard voices and the sound of men walking past the stalls toward him.

He turned as two men materialized out of the gloom.

"That you, Alf?" one of them asked.

"Where the hell you going with them horses?" the other drawled.

"Going for a ride," Longarm replied, as he pulled the Colt from his holster and leveled it at the two men. There was enough light for both men to catch the gleam of Longarm's gun barrel.

"Jesus!" the first one said. "It's that damn fool Deputy U.S. Marshal!"

"Yes," Longarm replied, "and he's got a Colt centered on your belly button. Just stand easy." Both men were too astonished to say much. Longarm frisked them swiftly. Neither one of them was carrying sidearms.

Longarm stepped back. "Get on past me to the rear of the barn. You're going to be a great help in a minute or two."

"Help? What do you mean? We ain't going to help you!"

"You'll see." Longarm waggled the barrel at them and they moved past him.

He herded them into the feed room and placed a beam against the door. They would be able to dislodge it, but it would give them a battle. Then Longarm went back to the lantern, lifted it down from the wall, and

100

lit it. He turned the wick up all the way, then tossed the lantern up into the loft. He heard the chimney shatter against a beam. As smoke began to coil down out of the loft, he hustled from the barn, leading the two horses.

The men inside the feed room began shouting. Longarm swung into his saddle and galloped across the compound toward the roadway. "Fire!" he yelled, shooting twice into the night. "The barn's on fire! Save the horses!"

Reaching the rocks, he pulled to a sliding halt in front of them and waited as Emilie raced out and tried to swing into the saddle. But she was too firmly corsetted and could not ride astride. As dark figures began racing from the buildings toward the barn, Longarm dismounted and told Emilie to get out of her corset. She was aghast, but pulled off her dress, then her petticoat. She turned her back to him and he ripped at the lacings on her corset and yanked it brutally off her. She gasped, then laughed nervously as she climbed back into her dress, leaving the petticoat and corset on the ground. In a moment she was astride her horse and the two were galloping down the road away from the rising clamor behind them.

Glancing back as they reached the fields, Longarm saw the roof of the barn just catching fire. The flames were leaping skyward, making the yard and the buildings surrounding it as bright as day.

"The poor horses!" cried Emilie.

"I left two men inside. They'll take care of the horses, I reckon." Even as he glanced back he saw the horses crowding frantically out of the barn, the two men driving the animals before them. Others were rushing into the barn for the remaining horses, and a bucket brigade was forming swiftly. Longarm could hear the frantic shouting as men issued orders and others tried to prevent the spooked horses from stampeding out of the compound.

As a diversion, his fire was working perfectly. But

101

he did not know how much time it would buy, and he would much rather have found the mules. Over the terrain they had yet to negotiate, those two army mules would have been more than sufficient. The two horses they were riding seemed hardy enough and were the best he had been able to find in the barn, but they would have to be babied if they were to go the distance.

Even then, it would be shaving it a mite too close for comfort.

Through the night they rode, Longarm having filled all six canteens when they rode through the canyon. Emilie explained the fountain gushing from the wall of the canyon as the work of Elder Wolverton. A revelation had told him that a source of unlimited water—enough to transform a small stream into a broad river—could be obtained at that spot after he had seen a small trickle oozing through a crack in the canyon's wall. Dynamite had done the rest. It was this proof of the infallibility of his revelations that had given Wolverton the leadership of Little Zion.

Daybreak found them riding into a narrow draw. Again Longarm used the presence overhead of birds to tell him whether a stream could be found within it, and again he was right. The two of them pulled up wearily and dismounted. Longarm hobbled the horses after letting them drink their fill at the stream, and then they set up their camp in the shade of a small clump of juniper.

"We'll have to keep going," Longarm told Emilie. "But the horses need this rest, and so do we, I reckon."

"I certainly do, Mr. Longarm," she replied.

"Just call me Longarm, Emilie."

She nodded and he looked her over. She reminded him of her sisters as well as her father. She had his long, patrician features and her eyes had the same appealing wide-eyed quality. Her hair was light. Done tightly into a bun under the bonnet she was wearing, errant strands of it had come loose during the ride and

102

now poked out from under the beak. The skin over her cheekbones was taut and smooth, her mouth firm, her chin strong.

She felt his eyes on her and began to do what she could to smooth her appearance. The dress was a mess and he remembered she no longer wore her corset or petticoat under it. It didn't seem to matter much. She was still as slim as a sapling.

"Sorry we had to get rid of your corset like that," he told her, smiling slightly.

"Oh, please, Longarm. To get out of there, I would gladly have emulated Lady Godiva, I assure you."

"No need for that, Emilie. You'd get a terrible burn in this country."

She laughed appreciatively. "Anyway, it is no chore to ride without that tiresome corset. I do think we wear them too tightly nowadays. I'm never comfortable, really, unless I'm in my nightclothes." She blushed suddenly, aware of what she was saying.

He grinned at her. "Guess I can understand that," he said. "I sure wouldn't want to go around tied up inside one of those things."

She frowned. "Are we safe now, Longarm?"

"Far from it, I'm afraid. We've got a ways to go yet, and most of it in daylight."

Longarm looked over at the horses. They had held up well enough, so far. But he was sure they would begin to wilt under the fierce heat this land generated. He decided he would let them set their own pace as long as their pursuers—and he was certain they were now closing fast—were not on their tails visually. His plan was to reach the desert around nightfall and then make a run for it through the night. If they could reach the water tower by daybreak, he was sure he could hold off his pursuers until a Central Pacific train arrived. The approach of a train would, by itself, insure that the Avenging Angels would have to pull back. A train-load of witnesses was the last thing Wolverton and his Saints would want.

103

He looked back at Emilie. In the first light of day she looked incredibly fresh, her eyes glowing with the excitement of their escape. Longarm did not want to see that look fade or that excitement turn to despair. In that instant he realized that it no longer mattered that he was here because the federal government sent him. He wanted to see Emilie Boggs leave this place because it was what she wanted. And that was all that mattered.

"Let's go," he said softly. "We've got a long ride. For now, let's just let the horses find their own pace. We can't push them. Not yet, anyways."

"I understand, Longarm."

And as he got to his feet and started for the horses, he knew that she did, indeed, understand.

Time was a searing sun boring first into their eyes, then drilling holes in the tops of their heads. They rode slowly, saving the horses, through the same broken land he and Sarah had covered the day before—a rocky, scrambling, treacherous place, with the skeletons of dead junipers gleaming in the sun. The earth was cut by winding, sheer-walled draws, deceptive and deadly as pitfalls. Flat-topped buttes propped up the sky on all sides of them. Carved by the wind and sand, rocky projections loomed menacingly over them as they rode by, resembling hunchbacked gargoyles, misshapen monsters frozen in the terrible glare of the sun.

Buzzards circled overhead, hopefully, it seemed. He tried not to notice their shadows as the buzzards passed between them and the sun, but they did have a way of making Longarm nervous. There were times when the buzzards seemed to know more than a man did. He hoped this wasn't one of those times.

They rode on, heads down, the sun beating mercilessly upon them. The air itself seemed to sear Longarm's cheeks. Only it was not the air; it was windborne sand. By midafternoon a hot wind had come up. His eyes became scorched and grainy. He looked over

104

at Emilie. She was trying to ride beside him, but kept falling back. The freshness was gone from her face, her eyes were slits. He had given her his bandanna and she wore it now, tied about the lower portion of her face, but her nose looked raw, and he wished he still had the goggles he had worn when crossing the Salt Desert.

He looked back to the trail before him, what there was of it. Only occasionally could he see dim signs of wagon tracks, but they were persistent and he never failed to find new tracks as long as he kept going. When he thought of what those Mormons back there had gone through to stock and supply their earthly paradise in the beginning, he felt a grudging respect for their tenacity.

"Longarm!"

He swung about in his saddle. The roan she was riding had halted, shuddering from neck to flank, head down and trembling. White ropes of lather dripped from his mouth. He hadn't realized how far gone her horse was.

Longarm pulled up. "We'd better rest them," he said, "but I was hoping for some shade, some grass, and some water."

Emilie dismounted. The horse seemed to appreciate that and straightened somewhat. Longarm dismounted, emptied some water from his canteen into his hat, and held it under the roan's mouth. The horse emptied the hat in a twinkling and then almost knocked his hat from his hands in his eagerness for more.

"Just hold it a mite," Longarm told Emilie's horse. "I got to tend to your partner over here."

When he had taken care of his own mount, Longarm led both horses into the shade of a rock outcropping, loosened their cinches and lifted off their saddles. The horses seemed to heave enormous sighs of relief. Then he and Emilie sat down with their backs against a rock. Though its face was now in the shade, it was still quite warm from the sun's rays it had absorbed earlier.

105

"Do you think we'll make it?" Emilie asked. Her eyes no longer held that excitement they had exhibited before.

"If we find water soon, and if—" Then he looked at her and realized he was singing the wrong tune for this time of day. He laughed. "I reckon it won't do us any good to cross our bridges before we come to them. We'll make it. And that is a promise."

She took a deep breath and leaned her head back against the rock. "I believe you, Longarm. But even if we don't, I want you to know that even this is better than waiting in that terrible hut for that Elder Wolverton to visit me."

"He didn't hurt you, did he?"

"If you mean did he touch me, force himself on me—no, he didn't do that. But he *imposed* himself on me. He harangued me mercilessly, read endlessly to me from the Book of Mormon. And then—when all that was to no avail—he got on his knees before me and pleaded with me, begged me to—" She stopped herself suddenly, unwilling to go on, but quite obviously as appalled by the memory of it as she had been at the time it happened. "I am sorry," she said. "I suppose I should not have revealed that to you. It must be very distressing for you to contemplate the indignities I suffered at their hands."

"It is."

She looked at him and frowned. "I suppose I should have had pity on the man. He seemed in such dire need of me—of the love he craved from me. But I would be his fourth wife—and I am so certain that he must have told every single one of them the same thing." She shook her head in sudden perplexity. "How can a man that old, with that many wives to ease him, still be so needful of a woman?"

"Begging your pardon, Emilie, but I wouldn't want to shock you."

"I want to know, Longarm. It puzzles me deeply. Elder Wolverton seemed in great distress."

106

"Well, now," Longarm began hesitantly, "seems to me a lot of his problem might be a craving for variety, so as to keep his juices up, if you know what I mean. I guess some old folks just don't like to think they really are old. And like I heard tell once or twice, there ain't nothing that makes a man young again quicker than a young girl, if you'll pardon the expression, so to speak."

She laughed. "You are *so* circumspect, Longarm! It's really quite charming! But honestly, you know, you are not talking to a nun. I am a healthy, intelligent woman who knows a great deal about life—and appreciates every bit of it!"

"That's right sensible, Emilie."

"Yes," she said firmly. "It is. And that's why that old man . . . disgusts me so, may the good Lord forgive me for my lack of charity."

"I reckon He will, Emilie. He's let people go for lots worse, I hear."

She laughed at that and leaned her head impulsively on his shoulder. He liked very much the gentle feel of it and would have preferred to stay in that position until hell froze over—or at least until the sun went down—but he knew they had to keep going.

Gently, he straightened himself. She lifted her head from his shoulder and looked at him.

"Must we go so soon?" she asked.

Longarm nodded. "We've got to keep ahead of our friends, Emilie. They can afford to change mounts and press us hard. They've even got two army mules of mine to really make it tough on us."

He pushed himself erect, reached down, and helped Emilie up. She insisted on helping him saddle the horses, and in the sweltering heat he was grateful for her aid.

They mounted up and rode on for about an hour before Longarm's horse snorted and stomped.

"Smells water," Longarm said, turning back to the girl. "Must be just ahead."

Pure relief flooded the girl's face.

They rode around a bend in the trail they were following and saw the red mud bank of a water hole fed by a thin trickle of water lacing down the polished side of a rock face. They dismounted, filled their canteens, and watered the horses, then mounted up and rode on, the horses now moving at a shambling lope. The rock forms moving past them shimmered in heat waves like coals in a stove. The hot wind blew drifting streamers of dust at them. Longarm kept his head down, his eyes narrowed, but he could not keep the grit out of them. They stung powerfully. Red sand was piled in ribbed dunes against the bleached bones of downed junipers.

Misshapen hulks of rock shoaled out of the earth, their surfaces pitted, potholed. The horses stumbled going around them, their shod hooves sliding whenever they tried to cross them. It was tedious going and the horses, Longarm now began to realize, were not going to make it to sundown. And yet they had to keep going.

Surprisingly, it was his horse that went first. Without warning, the horse shuddered and pulled up, head hanging. Wind wheezed from its exhausted lungs on a curiously high note, and the animal crumpled under him. Longarm swung free and landed on his feet beside the horse as it crashed heavily to the ground. The horse lifted its head, then fell back.

As Emilie hurriedly dismounted and stood beside him, he told her, "Best thing I can do is pull off the bridle and loosen the cinch. If he gets his feet under him again, he'll be free of the saddle, anyway."

She nodded, her eyes filled with compassion for the suffering animal.

When he had finished seeing to the horse, he instructed Emilie to sit behind the cantle on her mount while he rode in the saddle. They started up again with her cheek resting against his back, both arms snug around his waist. Despite the discomfort both of them felt because of the heat, Longarm felt surprisingly gentled by this arrangement.

Not long after, the impact of the sun's rays lessened

108

as the buttes now continually passed between them and the lowering sun. Soon Longarm found that the trail they were following had descended to the level of the Salt Desert. The dark, highly polished rock formations shouldering out of the ground were lower, less pocked from the wind and sand. Glancing down at these boulders as he rode past them, he was reminded that he was traveling over what had once been the beach of a vast inland sea. He could almost imagine the restless waters rushing between and over these rocks, smoothing them out, polishing them, while gulls and sea birds of another age rested upon them.

Within sight of the desert, Longarm pulled up. Off to his right, less than half a mile away, he saw a few small buzzards wheeling about a vaguely familiar rock formation. What little was left of Zeke Bannister was providing some nourishment still for the younger buzzards. It was a reminder of what would be waiting for him if he did not succeed in outdistancing his pursuers, and it made him somberly thoughtful on the loss of his mules, especially when he considered the condition of the horse under them at the moment.

He urged the horse into the shadow of some rocks and dismounted, Emilie slipping off the horse first to give him room to swing his leg over the cantle. She smiled wearily up at him as he began to loosen the cinch.

"Is it much farther? I was in a wagon when they brought me to Little Zion. Seems to me I remember a long journey over very flat ground. From the taste of salt in the air, I assumed it was the Great Salt Desert."

Lifting off the saddle, Longarm nodded. "You were right, Emilie—and it's waiting out there for us now. We still got a ways to go."

She peered then at what she could see of the vast salt expanse that extended unbroken as far as the horizon. She appeared to shudder.

"Don't worry," he told her. "If those men after us don't force me, we'll wait until dark before venturing

109

out onto it. There's a water tower on the Central Pacific tracks. We'll make for that."

"How far is it?"

"About thirty miles, I reckon."

"Do you think this horse can carry us that far?"

He looked at her for a long moment, then decided he would lie. "If we don't push him and give him all the rest he needs now. And maybe we can take turns riding him."

That seemed to satisfy her.

He turned his attention back to the horse—and her question returned to him with renewed force. The horse was streaked with dried lather and both his eyes were inflamed from the windblown sand and were running. The saddle-slick on his back was close to becoming one enormous sore. They had rationed their water and he had at least two canteens still set aside for the horse. He asked Emilie for his bandanna, then poured some water into it and squeezed it out onto the horse's slobbering lips and tongue until there was no more moisture left in the bandanna. Then he repeated the process until the horse was able to accept tiny doles of water directly from the canteen. When the horse had finished what was left in the canteen, Longarm hobbled him and let him find what grazing he could on the sparsely covered ground in among the rocks. On tottering legs the horse followed his nose.

By this time Longarm noticed how chilly it had grown. The suddenness of it warned him and he looked back the way he had come, to the west, and saw the long black curtain of a cloud that had drawn itself over the sky, like the wing of some monstrous bird. At about the same time he heard the distant muttering of thunder. Flecks of lightning gleamed in the bowels of the cloud. It was moving with desperate speed and the wind had changed direction. As if it too were confused, it began stirring up wicked dust devils, swirling tiny grains of sand up into their faces. Emilie had been standing beside him when the wind sprang up. She

110

looked at him in dismay. He reached out for her and she buried her face in his shirt. He held her close and moved as close to the rock face as he could, shielding her as best as he could from the sudden fury of the wind.

The chill that came with the storm was surprising in its intensity. Both of them had been wringing wet with sweat from their day's journey through the blistering sun. Now they both shivered from the cold as their wet bodies felt the descending chill. Thunder cracked overhead now. Longarm looked up. The cloud was almost directly overhead. White tendrils were reaching down. Just behind the leading edge of the cloud, he saw a dusty, hazy curtain being dragged along. Rain. Long, lashing tendrils of rain.

There was another crash of thunder and this time it was accompanied by a blinding bolt of lightning—and then another, and still another. The thunder came now in deafening detonations barely seconds apart with the lightning keeping the ground around them bathed in a wildly eerie, almost continuous blue glow. Longarm glimpsed the horse struggling against its hobbles, neck distended, eyes wide in terror, a couple of yards away. It was obviously whinnying frantically, but Longarm could hear nothing except the ceaseless crashing of the thunder.

Emilie cowered against him as both leaned into the rock face for support. And then the rain was upon them. They heard it crashing down upon the hard ground moments before it reached them, sounding like a great faucet had been turned on. At first the rain just stung, then it grew in intensity, causing Emilie to cry out in pain. He bent over her still more, taking as much of the brunt of the lashing rain as possible on his shoulders. He found it difficult to catch his breath, so heavy was the downpour. It was almost as if they were both under water. He heard Emilie gasping for air and pulled back from the rock face to give her a chance to breathe.

111

And then—almost as swiftly as it had begun—the rain slackened. Drenched completely, Longarm stepped away from the rock and looked around. The horse was some distance from them, but apparently none the worse for his scare. The rain still pounded down and in fact the water on the ground was up past his ankles, but the thunder and the lightning had swept on. A cloudburst, he muttered to himself, was a real fine way to describe these sudden, demented downpours.

Emilie was shivering, her teeth chattering. "Well," she said. "First I was too hot, now I'm too cold. Some country, this, Longarm."

"I guess I'll just have to agree," he said, admiring her spunk. "I'll see if I can find anything dry in the saddle roll."

He knelt by the saddle and undid the bedroll. A worn soogan was still dry on the inside. He threw it over Emilie's shoulders and soon she was no longer shivering. Then he sat down on a rock while the muddy water swirled about his ankles and watched her. She leaned back against the rock face, the soogan wrapped closely about her, only her face and head sticking out. The water was almost over the tops of her high-heeled, high-button shoes.

"Will this slow them down, do you think?" she called through the heavy rain.

"It should. A cloudburst like this can make those narrow atroyos pretty dangerous. We're lucky it caught us down here."

"Lucky!" She laughed and pulled the soogan tighter about her neck.

In an hour or so the rainfall had become a drizzle that gave way to a shower. The thunder became only a barely audible mutter in the east, the lightning just occasional flashes in the distance that lit up the belly of the storm clouds as they moved on to Salt Lake City.

112

And then the dying rays of the sun transformed the world for a few brief moments before night fell.

They saddled up and rode out onto the Great Salt Desert.

Chapter 5

They were a couple of miles out, at least, when Emilie asked him, "Does it ever end? It just seems to go on forever!"

Her cheek was resting against Longarm's still-damp shirt. He had packed away behind the cantle his sopping jacket and vest. The moon had come up, flooding the desert with its pale, somewhat bluish light. Though Longarm was used to the sight by now, for Emilie it was evidently a brand-new experience.

"Didn't you get a chance to see any of this when they took you to Little Zion?"

He felt her lift her head from his back to speak more easily. "No. Two men sat beside me inside the wagon and wouldn't let me look out once. But I knew we were riding over the Salt Desert. I could taste the salt in the air." He felt her moving her head as she looked all around. "Is that all it is—just table salt?"

"There's clay mixed with it, but not enough to kill the whiteness of it. The glare is fierce in bright sunlight. That's why it's better that we travel across it at night."

She nodded and rested her cheek against his back again, her arms tightening slightly around his waist. This action caused a slight protective urge to stir within him again. He didn't mind it all that much, but it reminded him that he would find it difficult if things went wrong to treat this as just another assignment.

114

And things could always go wrong; they had a habit of doing just that.

They were heading southeast by Longarm's reckoning and he had expected to catch sight of the Central Pacific's tracks before this. More than once they had had to skirt large puddles of water left by the storm. Riding through brine would raise hell with the horse's hooves, and as it was the ground was damp enough as a result of the rain to have caused the horse to stumble more than once as its feet broke through the dry crust. All that Longarm felt he could hope for now was for the horse to last at least until they were within sight of the tracks.

Abruptly, Longarm pulled up. The horse obeyed the reins, slowly, woodenly. He felt it tottering slightly under them. Ahead of them was a large pool of water left by the cloudburst. Moonlight flecked its smooth surface. They would have to go around.

"I'd better get off again," Longarm told Emilie, "and lead this feller a while."

Her muffled assent came to him and he felt her slide off the horse. He swung down and then held the horse while she mounted again. As soon as her feet were secure in the stirrups, he led the horse north, looking for an end to the sudden pond.

Twice within the next hour his boots broke through the salt crust into the water-softened mud beneath. Each time he was forced to use some of the precious water left in his canteen to wash off the brine. Otherwise, he knew, it would dry and soon eat through his boots. By the time he succeeded in skirting the water, he had traveled some distance due east, which meant they had not gotten much closer to the tracks. Cutting southeast again, he noticed how tardily the horse responded to his lead. He glanced back at the horse. His head was drooping. Long tendrils of foam hung from his mouth and striped his chest. He was trembling from withers to hocks.

"You'd better get off," Longarm told Emilie.

She swung off the animal just in time, as the horse went down onto his knees, then toppled sideways. Twice he struggled to regain his feet, his head and neck craning desperately. Then he gave up. Longarm was not surprised, and felt more than a touch of compassion for the horse. He had lasted a good deal longer than Longarm had expected he would, and his only concern now was that the animal not suffer unduly.

He loosened the cinch as he had with the other horse and took off his bridle. If he did manage somehow to get up, he just might make it back to the badlands and water. If he did, of course, and his condition told their pursuers what they wanted to know, that was just too bad. He could not see himself shooting the animal on the strength of that possibility alone. He reached over and pulled the Winchester out of the saddle boot.

Slinging the remaining two canteens over his shoulder, he turned to Emilie. "All we can do now is keep moving until we reach the railroad tracks."

Emilie just nodded as she took her place alongside Longarm. As she trudged beside him, she glanced back a couple of times at the horse. Soon he was lost in the luminous darkness, and then she kept her eyes forward, peering like Longarm into the moonlit, ghostly emptiness of the desert.

Dawn—then full daylight—found them walking across what seemed an ever-broadening expanse of blinding nothingness. They were flies crossing an immense tablecloth. The sun was a fearsome spider whose shimmering web they were trying desperately to escape. A constant wind blew out of hell, driving fine salt granules into their faces, down their necks, into every exposed crack in their clothing.

Though they had been extremely careful in their use of the remaining canteens, they were unable to keep the salt out of them; and soon this water not only failed to slake their thirst, it increased it. Longarm

116

suggested that they use what remained to cool their necks and wash the salt from their faces. Emilie accepted this without protest and kept on. He was amazed at her stamina. She was matching him stride for stride.

After a while she moved close to him and began talking in a low whisper. Since the only sound was the gentle slap of their feet on the salt surface, he could hear her without difficulty. He wanted to discourage her from wasting the energy that she expended in conversation. But she seemed to need to talk. It was as if she were afraid there would be no time for conversation if they waited much longer, and she felt a need to make a few things clear to him.

She insisted that she was as good a Mormon as Elder Wolverton, that she too had read and studied the Book of Mormon. She believed without question that the angel Moroni had appeared before the prophet Joseph Smith, and that he had died a martyr for all of them. Emilie's grandparents on her father's side had pushed handcarts from Iowa City all the way to Utah and had been among the first to settle in Salt Lake City.

"I can understand," Emilie said, "why plural marriages might have been needed in the beginning to help populate this empty land, but as father says, its usefulness is long since over. We can't expect to join the Union with this practice condoned. Besides, I don't like it—and I don't know many women my age who do."

"I met one who was all for it," Longarm commented dryly. "She was the one who led me to Little Zion."

That silenced Emilie for a while and she trudged along beside him without speaking for some time. At last she sighed. "I've been trying to think why I don't like it," she said to him. "Perhaps I *am* selfish, just as the elder told me I was. But it is something else too."

"And what might that be?" he asked, squinting down at her through the glare.

"I want it to be like it was with my mother and father. There was no one else for either of them. They

117

had no time for anyone else, and now that mother is dead. she is still enough for my father. They loved each other very much, and we live by the warmth of that love still, my sisters and I. But how can such a love develop among three or four people? Or even five? How can there really be any closeness? It's just an . . . arrangement, a convenience."

"Not very romantic at that," Longarm commented, smiling despite the heat and the awesome dryness of his face.

"Besides," Emilie continued, her voice hoarse now, but straining with eagerness to express herself to Longarm, "I want to choose my own husband, not have someone choose him for me. I want to have *my* revelations." She smiled up at him then, a brave effort indeed, considering how blistered her pale face had become from the heat.

"Well now, I reckon you will have, sure enough."

"If we can just keep on walking. Is that right, Longarm?"

He placed his hand in the small of her back and gently supported her as she walked. She had begun to stumble. "That's right, Emilie. If we can just keep on picking them up and laying them down."

She said nothing for a long while, and then sighed wearily. "Oh, Longarm, where *are* those tracks?"

"Just ahead," he told her. And he meant it.

For some time he had been denying the evidence of his senses. His tortured eyes had seemed to be torturing his brain, feeding him evidence of something out there on the horizon when all the while it was only another mirage, another shimmering lie. But this time he was sure of what he was seeing. The tracks seemed suspended in midair, but there was no mistaking the telegraph poles and the gleaming wires strung between them. The distortion caused by the heat mirage caused the poles and even the lines to appear uncommonly outsized for long moments at a time. But the tracks

118

remained, fading at times, then looming toward him—but remaining always, persisting.

"Yes!" Emilie cried. "I see them! I see them!"

They both pulled up then and took a deep breath. They still had a long way to go yet, though the distortion caused by the heat created the illusion that the tracks were much closer than they were. Nevertheless, they had something solid now toward which they could move.

"I tell you," Longarm confided in Emilie as he started up, "for a while there, I had the foolish notion I wasn't moving at all. My legs were going and I was leaving tracks, sure enough—but everything else was standing still and laughing at me."

Emilie laughed. "I know," she said. "That's just how I felt."

They walked on for what seemed another hour at least. The sun that had been searing the backs of their necks was sitting atop their heads. The glare had increased to such a level that they no longer tried to see through it to the tracks. It was when Emilie staggered for the third time and he reached out to steady her that he noticed something to the right of her.

"What's that?" he asked, peering into the glare.

She looked but did not reply, and he did not need her guess. He knew. It was just a crowd of moving dots for now, but soon enough he would see the individual riders. Longarm and Emilie stood there and waited for what seemed like an eternity, peering into the shimmering glare. At last the riders became separate images wavering in the heat. Abruptly, it seemed, they appeared enormously large, grotesquely misshapen as they loomed out of the trembling air. Longarm heard the jingle of their bits.

"Oh, Longarm!" Emilie cried. "It's them! They have caught us!"

"Get down," Longarm told her.

As Emilie dropped to the desert floor, Longarm

119

pulled out his Colt and fired into the air. The reverberation from his single shot was stunning in its intensity. The sound of it rolled like a cannon shot over the gleaming desert.

The riders pulled up in a sudden confusion of horses and men. Longarm heard discussion, but could make little of it. He heard the unhappy whinnying of impatient horses. And then at last someone disengaged himself from the crowd of men and horses and started to walk toward them, the curtain of heat causing him almost to disappear at times.

For a long while he walked and then, suddenly, he was in full sight, as clear as an etching, a white handkerchief attached to the barrel of his rifle. As he walked closer, Longarm saw riders pulling away from the group, spreading out to encircle him. The fellow continued toward Longarm.

"It's Elder Wolverton!" Emilie cried.

"Stop right there!" Longarm called.

The elder pulled up obediently. "We've been following your trail for miles," he called. "Now we're between you and the tracks and in a moment you will be surrounded! Surely you must see the futility of your present position."

"It ain't futile as long as I got this Winchester and sixgun."

"There are more than two dozen men at my back, Longarm. You'll get some of us, but we'll surely get you."

Longarm could not deny the logic of Wolverton's assertion. With his rifle he could keep them well back, but they had rifles also. And in this blasted heat and glare, he could not be sure of distances. It would be like shooting smoke. They would have the same difficulty, but it would be madness to think he could outshoot all those men now encircling him.

And in such an exchange the chance of Emilie taking a bullet would be alarmingly high. Longarm assumed that the reason the Avenging Angels hadn't al-

120

ready opened up on him as they had on Zeke Bannister was the presence of the elder's bride-to-be.

Still, Longarm liked to play poker, and a good poker player should know how to bluff. "I don't care about that!" he called back. "I'll be happy to take a few of you with me—if that's the only chance I've got! And you'll be first, Elder!"

"And what of Emilie? Do you want her shot in the exchange? Is this how you rescue her from us?"

"She doesn't want to go back and I don't blame her. You can solve this nicely, Elder Wolverton, by simply backing off. Let Emilie and me go!"

"She is to be my bride! I have seen it!"

"Well, she ain't seen it—and she won't. You'd best try and have another revelation, Elder."

"Emilie!" the elder cried. "Listen to me! It is written that you and I will wed! We are destined for each other! Stop this foolishness and come back with me. I will make you first among my wives! You will stand by my side as I sweep the apostates from our church!"

Emilie got to her feet. "Does that mean you will sweep my father from the church's councils?" Her anger was fierce.

"Your father will be one of us. He will be my father-in-law! You see, it will all be well if you will just come back with me."

Emilie looked with despair at Longarm. She was torn. He shook his head at her.

"Get back to your Eden, Wolverton," Longarm called, "and take your Avenging Angels with you. This is one Mormon girl you ain't going to buffalo."

"Stay out of this, Longarm!"

"I'm in, Wolverton. All the way."

"You are a fool!"

"Maybe. But at least I don't go having dreams about women I want and then go out and kidnap them—and call it revelation!"

"You are an apostate—a godless gentile and you do

121

not understand. I forgive you, Longarm. But my patience is wearing thin!"

"Hell, Wolverton, mine's already run out." He lifted his rifle. "I've got a bead on you right now. You call off your so-called Angels and I'll let you walk back to your horse and ride out of here."

"Pull that trigger and you and Emilie die with me. My men have their orders. But you see, it will not come to pass that way. I have already seen how it will be, and nothing you can do, Longarm, can alter that revelation. You're bluffing, Longarm. But I am not!"

Longarm looked around him. The riders had circled them completely by that time, and there were indeed more than a couple of dozen. Elder Wolverton was not taking lightly this expedition to retrieve Emilie. "Well, hell," Longarm said, levering a cartridge into the firing chamber of his Winchester. "I might as well take you with us, then. I sure ain't going to let you talk this young woman here into going back to a fanatic like you!"

As he raised the rifle to his shoulder, Elder Wolverton raised his hand to stay Longarm's trigger finger.

"Now, just a minute, Longarm! Let me speak again to Emilie! This is her decision to make. It is, after all, her life we are bargaining for!"

Longarm let his rifle down a little and turned to Emilie. "You want to talk to him?"

She nodded.

"Talk, Wolverton! But you'd better make it good."

"Emilie, listen. This man, you, and I myself will soon be dead if you do not let good sense overcome your natural reluctance to wed a man my age! If you will not think of yourself or of me, think of him. He has come far to save you and is a brave man. I promise you I will not have him killed if you will step forward now and return with me."

"It is not your age! It is everything about you! I prefer to die here!"

"You prefer that he die as well?" Wolverton asked.

122

Emilie looked up at Longarm, her face revealing how torn she was at that moment.

"Damn you, Wolverton!" Longarm said, bringing up his rifle again.

"His freedom!" Wolverton cried. "I promise you, Emilie. He will live! We will not kill him if you will return with me. My patience is nearing its end. I am not accustomed to begging. It is only because of what I know that I persevere in this matter. Think of that man standing beside you. Think of him if you will not think of yourself."

"I will go back!" she cried.

"No," Longarm said.

"It is all over, Longarm," Wolverton told him. "Put down that rifle. Be a gentleman. Stand aside. The woman has made her choice. She still has not accepted me and she may never do so. That will be her choice to make. But no matter, it is no longer your concern. Be sensible and stand aside."

"And if I do?"

"You have my word that no harm will come to you."

"Your word?"

"Do you imagine that I would break my word with Emilie on hand to witness such a deed? It is a foolish way, indeed, to impress the woman one wishes to join in Celestial Marriage. She has my word—as have you."

"You'll let me return to Salt Lake City?"

"I did not say that. I said I would not kill you. And I will not."

"What will you do?"

"I will leave you alone on this desert at some distance from the railroad tracks. You will, in short, have very little chance of making it to safety. But this way you will have a fighting chance. Otherwise, Longarm, I would not give much for your chances of surviving this adventure."

"No!" cried Emilie. "You can't just leave him out here to die! I won't go back with you!"

"Let *him* decide."

123

Longarm looked at Emilie. He smiled and spoke quietly to her. "You can still refuse him when you get back there. I'll take this chance. It's the best deal we can get, I'm thinking."

"You might die out here!"

"I won't die. And I promise you, Emilie, I'll come for you again. And this time I'll make it stick."

"That's a promise?"

He nodded.

She looked then at Wolverton. "All right," she said wearily. "I'm thirsty and very tired. Do you have a horse for me?"

Wolverton smiled at Longarm. "We have better than that. We have two fine army mules you were kind enough to deliver to Little Zion personally."

Longarm's captors not only had his two mules, they also had a wagon filled with water barrels and a remuda of spare mounts. They took Longarm's Winchester, his Colt, and his derringer, the latter along with his watch and chain. Then he and Emilie were allowed to mount the mules. For the rest of that day they rode steadily due north into the heart of the Great Salt Desert. By nightfall they had covered close to thirty miles.

They pulled up then and Longarm was told to dismount. As he got off the mule, he asked for a couple of canteens filled with clear water. He addressed his request to Wolverton and for a moment the man looked as if he was about to refuse it. Then he looked at Emilie. Her face was livid at his indecision.

"All right, Longarm," the elder said. "You may have your water. Fat lot of good it will do you."

At that Emilie slid down off her mule and ran to Longarm. "I'll stay with you," she cried. "Let me!" She flung both arms around him and hugged him fiercely, pressing her face into his chest.

He disengaged her gently and looked into her face. Tears were in her eyes. "You just go back with that old man and wait for me, hear?"

124

She nodded bravely, aware as he was just how far-fetched such a hope had to be. But Longarm understood. Sometimes a man needs a big fat lie to believe in. And both of them needed this lie in particular.

Impulsively, she reached up, pulled his face down, and kissed him on the lips. Then she turned and ran back to the mule. Longarm caught the face of the elder in that moment and saw it go raw with shock and jealousy. The old goat probably had all kinds of notions as to what had gone on between the two of them since leaving Little Zion, but there was no way to prevent him from thinking that. And protesting that it wasn't so would not help Emilie much.

A sweat-streaked rider urged his horse close and dropped two full canteens at Longarm's feet, then pulled his horse around and rode back to the wagon. Emilie climbed back up onto the mule. Longarm's mule was caught up by another rider and led to the wagon, where its reins were tied to the rear of it.

"Goodbye, Longarm," said the elder. "May this be a foretaste of the hell and damnation that will be your certain reward!"

He pulled his horse around and with a stroke of his arm, turned the rest of the riders about. Longarm watched them ride off for a long while. It took almost forever, it seemed, for them to grow smaller in the distance, and their presence on the flat expanse was a comfort of a kind. And then, with a suddenness that startled him, the entire party was swallowed up by the horizon, though occasionally the clean sound of a bit jingling, the squeak of the wagon's axle, came sharply across the vast emptiness.

He looked about him. The westering sun was sitting on the horizon, a monstrous, swollen red eye. The crimson light it shed turned the desert floor and the sky overhead a salmon pink. A cool breeze touched his face and neck. Slowly, he turned completely around, his eyes searching an incredibly flat horizon that for the first time was not a maddeningly undulating, shimmering mirage.

He paused a moment and squinted. There was something on the horizon, almost due north of his present position. He waited for it to disappear, to flicker. But it sat there solidly. He took a few steps toward it in his eagerness to see it more clearly, but it made little difference. Then he stood stock-still and concentrated on picking out details.

At last he was fairly certain what it was he was looking at—the roof of a building. It was incredible, but that was precisely what it looked like to him. The sun was dropping rapidly now, but its rays still enclosed the projection and for just an instant the roof stood out clearly. Then the sun dipped out of sight and whatever it was vanished, winked out like a lamp being turned off.

Longarm went back for the canteens. He hefted them. They were full. He opened one and took a tiny sip. The water was clean; that much, at least, the elder had given him. He frowned and looked once more in the direction where he had seen that roof. Could the man have been more human than Longarm had thought? Had some sense of decency convinced the elder to leave Longarm within sight of help? There was no doubt that whatever it was Longarm saw was one hell of a distance from where he was standing at the moment, but if he was careful with his consumption of these two canteens, he just might make it. Had the elder given him at least that much of a sporting chance?

There was, Longarm realized, only one way to find out. Slinging the two canteens over his shoulder, he set out due north, hoping that as the night fell, he did not begin to trace a vast circle. He would have to rely on the stars.

Longarm drove himself on through most of the night, but well before dawn he had collapsed to the moonlit floor of the desert, a stumbling, shambling wreck,

126

curled into a ball to keep out the bone-deep chill, and fallen asleep. When the sun reappeared on the other side of the world and sent its fingers of light probing at him, Longarm stirred, feeling like some worm that had been caught on a vast boardwalk after a night's rain.

He pulled his canteens to him. One was nearly empty. He shook it unhappily and struggled to his feet. For a moment he experienced some difficulty in standing erect. It was as if the sun were pushing him back down. He realized his hat had fallen off. He bent over to get it and put the hat carefully back on his head. He felt a little giddy and drank what was left in the nearly empty canteen.

And almost threw it back up. The pain in his stomach was knifelike. He doubled over and fought to keep the water down. At last the gagging subsided. For the first time he realized how hungry he was, how dried out. He wiped the tears out of his eyes and tossed away the empty canteen. That left him with only one full canteen of water to make it to . . . where?

The night before, he had been heading for a rooftop he had glimpsed on the horizon. Looking around him now, his narrowed eyes saw nothing but shimmering heat waves and the reflections of the blue sky just below the horizon line. Water. Cool water. Of course it wasn't. There was nothing out there. Nothing.

Except death, in the form of a fiery hand that was waiting to squash him with one merciless swat.

How you do run on, he told himself sardonically. *Now just brace yourself and remember what you told that girl—and get after that there roof. It's out there somewhere. You saw it, and it's there. And where there's a roof, there's a settlement.*

Perhaps he was looking in the wrong direction. What *was* the right direction? The sun hung halfway up the sky, not quite at full blast yet. So that was the east. Turning carefully, Longarm looked back, squinting into the white glare. He saw how his tracks had been tracing a pronounced drift westward, instead of due north. He

127

turned himself carefully, as if he were steering a stubborn mule, and began walking.

He found comfort while he walked in looking back every now and then to see how straight a track he was leaving—and to assure himself that he was indeed covering ground, that this was not some nightmare in which no matter how far you walked, you found you were still in the same place. The passage of time was marked clearly by the steady climb of the sun until at last it was almost directly overhead. The glare caused the ground around him to fairly dance. He kept his eyes as narrow as possible in an effort to keep out the glare. But it was impossible. He walked for a while with his eyes closed, but he began stumbling and the white glare beat upon his closed lids like a fist.

He took a sadistic delight in not drinking any of the water in his remaining canteen. He told himself he would not take a sip until he was sure he was on the track of that settlement he had glimpsed. At last, as the sun began to slip down the western portion of the sky, he saw once again—and this time with much greater clarity—what appeared to be a portion of a shingled roof. It now seemed to hang there in front of him just above the horizon. He even imagined he could see light gleaming through chinks in the roof. He attributed that to mirage, however. He did not want the roof to be anything but solid.

He stopped then and slowly, dramatically unscrewed the cap of his canteen and carefully allowed a few drops of the water to fall upon his tongue. He swallowed this carefully, then allowed himself a small trickle. With a smile, he screwed the cap back on and continued his trek, his steps firmer, his shoulders back.

It was close to midafternoon before he reached the buildings. Well in advance of getting there, he realized he had been the target of a devilish humor, the butt of a malicious, possibly fatal joke. He would have reached the place a full half-day sooner, he realized, if he had

128

not drifted almost due west during the night, for when he finally approached the place, he found himself coming at it from the west. But that didn't matter at all. It made no difference whether he came at it from the south or from the west.

There was nothing for him to reach, only a battered cluster of frame shacks with all the roofs but one fallen in, the walls leaning, the window frames out. He had been thinking about it during the last quarter-mile of his trek, trying to figure out what it could once have been, standing out here in the middle of the Great Salt Desert, and he wondered if perhaps it was an old Pony Express station, one of those that had been abandoned back in the sixties when the telegraph lines had been put through to the coast.

The closer he got, the more certain he became that this was indeed what he was approaching. He saw what was left of a Conestoga freight wagon behind one of the three frame buildings still standing, and through one of the open sides of a barn, he could see the horse stalls, a single wooden bucket hanging on a nail.

Hope stirred within him that this station had not had to have its water supplied by tank wagons, that this one had managed to dig a well and that the well might still be functioning. At last, stumbling into the station, he reached out and grabbed hold of a corner of the most solid building, and hung on. The shade provided by the building was blessed. He felt better at once and looked around, hoping for some sign of that well. He circled the station.

No structure was solid. No wall was straight or without its gaping holes. Sun-bleached timbers and warped planking leaned crazily one way or the other. The buildings were ghostly skeletons, through which he looked in vain for any signs of a well. At last he admitted the futility of such a hope. There was no well.

He slumped slowly to the ground, his back to a wall facing the Conestoga wagon, and listened to the aimless flapping of the wagon tarp as it beat against the ribs of

129

the battered hulk. The freight wagon was buried up to its hubs in drifted salt dust, the flapping canvas half rotted away. As he looked at the wagon, the hope within him died. He had only the water left in his canteen. By leaving him within sight of this abandoned Pony Express station, Elder Wolverton had cunningly managed to see to it that all of Longarm's remaining energy would be expended in going the wrong way.

It galled Longarm to realize how effective the elder's strategy had been. And when he recalled his brave words to Emilie, he stirred fretfully, then slowly, judiciously, unscrewed the cap of his canteen and let the smallest possible amount trickle onto his swollen tongue. He would husband every drop. He would hang on as long as he could. He would not join the ghostly hulk rotting in front of him until the last possible moment. Somewhere he had heard that where there was life there was hope, and Longarm believed it.

He had been in worse scrapes than this, he told himself. Then he chuckled softly, dryly. If he had, he really couldn't remember when or where.

Night fell like a benediction. The flapping of the canvas ceased, finally. The stars gleamed brightly, swarming like dust across the heavens. He leaned his head back against the wooden wall and drank in the sight. After a moment he took another sip of his water and just managed to secure the canteen before he fell into an exhausted sleep.

It was the flapping of the canvas that woke him. The eastern sky was bright with the coming sun. He watched it for a moment, then pulled himself to his feet. Perhaps there was something in one of the buildings he could use to fashion a signal with. He thought then of a fire, smoke signals.

This thought gave him a fleeting hope, but even as he considered it, wandering hopelessly through the ravaged buildings, he knew it was a foolish plan. Who would see the smoke? And seeing it, who would care?

130

And if anyone cared, how would they get out to where he was? How many could invest in army mules for the sole purpose of rescuing luckless Deputy U.S. Marshals who got themselves stranded in the middle of the Great Salt Desert?

They would need a magic carpet, he told himself, his thoughts moving sluggishly, foolishly inside his addled head. Bending, he found an old, rusty tool box. With nothing better to do, he managed to pry up its rusted lid. He found a hammer, two screwdrivers, a bent square, a plane with no razor in it, a couple of boxes of nails, and a small hand ripsaw.

He straightened and looked around him. If he wanted to, with all this loose lumber lying about, he could build himself an outhouse. If he had a shovel, that is, to dig the hole.

He did not like the joke. He kicked shut the tool box and worked his way aimlessly out of the shed where he had found it. The shed had obviously served as a makeshift blacksmith shop when the station had been in operation. He found a coal shuttle, and under salt drifts, pieces of coal. If he got cold, he would be able to warm himself. Moving out of the shed, he investigated the two other buildings. He imagined that what had been the stable still smelled, however faintly, of horse manure, but the drifted salt, like ageless snow, covered everything.

The sun was higher when he returned to the freight wagon and inspected it. The canvas tarpaulin slapped at him a couple of times, catching him across the face and neck, aggravating his scorched and blistered skin. He tried to rip it down, but could not in his weakened state. The wind, blowing steadily toward the center of the desert, tugged on it relentlessly. He inspected the axles idly. Without a horse, it made no difference what the condition of the axles was. The rear axle, he found, was broken, the spring hanging from the wooden frame and almost completely buried in the salt dust.

As the sun climbed higher, he crawled in under the wagon for the shade.

He was going to die, he thought finally, without fear or panic. It was just a cold, solid, uncompromising fact. Perhaps he would die under this wagon, with only the flapping tarp to protect him from the buzzards.

Only there were no buzzards this far out. They weren't as foolish as Deputy U.S. Marshals.

He closed his eyes and tried to ignore the dryness of his mouth, the ache in the pit of his stomach—and the damned flapping of that canvas. He opened his eyes. If only the blamed thing would flap with some kind of regularity, like a clock. But it would be still for a while, perfectly still, then it would start flapping rapidly, causing the entire wagon to shudder along with it. With a sigh, Longarm crawled out from under the wagon and found a spot inside one of the buildings. He doled out a small taste of water, rolled it luxuriously around in his mouth, then swallowed it. For a few moments he wondered if it wouldn't be a good idea to swallow the entire contents of the canteen and be done with it. What was the sense in prolonging matters?

But he didn't like himself when he started thinking like that and slowly, firmly screwed the cap back onto his canteen and placed it carefully down beside him. The heat was stifling in the building and large, irregular bands of sunlight traversed his body as he lay there—but at last he slept.

When he awoke, the sun had almost set—and the flapping tarp was silent. It was the absence of that constant flapping that had awakened him. And it had stopped because the hot wind had ceased to blow.

He reached for his canteen—and frowned suddenly.

Without touching the canteen he struggled to his feet, stepped over the rotting timbers and planks, and left the building to stare at the freight wagon—and the now limp tarpaulin.

Hell! Sails drive ships! Windmills pump water out of the ground. Maybe he couldn't build himself a magic

132

carpet, but he sure as hell could build himself something a whole hell of a lot more sensible—a land yacht!

He laughed, and found he couldn't laugh. He didn't have enough moisture in his mouth. All he succeeded in doing was cracking his lips. He went back into the building for his canteen. Sipping carefully on the neck of the canteen, letting the moisture seep into his mouth, he considered once again his brainstorm.

Did he have tools? Yes, he had tools. How many wheels would he need? He could get by with two, and those he had—plus an axle. And of course he had the sail—a stubborn tarpaulin that had been nagging him since the moment he arrived. Yes, if he had the strength left, he could build it.

He went looking for that tool box. God damn it! Of course he had the strength to build it!

Chapter 6

Longarm worked by the light of the moon, preferring it without hesitation to the fierce impact of the sun. It made things difficult at times, however, since he had trouble making accurate measurements in the dim light and cut himself repeatedly whenever he wielded the saw. Though the saw he had found in the tool box was next to worthless, it was a saw and it did cut, and with it he was able to cut through the wagon's struts, freeing the tarp.

After that, his biggest problem was digging out the wheels from the drifts of salt and sand and beneath that, the clay. He broke the handle of the hammer while using it to free the spring, but with the spring he was able to gain enough leverage to lift the bed of the wagon off the broken rear axle. The rusted spring was an awkward crowbar and its rusted, pitted surface cut into his hands. His blood turned the rust into a sticky mess that made it almost impossible for him to handle the spring. But he persisted, and when at last he had swung the bed of the wagon free of the rear axle, he was so weak he was trembling from exhaustion and decided to take a break.

He slumped down against a wall and studied his progress so far, contemplating what he had yet to accomplish.

As near as he could figure, one of his biggest problems would be the mast. He would have to get rid of the wagon's sides to lighten it and strip the bed as

134

close to a triangle as he could get it. The front wheels of the wagon he could still use. For a rear caster he would have to contrive a springy pole of some kind. Without a rudder or the ability to tack, he would just be able to sail downwind, but downwind should take him to the Central Pacific tracks. Yessir. That tarp, rigged as a square sail, would sure carry him along. For braking he would just have to use both feet on the rims of the wheels as long as the soles on his boots held out. But he would worry about stopping after he got the damn thing to go.

That mast, now. How the hell was he going to fasten it to the floor of the platform? How was he going to anchor it? He would need guy wires to steady it and a spar from which to hang the tarp. And nails. He would need sturdy nails that could be driven. Those he had found so far had crumbled into red powder at the slightest handling, or snapped or bent double when struck. He was sure it was the incredibly corrosive effect of all this salt. And that hammer bothered him. He needed it. He would have to construct a new handle for it, first thing.

Longarm closed his eyes, letting the cool wind blow over his brow. Thoughts of his eventual ride aboard his land yacht crowded in upon him. His mouth was as dry as old tinder and he meant to reach out for his canteen. But his arm was heavy, his will weak. Longarm slept.

When he awoke he felt as light and insubstantial as the tinder-dry boards flapping in the hot wind about him. The sun was well above the eastern horizon, impaling him with its relentless eye. Longarm struggled to his feet, as weak as a kitten. Any movement of his lips caused them to crack. He felt of his face. It was blistered and painful to touch. Both of his hands were swollen and raw from the night's work.

Steadying himself by reaching out and grabbing hold of the wall, he looked through the glare at the freight wagon and tried to regain the enthusiasm he had felt the night before. It was difficult. All Longarm felt at the moment was an incredible weariness. And thirst, a terrible, unslakable thirst.

He might as well be attempting to finish that Mormon temple singlehanded.

Finding a shady spot in one of the buildings, he slumped down, unscrewed the cap to his canteen, and took small, careful swallows. He felt a little better after that and looked about him. He was in the building that had served as the horse barn. Hanging on a nail from the wall facing him was the wooden bucket he had spied earlier. It was in surprisingly good shape and was a large bucket with sloping sides. It looked reasonably tight and still well-caulked.

The idea didn't come to him all at once—but it came, and that was the important thing. He would knock a hole in the bottom of the bucket, stick the mast through it, and nail the bucket to the floor of the wagon. The bucket would serve as an anchor for the mast, and strips of canvas could serve as guy lines.

He struggled to his feet and lifted down the bucket. As he examined it and felt its solidity, he regained some of his enthusiasm. He took a deep breath and looked around him with eyes inflamed, and realized that he had damned well better be enthusiastic about this crazy idea of his. The alternative was to finish the canteen and die here, with not even the buzzards caring enough to pick his bones clean.

Slowly, doggedly, Longarm set to work. His first task was to find a piece of wood he could use as a new handle for his hammer. It was a maddening job. The handle had broken off inside the head and clearing it was almost impossible. He had to use the wagon spring to drive the new handle through the head opening. By noon, however, he had himself a new hammer and had found enough nails—from the roofs, mostly—to begin to fasten the mast onto the bed of the wagon.

First he knocked a slit in the bottom of the bucket through which he intended to slip the board he would

136

use for the mast; then he nailed the bucket, top down, to the bed of the wagon. The board he selected for the mast was hanging loosely from one of the walls and was more than twelve feet long. He nailed a spar across it to hold the sail, narrowed the board somewhat with his wretched saw, then drove the board down through the slit in the bucket's bottom. He contrived it so that the tip of the board would wedge itself between the boards used as flooring for the wagon. Though the mast leaned slightly forward, it stood solidly, already tugging slightly in the hot wind—an encouraging sign.

It was well past noon by this time and Longarm clambered down off the wagon to look at his mast and take another sip of water. He did not like the light heft of the canteen as he lifted it to his lips and forced himself to take less water than he had counted on.

He wanted to rest, to lean back in the shade and contemplate what he had already accomplished, but he did not allow himself this luxury. From somewhere in his past came the words of an old prospector: the only way to get an impossible job done is to go at it like you never figured it was going to end—and don't expect it to now. Then one day you'll look up and find it finished. And you hadn't even noticed.

Deciding he would tear strips from pieces of the tarpaulin for guying the mast later, he headed resolutely for the wagon spring and picked it up, climbed back up onto the wagon, and began swinging the spring like a crowbar, knocking out the sides of the wagon. He was so weak by this time that he sometimes had to swing twice at the same spot to break through. He kept at it doggedly, however, and when he had cleared away the sides, he sank to the floor of the wagon, the rusty, bloody spring leaning across his shoulder, and contemplated what he had yet to do.

The back corners of the wagon, he realized, would create too much drag and would prevent him from moving straight before the wind. In addition to the rear caster he still had to fashion, he would have to

137

cut back the rear width of the wagon bed. That meant sawing it, and failing that, simply knocking the boards off. He stood up shakily, and heaving the spring over the side, let himself gently down from the wagon and went in search of the saw.

He found it with no trouble and clambered weakly back up onto the bed of the wagon and began sawing. The saw bucked and caught and behaved like a wild thing infuriated with the use to which it was being put. With his tortured eyes shut most of the time, his face baking in the torrid rays of the westering sun, Longarm persisted and by sundown had hacked and sawn away the left side of the wagon. Remembering grimly those words of the prospector, he continued sawing—his hands bloodied, his wrists and the lower portions of both arms lacerated—until he had cut away the right portion of the wagon bed as well.

Flinging the saw from him, he jumped down from what was left of the wagon and turned to look at his handiwork. The moon was no longer as high or as bright as it had been during previous nights, and in the dim gloom Longarm could see only that he had managed somehow to hack and tear the wagon to pieces. The result of his day's labor gave him little hope. Only the mast, no longer as straight as when he had first set it into the bucket, gave him any cause for optimism. Still, what was left of the wagon bed did indeed resemble a kind of ragged triangle—and that, after all, was what he had intended.

So what's next? He asked the question of himself in a kind of raw fever, standing in the cool night and trembling slightly from head to toe. The hacked wagon and the leaning walls of the station appeared to be dancing slightly, while the night air seemed almost palpable with ghostly forms. He kept thinking he was not alone—that some malevolent force was just waiting to pounce on him from out of the vast, pale darkness that surrounded him. He twitched nervously whenever a slight wind caused a hanging board to creak or slam.

138

He knew he was alone. He knew he was imagining things. But it did him no good to reassure himself in this fashion. The way he figured it, his brain was drying out just like every other cell in his body.

So what's next, old son?

Tear strips from the tarp and use them to steady the mast. But be sure you leave some of the tarpaulin, since you've been thinking of it for your sail. Remember? Yes, I remember.

He realized he was talking to himself.

He shook his head in disbelief and walked over to the tarp where it was lying on the ground. Tearing the strips was not easy. The damned thing was a lot tougher than it looked. He stuck to the torn sections, and staggering about drunkenly, finally managed to rip free enough strips to use for the lines. He twisted the canvas strips to strengthen them and then tied them around the mast until he had four strips hanging from the mast, two on each side. Then he went looking for his hammer and the pile of nails he had gathered.

He got lost.

Chuckling to himself, he straightened up and looked back at the station and the crazy land yacht out in back of it. He knew the hammer and nails were not out here in the middle of the Great Salt Desert, unless someone had sneaked in and taken them out here to confuse him. He pondered that notion for a while, then shrugged and shambled back to the station.

It was luck—sheer luck—when his disintegrating boots struck the hammer as he returned to the station. Feeling around on the ground, he found five nails. He clambered wearily up onto the deck and hammered the four strips to the floor, securely guying the mast.

He didn't want to fasten the tarpaulin to the yardarm. Not yet. He didn't want it hanging lifelessly while he worked on the tail skid. He had been considering for some time in the back of his mind what he should look for and had wondered if there might not be some old pitchforks, or at least some handles, buried under

139

the drifts of salt in the stable building. Such a handle would provide just the right amount of spring.

He went inside and began kicking at the salt dust with his boots. He thought he felt something and dropped to his hands and knees and began digging with his hands. The salt ate into his torn hands and he pulled back, finally. He leaned against the wall of the stable, closed his eyes . . . and slept.

He awoke with the sun almost directly overhead. Every muscle and bone in his body was sore. He didn't dare move his lips. He felt like he was burning up, and when he looked at his hands, he saw they were shaking. He figured maybe he had the St. Vitus' Dance.

Well now, we'll see about that, old son.

Feeling like he was a hundred and sixty years old and being asked to run to California and back for his breakfast, Longarm struggled to his feet, tried to blink the blinding sunlight out of his eyes, and looked around, recalling dimly what he had been up to for the past two or three days. How many days had it been, at that?

Two? Three? A week?

He shook his head to rid himself of the nagging riddle and forced himself to remember what he had been doing when he fell asleep. That crazy sonofabitching land yacht. That's what he had been up to—and now all he needed was a nice, long, springy pole for a rear caster. Well now, nothing to that. Let's see now. No problem at all.

Longarm spied the canteen lying in a patch of brilliant sunlight. So bright was the glare off the canteen that he had to avert his eyes. He forgot about the land yacht, then, and stumbled for the canteen. Snatching it off the ground, he shook it, a sinking sense of disaster in the pit of his stomach. The canvas covering had long since rotted off it and the canteen had been sitting in the blazing sun—with its cap on the ground beside it.

140

Lifting it to his mouth, Longarm felt only a tiny trickle of warm moisture fall upon his tongue. He held it up a moment longer, waiting, but nothing more came out of the hot, empty canteen. He flung it from him. It bounced off the front wheels of the wagon and came to rest in the broiling salt dunes.

He slumped down in the shade of the wall he favored and stared listlessly before him. He knew he had to get up and told himself that soon he would. Not really certain how long he sat there, he found himself moving sluggishly at last, as the sun probed at his face from a different angle. He shook his head and looked up at the deck and the crooked mast.

What was it he had to do next? The answer came slowly. He had been looking for the handle of a pitchfork, or some other such implement that might have been left behind when the former occupants cleared out of this place. The night before, he had thought he felt something beneath his feet over there where the stable had been. He pulled himself erect and went back to the spot. He kicked at the ground with his feet. A small handle was protruding from the salt dust. He reached down and yanked it loose. The tines had all been broken off, but five feet of the handle remained.

It wouldn't be long enough unless he attached it to a board. He went looking for one, stumbling, shambling, forgetting at times what it was he needed. He found a board that would do nicely and then spent an interminable time looking for a hammer. After he had found the hammer, he realized dimly that he needed nails. That stumped him for a while until he remembered how he had gotten the other nails he had used before. He clambered up the side of a building, and with the claw of his hammer, pulled from the boards a few more nails that had escaped the salt and the moisture. He must have lost more than he kept as they eased out of the dry wood, but he paid no heed and it seemed for a while that he had been performing this strange activity as long as he could remember. At last he came

141

down and counted the nails more than once, unable to remember clearly what he wanted to do with them.

At last, in a kind of daze, during which he had to remind himself repeatedly what he was doing, he sawed off the broken tines from the handle, then nailed the handle to the board he had found, bending the nails around the handle to secure it. Then he thought a long while, considering his next move. It was, he finally decided, necessary to lift the rear of the deck, using the spring as a lever, so that he could attach the caster to the deck. It took an interminable time for him to work the spring in under the deck and prop it up, using one of the rear wheels. But he couldn't keep it up. At one point he found himself lying on his back on the salt crust, looking up at the bottom of the deck, the spring lying across his midsection.

Finally he managed to fasten the board to the back of the deck with a few minutes of hard hammering. He kicked the spring to one side and the deck sagged down onto the caster. The caster held, the end of the handle sinking only an inch or so into the hard salt surface. The greatest amount of sag, however, was where the handle was joined to the board. If it snapped, that would be the place. But he realized it was no good thinking of that.

Now it was time for the sail. He had some difficulty locating it, even though it was where it had been ever since he had removed it from the wagon. When he found it, he grabbed the edge of it, pulled it up onto the deck—and stood there looking at the spar, feeling foolish, empty of direction. Something was wrong and he didn't know what it was. And then he remembered. How in hell was he supposed to attach the sail to the yard? He had no lines.

For a moment he sagged under the weight of the heavy, salt-laden canvas and fought an impulse to throw the sail down and retreat into one of the buildings, to get away from the withering heat. Instead, he found himself putting aside the sail and jumping care-

142

fully down from the deck. He was looking for his saw. It was at his feet when he left the wagon, but he went past it twice until he realized what he was stepping over. Then he pondered a while until he remembered what he had planned.

He returned to the sail, slashed holes in its four corners, then tossed away the saw. Reaching up, he hung the sail on the spar, sticking both ends of the yardarm out through the holes. Then he took off his shirt, tore it into strips, and tying them to the holes in the lower corners of the sail, fastened the makeshift lines to the deck with a few well-driven nails.

At once the sail bellied out with a soft *whump*. But almost at once, the sail lost its belly and flapped loosely on the spar. Longarm looked to the west. It was hard to believe, but the sun was going down. And the hot wind was dying with its setting.

Longarm jumped off the deck and shook his head in wonder. Time had no logic, it seemed. Only a little while ago it was high noon. He frowned and tried to trace back, tried to understand where all the hours had gone—and realized that time, like everything else, was out of kilter for him.

And there was no getting around it now. No matter how hard and how fast he had worked this afternoon, he would have to wait until the next day.

He stumbled into the shade of one of the buildings and as the sun set and the long blue shadows crept over the salt wasteland, he tried to quiet his racing thoughts, tried to settle himself down. He glanced down at his hands—and was astonished at what he saw. They had long since stopped bleeding. But only because they, too, no longer gave a damn. They were like the claws of a hawk—bony, ridged, and frozen into one position. They didn't sting any longer. They buzzed. He turned them slowly so that he could look into their palms. Long, hardened ridges crossed them.

It had been, he realized dimly, one hell of a time to

143

learn the trade of a boatwright—and one hell of a place to learn it.

Longarm leaned back to wait for the next day—and was asleep almost at once.

It was the flapping of the square sail in the hot morning wind that aroused Longarm. He looked at the tugging sail and got to his feet. The wind was strong and the sail was holding the breeze beautifully. So what was wrong? Why wasn't it moving?

Longarm looked at the front wheels. They were deeply mired in the drifted salt sand. He would have to dig them out.

He used the spring to break the wheels loose from the salt drifts and the hard-packed clay underneath. Once the wheels were free, he got behind the wagon, lifted the caster, and pushed the wheels out of their ruts. As soon as he let the caster down upon the smooth crust of the desert, the contraption began to move slowly forward. Longarm stood where he was and watched it go, pleased in an odd, objective fashion that what he had been laboring at all this time really did have some sense to it after all. Was he finally about to take this magic wind vehicle and sweep across the desert?

Longarm felt giddy, lightheaded. He knew he should feel elated at what he had done, but he was aware only of an immense fatigue, so that everything came to him through a kind of hazy screen. It was difficult for him to think logically, or to concentrate on what he had to do next. But he knew he should be pleased. That much got through to him.

And then he realized that his land yacht was moving not south, but southwest. He stumbled after it, lifted the rear caster, and swung the craft to the left so that it was pointing due south. He let down the drag and almost at once the craft began to pick up speed. For a moment he just stood there, watching it move faster

144

with each passing second—until he realized that he would have to run like hell now to catch up with it.

As soon as he overtook it and stumbled, sprawling, onto the deck, the craft slowed to a crawl and for a moment Longarm thought it would stop altogether. Then, once again, it began to pick up speed.

Longarm pulled himself around the mast, and leaning his back against it, positioned himself on the leading edge of the vehicle. He reached out with both feet. As the soles of his boots came down on the rims of the wheels, the craft slowed almost to a halt. Longarm let up. The craft began to pick up speed almost immediately. The trick, he realized, was not to use too much pressure. He pulled his feet back and rested his head against the mast. Though a hot wind was pushing him across the desert, there was a stiffening breeze striking his face. He was aware, too, of the baking sun on his bare arms and torso.

He reached out with his feet every now and then to slow himself down, but the buffeting his feet took discouraged him. Besides, he thought, why did he want to slow down? He wanted only to get to that railroad track. Pulling his legs back, he turned sideways so that he was lying athwart the deck. Glancing behind, he saw the thin line, almost perfectly straight, that was left on the clean desert surface by the trailing caster.

It was working just beautifully—as slick as a tallow factory.

Soon, however, he found that he was beginning to drift westward. Rousing himself, he braked the wheels with his feet until he had straightened his course once again. He was happy to pull his boots off the wheel rims. The heat generated by them was beginning to cook the bottoms of his feet. He was surprised that his boots were lasting. He figured they would not last much longer.

What he reckoned to be an hour, and then another hour, passed. Twice more he had had to brake and

145

steer the craft with his feet on the rims, and the sole of his right boot—or what was left of it—went tailing off behind him a second after he pulled his foot back. That left him with one foot for braking and steering, but he wasn't worrying. His elation at his coming deliverance as a result of his contraption had faded now to a sober awareness of what had to be done when he reached the tracks. There would be no protection from the sun except for his hat and his pants. Yet he still had to wait for a train, and how long that would take he had no idea; he was only roughly certain of the time of day and he had no handy rail schedule to consult.

It was conceivable that after reaching the tracks and even after staying alive long enough for a train to come by, it would be too late to do him any good, or too dark for the train's engineer to see him.

Hell, why should they stop anyway for some crazy, ragged, burnt-out codger waving hello to them as they clacked past? The thought didn't comfort him at all, but he could not deny a kind of sardonic amusement at his predicament.

"Who's that fool out there on the 'desert waving at the train, Marybelle?" some passenger might ask his wife. "He's going to get an awful sunburn!"

"He's probably drunk, Alfred," Marybelle would reply with a sniff. "Don't encourage him by waving back!"

Longarm would have chuckled aloud at this imaginary exchange, but his mouth was so dry he thought it would break if he tried to use it. Funny as the imaginary conversation was, it could happen. The train could charge right on past him if all he did was stand on the desert and wave.

No. He would have to do something more dramatic. But what?

And then he saw the tracks, shimmering on the southern horizon. By this time he was rushing over the dead, flat, hard surface of the desert as fast as a galloping

146

bronc, perhaps even a little faster. Longarm began to think of ways of slowing down. He could not use his only remaining shod foot without tipping the damned thing, maybe throwing him out and breaking his fool neck.

The tracks were no longer just a wavering line on the horizon. With gratifying and surprising speed, they were becoming solid, gleaming rails of steel, neatly placed atop the gravel roadbed. Longarm had now to think seriously of stopping. For a moment he thought of scrambling to his feet and perching on the deck above the wheels so that, on the moment of impact, he could jump. But that idea did not please him. He turned then to the sail. Since this was the source of his speed, all he would have to do was rip it down.

He turned to it, grabbed the mast and pulled himself upright. He was reaching up for the sail when he heard a loud crack, like a pistol shot, and the deck abruptly pitched downward, hurling him past the mast. He reached out and tried to grab it as he went past and then found himself spinning drunkenly on the hard surface of the Salt Desert. He spun only a second, his momentum causing him to lose his balance, and the next thing he knew he was sprawling face-down across the hard packed surface of the ground while the land yacht, slowing swiftly, began to describe a sharp turn to the left.

It never completed the turn as it crunched with surprising force into the gravel roadbed of the train. The deck shattered, the mast cracked forward, but one wheel continued up the steep embankment, skipped lightly over the rails, and disappeared beyond the tracks.

Longarm got slowly to his feet and inspected himself. He was a sight. His chest hung in ribbons of bright flesh, the salt that had been ground into the open lacerations beginning to sting already. He felt his chin. It, too, had lost some skin. But the palms of his hands, toughened now to the consistency of cement, showed

147

little blood. He walked slowly the remaining distance to the tracks and inspected the shattered craft.

He saw at once what had caused him to be spilled from the deck. The caster had snapped at the point where the pitchfork handle had been joined to the board. Perhaps his standing up and moving his weight back onto it had been what triggered the break. Whatever, he was at his destination, and when he saw the wreckage, he knew how he was going to be able to bring the first train from the west to a halt.

It took Longarm the rest of that day to drag just four beams up from the desert floor and drop them over the eastbound tracks. Then, as darkness descended, he gathered a pile of the tinder-dry remnants of the deck alongside the tracks on the desert floor. Pieces of one very dry board he ground under his remaining boot until he had reduced the wood to a powder. Placing this with burning, shaking fingers under the pile of wood, he waited with his two remaining sulphur matches.

He sat down then, crosslegged, in front of the pile of wood and waited for the train to come. If this bonfire didn't stop the train, then maybe the beams from the wagon lying across the tracks would do the trick.

But the moment he sat down to wait with his two matches, a fatigue he had hidden from himself the moment he had started to run after the land yacht returned and smote him like a sledgehammer. He found he could not keep his eyes open. He could not sit upright. He began to weave. In less than a minute after sitting down, he slipped sideways and sprawled face-down on the desert floor beside the pile of wood.

He must have slept at least four hours. When he stirred, he saw the train chugging toward him silently, the flames from its fire box illuminating the belly of the black cloud of smoke pouring from its stack. It was still too far down the tracks for him to hear the sound of its passage or its whistle. He was fully awake in an

148

instant, however, and realized that he did not have much time to get the bonfire going. But he had dropped the matches. He began patting the ground frantically around him in hope of finding them, but the train kept on coming and now he could hear its rapid puffing, the clack of the wheels singing over the rail joints.

He gave up looking for the matches and stood on his feet. It was surprising how light he felt, how rested he was. He began waving his arms. The train showed no sign of slowing down. At the speed it was going, it might not be stopped by the four beams. The cowcatcher might just fling them aside into the night. Longarm scrambled up the embankment and started to race down the tracks toward the train, waving his arms. The headlamp impaled him with its beam. He heard the *whoosh* of sand dropping to the rails and the screech of flanged wheels grinding the sand into the rails. The train's whistle shattered the desert night. Closer and closer came the thundering engine, the sound of its screeching wheels tearing at Longarm's ears, its whistle pushing at him shrilly—until at the last moment he dove off the tracks, the train grinding to a halt well beyond him.

But a good five yards from the barricade he had erected.

Longarm rolled over and looked at the halted train. He tried to get to his feet, but couldn't seem to manage it. The six coaches were lit and he could see silhouetted heads peering out at him. He heard the freight door slide back and the sound of feet striking the ground as someone dropped from the freight car and scrambled down the embankment toward him. He could see a lantern swinging from the dark figure's hand.

Again he tried to get to his feet, but it was no use. He seemed to be watching the whole show from a box seat. A part of himself smiled at the idea.

And then a fellow wearing a conductor's hat was leaning over him. He lifted the lantern he was carrying

149

to get a better view of Longarm's battered torso and face. Then he shook his head and spoke to Longarm.

"What happened to you, mister? You look like you got run over by a sawmill."

"Barricade . . . on the tracks . . . "

"We saw that. The engineer and the fireman are taking care of it now. Who are you, mister? What happened?"

"Name's Custis Long . . . Deputy U.S. Marshal. Take me to Salt Lake City . . . to Quincy Boggs."

"I don't know no Quincy Boggs. And how do I know you're a law officer?"

"Just get in touch with Boggs . . . Salt Lake City."

Longarm felt his senses leaving him, and he could see that the conductor was not really interested in helping Longarm, apart from getting him to Salt Lake City. Longarm summoned his last remaining ounce of strength.

"One hundred dollars . . . reward. Quincy Boggs! One hundred . . . "

The last thing Longarm saw that night was the look of pure, undiluted greed that animated the conductor's face. As Longarm slipped into unconsciousness, he heard the conductor call for help, and felt the man's arm around his shoulder.

Chapter 7

Longarm awoke in heaven—that is, with the distinct impression that he was being tended by two angels. When Marilyn saw his eyes flicker open, she brightened and pulled back excitedly.

"Audrey! He's awake!"

Audrey appeared and peeked over Marilyn's shoulder. "How do you feel, Mr. Long?"

"How do I look?" he grated hoarsely.

"Awful!"

"Simply awful!" cried Marilyn in happy agreement. "But we know how to fix that!" She turned to Audrey. "Tell father—and Molly!"

As Audrey fairly flew from the room with her news, Marilyn sat back down in the chair she had pulled up to his bedside, reached back to a basin, and pulled from it a dripping cloth. She wrung it slightly and then leaned close and dabbed soothingly at Longarm's face and mouth. "Thirsty?" she asked.

"Don't know what ever gave you a notion like that."

"Open your mouth a little wider and keep it open," she instructed.

He did as she told him, and Marilyn squeezed drops of water into his open mouth. After a while the drops became a trickle, and then she pulled back and proceeded to wipe his face.

"More," he croaked.

"Just a little at a time," she warned him.

"More, I said."

151

She smiled impishly. "For more than two days now we've been carefully dripping water into that mouth of yours, waiting for you to say just that." She leaned back and poured water out of a pitcher into a tall, clear glass. "Sit up—if you can," she instructed.

"Of course I can."

But as he leaned his weight on his arms and tried to push himself upright, he was astonished at how little progress he was able to achieve. Either he had grown very heavy or he had grown as weak as a tabby—and he knew at once which it was.

"I'll need some help," he confessed.

She took him by the shoulders and pulled him upright, then told him to scoot back so that he could lean against the headboard of his bed. He did as she commanded and felt somewhat proud of his accomplishment as he took the glass of water Marilyn handed him. He sipped at it slowly, as carefully as he had at the dregs that had remained in his canteen out on that damned salt desert.

He got a little carried away and had to go a trifle more slowly, but by concentrating furiously on each swallow, he had almost finished the glass when the door burst open and Boggs entered, with Molly and Audrey right behind.

Molly did not seem at all pleased, and Longarm noticed that she simply moved to one side of the bedroom doorway, and with her back to the wall, watched the proceedings. Boggs, however, was alive with pleasure and approached Longarm's bed with a wide, pleased smile on his face. "You're better!" he exclaimed. "I can see that at once! You have no idea how—dried out—you were when they brought you to me." He frowned at the thought. "Dried out and—in just terrible condition!"

"Did they do that to you?" Audrey wanted to know.

"The Avenging Angels?"

She nodded.

152

"Yes, I guess you could say they had a hand in it. My own foolishness was no help, either."

"Well," said Boggs, "tell us about it as soon as you can. But you need rest now—and nourishment." He turned about and addressed Molly. "Molly! That broth! Bring it at once!"

The woman did not acknowledge Boggs's instructions, but she sidled out the door in an instant.

Boggs smiled down at Longarm. "That woman has spent long hours tending you," he said. "All through the first night. She cut off your clothes and bathed you from head to foot. Your back and shoulders were baked to a turn, and you gave her quite an argument as she worked over you."

"I don't remember any of it."

"That's a blessing. You were unconscious most of the time. And delirious."

Longarm looked at the man. He knew how anxious the fellow was to learn of his daughter, and it pained Longarm to have to tell him what he must. "Let me finish this here glass of water," he said, "and I'll tell you about Emilie."

"Of course."

The three settled back as he swallowed the water. It was incredible how much better it made him feel. He handed the glass back to Marilyn.

"I found Emilie and we were free for a while—until they caught up with us on the Great Salt Desert. It was my fault. I had gone after her with mules, but when we left Little Zion, we were riding horses."

"We know all about that, Longarm. I mean the fact that you left Little Zion with Emilie and that they went after you and brought her back. But how did you find her? Was she well? How were her spirits?"

Longarm frowned. "They were fine. She's a brave, resourceful young lady. But what do you mean, you know what happened?"

Marilyn spoke up. "We've had visitors, Mr. Long."

Longarm looked to Boggs for an explanation.

153

The man shrugged. "You did quite a bit of damage when you visited their settlement, Longarm," he explained. "It angered Elder Wolverton and the others. They came here at once to remonstrate with us—to warn us never to send another federal officer after one of their women."

"They came *here?*"

"Yes."

"And they said *you* were dead," said Audrey.

"You broke away from them when they were taking you back to Little Zion," said Marilyn, "and got lost in the desert. They said there was no chance you would make it back to civilization. Not alive, anyway."

"And for a while," said Boggs, "it appeared they might be correct. You were more dead than alive when that fellow from the Central Pacific pounded on our door and demanded his reward."

Longarm took a deep breath. He remembered now. He had promised the conductor a hundred-dollar reward if he would take Longarm to this house. "About that money," Longarm began, "I am sure I—"

Boggs stopped him with a gesture. "I paid him on the spot—and gladly! You need not trouble yourself further about the matter. And I will hear no more about it. I am sure, however, that if you hadn't had the wit to wave pecuniary temptation before that grasping mortal, he would have left you where he found you."

At that moment Molly entered with a steaming bowl of soup on a tray. Longarm could smell the broth the moment she entered. He was, he realized immediately, famished. As she set it down on the table by the bed, Marilyn and Audrey both pulled back.

Boggs said, "Molly will help you get that down, Longarm. We'll talk later. Come along, girls."

"I don't need no help eating," Longarm protested. "I been doing it for some time now, and I learned how just fine. Just give me the spoon."

Boggs laughed softly and ushered the girls out of the room ahead of him. As the door closed behind

154

them, Longarm glanced at Molly. Her gimlet eyes regarded him coldly. "I understand you cut all my clothes off, Molly."

She said not a word. A spoonful of broth was heading remorselessly for his mouth. He opened it just in time. It was scalding hot and he tried to protest, but another spoonful came at him with all the relentless inevitability of time's passing, and he gave up the battle and submitted to Molly's ministrations.

In his present condition he was no match for the woman anyway.

Longarm was standing in his longjohns three days later, inspecting the new outfit Boggs had bought him, wishing he knew of a way to get back his derringer and watch from those jaspers in Little Zion, when Marilyn stole swiftly into the room, paying no attention at all to his lack of formal attire.

"Now, Marilyn," he said, "I'm plumb wore out with all your hospitality—and besides, this ain't no time—"

She placed her hand gently against his mouth. "It's not that," she told him softly. "I only wish it were! We've got visitors. I saw them outside. Come to the window!"

It was early in the evening. Marilyn turned the lamp on the dresser off and joined Longarm at the window. They were in the third-floor guest room in front and could see down onto the wide street in front of the house. Two carriages had pulled up and there were riders—an escort, it appeared—in front and back. The riders seemed a grim lot, with dark wide-brimmed hats pulled low on their heads, their coats and jackets as somber and depressing as their hats. He felt a slight chill as he watched them. As the riders dismounted, Longarm thought he recognized one of the men getting out of the lead carriage. He did. It was Wells Daniel. Behind him came Meeker and Job Welling.

One of the riders who had dismounted was waiting by the carriage for Meeker and Job Welling. He turned

155

as the two men approached him and then the three walked toward the house, Wells Daniel in the lead. Longarm felt a sharp thrust of anger. The rider who had joined Meeker and Welling was Elder Wolverton.

"What's going on, Marilyn?" Longarm asked. "That's Elder Wolverton down there—the man who kidnapped Emilie."

"I know," Marilyn said. "Molly told us. They're coming for you, Longarm."

"Molly told you?"

Marilyn nodded miserably, looking away from the window. "She's one of them, Longarm. Everything we've said, everything we've done all these years, she's been reporting to them. In our own home. A spy! Father didn't want to believe it. She had cared for mother in her last illness, and to us she's been . . . like a second mother. Yet all this time . . . "

Marilyn bowed her head and began to sob quietly. Longarm moved to her side and put his arms around her shoulders to comfort her. He led her over to the bed. She sat down on the edge of it and looked up at him, tears streaking paths down her face. "We used to be persecuted, Longarm. I remember mother telling us about it. But now we're persecuting our own people! There are secret courts now. Secret places of execution! I've heard of good church members as outspoken as father, but not as powerful, who have just disappeared! And none of us knows who is a member of the Avenging Angels, and who isn't."

She paused and looked toward the window. "And now . . . we find that Molly is one of them!" Marilyn looked back at Longarm. "Oh, Longarm, what's to become of us? I'm frightened. Do you think they'll take Audrey and me away like they took Emilie?"

Longarm began to button his shirt, trying to think of a response that would comfort Marilyn, when the door swung open without a warning knock. Marilyn got to her feet and the two of them turned to see who it was.

156

Molly swept into the room with another woman on her heels. "As I suspected," said Molly. "You two are shameless!"

To Longarm's astonishment the woman behind Molly was Sarah Smithson, Elder Smithson's latest wife. She recognized Longarm, of course, and there was a malignant gleam of triumph in her eyes as she saw Longarm standing beside Marilyn, his shirt still not completely buttoned. Sarah glanced swiftly at Molly.

"You were right, Molly," she said. "We did find them together!"

"Apostate!" hissed Molly at Marilyn. "He's a gentile! And you're no better than he is!"

Longarm saw Marilyn fall back as if Molly had struck her. He did not blame the girl. Molly seemed to have been storing up all this bile for quite a spell. Now it was just boiling over, taking the cork with it. And poor Marilyn was getting all the worst of it. Molly's words must have hit her like a mule's kick. Only it was probably even worse than that. Marilyn had come to love the old battle-axe, Longarm realized.

"Back off there, woman," said Longarm to Molly. "You got no call to go on like that. Do what you come in here to do, then get out."

It was Sarah Smithson who replied, a cold, thin smile on her face, "You are wanted downstairs, Mr. Longarm. You and the apostates infesting this dwelling. It is time now for all of you to meet your judges!"

Marilyn gasped and looked at Longarm. He reached out and put his arm on her shoulder. "We'll be down," Longarm said, "as soon as I finish dressing."

"We'll wait," said Sarah.

"Oh, no, you won't!" snapped Marilyn, straightening her shoulders in sudden anger and advancing on the two of them. "Both of you get out of this room! This is still my house! You're intruders! You especially, Molly! Now get out of this room this instant or I'll scratch your eyes out!"

Molly took Sarah by the arm and pulled her back through the door. "We'll be waiting for you both!" she said with grim finality. "And don't try to escape. There are guards at the foot of these stairs—and others surrounding the house." She pulled the door shut behind them.

Marilyn turned back to Longarm, then. Her fury vanished in the instant, and she collapsed, sobbing, in his arms.

Their trial was to be held in the library. As Marilyn and Longarm entered, Audrey ran to throw herself into Marilyn's arms. The two girls then joined their father, who was sitting in one of his leather chairs before the window. A grim-looking Avenging Angel stood behind him, the brim of his black hat pulled low, his arms folded across his chest. In the growing dimness Longarm could not make out the fellow's features, so well did the hat brim cover his face. Longarm saw only an implacable jaw, a straight, grim, undeviating line for a mouth, and eyes hidden in darkness. The other Avenging Angels stationed around the room, especially the two that had herded them silently into the library, were just as grim, just as expressionless. They were all cut from the same fearsome doctrinal cloth.

Longarm paused in front of the long table that had been pulled around to face the door. Behind the table were Elder Wolverton, another elder—a short, stocky fellow who was vaguely familiar—and Meeker, Welling, and Wells Daniel. Wolverton held the center of this imposing group, his pink, cherubic cheeks fairly shining in the gloom, his eyes grimly alight. He stroked his snow-white beard and spoke to Longarm.

"You have a charmed life, it seems, Mr. Long."

"I told you before, you can call me Longarm."

"Before we go any further," spoke up Wells Daniel, "I think we should give Longarm this telegram."

The elder shrugged. "Give it to him, then. But I

158

warn you, Daniel! It wil have no bearing on this trial. The judgment of this court is well outside the jurisdiction of that accursed federal despotism. Whether he has a legal right to be here or not is unimportant."

Wells Daniel appeared to flinch visibly under the weight of Wolverton's measured scorn, but he rose from his seat, nevertheless, and leaning over the library table, handed Longarm the telegram. "It's from your superior, I believe," he told Longarm.

Longarm took it. "I could read it better if someone would turn up a few lamps. This place is as dark as a back room in hell."

Audrey and Marilyn darted swiftly but noiselessly about the room lighting lamps and turning them up. Marilyn placed a lamp on the table. Wolverton immediately placed it on the far end, his eyes holding a stern rebuke for the girl. She looked quickly, fearfully away from his angry eyes and retreated back to her father's side.

Longarm held up the telegram and read it.

WASHINGTON RAISING HELL RETURN TO DENVER I AM CALLING YOU OFF THE CASE RETURN TO DENVER YOU NO LONGER HAVE AUTHORITY IN UTAH TERRITORY

VAIL

Longarm glanced at Wells Daniel. "Guess that cuts the rug out from under me, all right. You fellows behind this?"

"We had no choice, Longarm," said Burns Meeker, his small eyes weary, his round face no longer florid. "My brother . . . has already disappeared."

Job Welling spoke up then, his voice frail, distraught. "My daughter Marylou has left with them, Longarm. She insists it is her wish." He shook his head. "But I cannot believe that."

159

"Oh, ye of little faith," said Wolverton, his voice laced with contempt.

"They've put the screws to you, have they, Welling?" Longarm was sorry for the man.

"Longarm," said Boggs from his chair, "Elder Wolverton insists that Emilie has consented to join him in Celestial Marriage. He says she wants her sisters to join her."

Longarm looked back at Wolverton. His dander was up, and for a little while he considered quite calmly what his chances would be of surviving if he leaped across that table and strangled the old goat. Wolverton smiled at Longarm.

"Go ahead, Longarm. Try it. You will expedite matters beautifully."

"Can we get on with this?" said the other, smaller elder.

At once Longarm turned to look at him. In that instant he recognized the voice—and the man. This was the tormented elder who had visited him that night when he was a prisoner at Little Zion—the man who still lived the nightmare of the Mountain Meadows Massacre.

"Yes," said Wolverton. "You are right, Brother Smithson. We should get on with this." Wolverton looked at Longarm, then picked up some notes and began to read slowly, deliberately. The man needed glasses, but was too vain to wear them.

"Custis Long, you are hereby accused of willful destruction of property, of arson, and of the resultant homicide of one Linus Tarboot. How do you plead?"

"What was that about Linus Tarboot?"

"He was killed in the fire you set," said Wolverton. "Or do you deny you set fire to the stables in order to cover your flight with Emilie Boggs?"

"I don't deny it. I'm sorry about Linus Tarboot. I didn't think anyone but those two jaspers I locked in the feed room were in the barn at the time. And I saw them get out all right when I was riding off."

160

"Linus was the man you trussed and left in the arms and powder room. The fire spread to that structure, and before we could extinguish it, the building blew. We did not know until some time after that Linus had not escaped the flames. We assumed he was with the rest of the bucket brigade, trying to stem the fiery destruction you visited upon Little Zion. I did not know of the death of this man before I set out after you and Emilie Boggs. Had I known, I would not have dealt with you so leniently on the desert, I assure you."

"Your earlier defense of your shooting of Sheriff Barker and your explanation of the death of Jason Kimball we accepted," said Smithson. "But the death of Linus we cannot condone, no matter what the circumstances. He leaves four wives and sixteen children."

Longarm remembered leaving the man trussed on his cot, his face to the wall. He did not like to think of the man trapped like that in a burning building, and he had a powerful wish that what had happened to Linus had not happened. But he saw no way that he could have foreseen it. A burning ember must have carried to the roof of the small house, igniting it. With everyone either rushing around trying to corral the horses or busy carrying water to the fire, the flames could have spread from the roof with startling suddenness. Longarm moved uncomfortably under Smithson's gaze.

"I'm sure sorry about that fellow Linus. I never had anything against him, and he did just what I told him to do. I am sorry for his wives and his children, too. But I did not kill Linus deliberately, and if I could have stopped such a crazy piece of bad luck from falling on that man, I would have. But maybe you all, sitting there so righteous, ought to think on what I was doing in Little Zion to begin with. I was there because you had taken a young lady—without her permission—from her home at night, piled her into a wagon, then shut her up in a shack until she agreed to do what

161

you wanted her to do. If anyone is guilty of Linus's death, it's you, Elder Wolverton."

Longarm stopped then to take a breath. He hadn't talked that long at one spell since the time he'd cussed out a bronc that had thrown him halfway down a mountain because he'd heard a rattler.

"I am not on trial here, Longarm," said Wolverton. "You are—as are those here in this room who sent you on your ill-advised mission to Little Zion."

"How do you plead?" asked Smithson. "Guilty or not guilty?"

"If you think I'm going to play along with you silly jaspers, you really are chewing on loco weed. This ain't a court of law. You fellows remind me of little kids out in back of the barn playing secret society and worrying yourself to death over secret passwords. You're *older* kids, that's for sure—and you've got the chance to play with real guns and real lives—but you're still kids living in a make-believe world all your own. I think you ought to pack up your silly game and go home to mama."

"Good for you, Longarm!" said Marilyn.

"Shut up, hussy!" cried Sarah Smithson.

Marilyn recoiled, but her father comforted her and said, his voice quivering with anger, "I agree with my daughter. This man Longarm speaks the bitter truth! You are all dangerous children playing a dangerous game with real lives at stake! Well said, Longarm!"

Elder Smithson looked at Elder Wolverton, as if to say he should be the one to answer this challenge to their authority.

Wolverton leaned forward, his eyes fixed on Longarm, a zealot's fury burning in them. "It does not matter what you think, Longarm! Or the rest of these misguided fools who sent for you. It is what we think that matters."

"Why bother asking me, then?"

"You are right," the man snapped. He looked at

162

Smithson. Smithson nodded and looked back at Longarm.

"U.S. Deputy Long, we, the chosen Elders of Little Zion, pronounce you guilty of homicide in the death of Linus Tarboot. You shall be taken from this place and executed before this night is out."

"Swift justice," intoned Wolverton. "And this time, Longarm, you won't be given any loopholes."

"See here," broke in Wells Daniel. "We have this telegram calling Longarm back to his office in Denver. There's no need for this drastic action. The man will soon be out of the territory—and that by order of his superior!"

"We will accept this verdict of his guilt," said Job Welling, hunching his huge shoulders forward angrily. "But we demand as his punishment that he be exiled from the Territory of Utah. Surely that would be sufficient. You can't summarily execute an officer of the federal government of the United States."

Wolverton glared at them. "The United States is a foreign power still. Its citizens are rabble, gentiles who have persecuted our forefathers and would destroy us now if they could. Be meek with them and they will take everything we have built, everything Brigham Young brought forth upon this wilderness—and which you tiny men would forfeit for the paltry prize of statehood!"

"There must be another reason," snapped Boggs from his chair. "I've heard that political tirade used before to further other equally absurd proposals."

"Yes there is," said Wolverton, "and I admit it freely. This man must die because he is an enemy of Little Zion—as are all of you—and because he knows where our settlement is. Once back in Denver, allied with federal agents of a like mind, there is no doubt in my mind that this man will invade and ravage our settlement, as he has done already."

There was a gavel in front of Smithson. Smithson glanced at Wolverton. Wolverton nodded curtly. Smith-

163

son took up the gavel and brought it down smartly. It rang out like a pistol shot in the crowded room.

"This court is adjourned," said Smithson. "The prisoner will be taken from this place and executed. It is so ordered." Once again the gavel came down.

Wolverton stood up and moved out from behind the table with Smithson following on his heels, and Daniel, Meeker, and Welling right behind them. As Longarm started to look across the room at Boggs to say something to the man, he was spun quickly around by two Avenging Angels and prodded from the library.

Sarah and Molly were standing by the front door of the house, smiling with great satisfaction as Longarm was led out past them and down the walk to one of the waiting carriages. As Longarm ducked his head and climbed into the lead carriage, he tried to figure out what it was that made those two women hate him so much. Maybe he could understand why Molly felt the way she did, for she could not help but notice how nicely Longarm had gotten along with Marilyn. But Sarah he had rescued from Zeke Bannister and then taken back to Little Zion, without once laying an improper hand on her.

And then he remembered that conversation they had had about pretty ankles and how he had narrowly escaped her amorous attentions. Her anger, he remembered, had been intense, bitter. He thought he had pacified her and gotten her to thinking of poor Zeke Bannister, but he saw now, as he settled back in the seat between two grim-visaged Avenging Angels, that Sarah Smithson was still furious that he had been able to restrain himself so easily where she was concerned.

This was why she must have egged her husband on to join Wolverton in this business, and why she must have insisted on coming along as well to witness Longarm's comeuppance. Longarm recalled a proverb: *Hell hath no fury* was how it began.

With the two Avenging Angels on each side of him and another sitting opposite him in the enclosed car-

164

riage, Longarm was driven off through Salt Lake City. The broad streets seemed to him to have been mysteriously cleared of other carriages; they were surprisingly empty of traffic. It was not late in the evening, and yet the entire city somehow appeared to have lost its population as the grim, cheerless caravan wound its way through the streets.

The building into which Longarm was led was some distance from the heart of the city on the other side of a set of railroad tracks. Longarm clearly had felt them under the wheels of his carriage. The building's walls smelled of coal oil and kerosene. As he was being led into a small room, he heard the chuffing of a steam engine on the other side of the outer wall. There were two wooden chairs and a table, a potbellied stove, a foul-smelling chamber pot, and no windows. He saw all this in the light of the smoking lantern placed on the table by the Avenging Angel who pushed him unceremoniously into the room.

The dark-clad fellow left him alone in the room, locking the door behind him. At once Longarm set about trying to find a weak spot in the cell. The walls, especially the door, were quite solid. He cleared his throat loudly and realized with some apprehension just how soundproof the Avenging Angels' detention cells were. The fact that there was no cot indicated that he was not expected to spend the night. This had a chilling effect on him, but he promised himself not to panic.

Someone approached the door. He heard the key in the lock and then the door was pulled open. Elder Smithson entered warily. He saw Longarm standing within a few feet of the door and waggled an enormous Walker Colt at him.

"Get back, Longarm," the elder said. "Back!"

Longarm moved back as far as the table. Smithson entered and pulled the door shut behind him. Someone outside in the corridor promptly locked it.

165

"We could sit at that table," Smithson suggested. "No need to stand around like adversaries waiting to strike."

"Ain't that what we are? Unless I'm here under false pretenses, you just came in to execute me—judging from the size of that cannon you're packing."

"Yes. I am your executioner. Because of my earlier indiscretion, my weakness in coming to see you in Little Zion."

"I didn't tell a soul, Smithson."

"I know."

"Then who did?"

"My wife, Sarah—the woman you rescued from Zeke Bannister and brought back to Little Zion. She followed me that night and listened at the door. She confronted me, then went to Wolverton." There was no mistaking the touch of bitter irony in the elder's voice. Longarm did not pursue the matter. The man was obviously sorely troubled by his present assignment, and when Longarm considered what he had done for the elder by bringing back his third wife, he realized the man had one corking good reason for shooting Longarm with that Walker Colt.

"This execution is supposed to put you back in good standing. Is that it?" Longarm asked.

"*Rehabilitation* is what it is called," Smithson replied, a pained, ironic glint in his eye.

"That's one hell of a jaw-breaker for something as basic as murder. The only difference between this and that Mountain Meadow Massacre, Smithson, is the highfalutin words you jaspers are attaching to it."

"Yes," the man said softly, "you are right. Murder is just what it is."

"Then let me go."

"I can't do that, Longarm."

"Why not?"

"This place is guarded heavily at the moment. Sarah is outside the door. She is to watch me—to see that I perform this business properly."

166

"But you don't want to kill me, do you, Smithson?"

"Yet I must." His voice lowered. "And, indeed, Longarm, one of us must not leave here alive."

"Smithson, you said before that you wanted to expose this fellow Lee. If you let me get out of here, I'll help you do just that. You can go to the courts, the newspapers."

Smithson shook his head sadly. "That's utterly impossible, Longarm."

"*Why* is it?"

"My children. They would be his hostages."

"You mean Lee would—?"

"Yes, he would, Longarm."

"I think you're exaggerating, Smithson. Your wives would sure as hell protest something fierce. And how could Wolverton stand by and let Lee do something like that? He'd lose any authority he had over Little Zion. The other elders would not stand for it."

Smithson smiled sadly at Longarm's assurances. "There is something you don't know, Longarm."

"What's that?"

"Lorenzo Wolverton *is* Mordecai Lee."

Longarm blinked, astonished.

"Now, you'd better let me take this one bite at a time, Smithson. You think you can explain that?"

"Lorenzo Wolverton—the *real* Lorenzo Wolverton —died after the Mountain Meadow Massacre. Lee and I knew this, but no one else, because Lorenzo was being taken care of by the same band of friendly Indians that fought the settlers with us at the Meadow. Just before Lee and I visited their village to check on Lorenzo's condition, Major Higbee received a letter from Brother Brigham forbidding any interference with the immigrant train. When Lee saw that Lorenzo had died while in the care of the Indians, he decided then to leave that area of Utah carrying with him the name of Lorenzo Wolverton. We buried Wolverton with Mordecai Lee's name on the marker. In this way did

167

Lee escape what he feared would be the wrath of Brigham Young."

"What good did that do? Hadn't Wolverton done as much mischief as Lee at the massacre?" Longarm asked with puzzlement.

"No. Wolverton had been wounded before that. He played no part in the massacre. But Lee had been prominent. It was he who directed the fire on most of the children."

"The children?"

"Ten of them—from ten to sixteen years of age."

Longarm sighed. "I reckon I get the picture, all right. Your children would only make it a few more."

"And my wives," Smithson said with a weary sigh. "Except for Sarah, of course, he would not go easy on them. Naturally, there would be a trial—to make matters look perfectly legitimate."

There was a sudden pounding on the door. "Hurry it up in there, Elder! We must be riding soon!" called a powerful voice through the heavy door.

Smithson turned to the door, his face grim, as if he had come to a sudden, irrevocable decision. "Open the door, Grimsby! I want the burial shroud!"

The door swung back and a hulking figure loomed in the doorway and caught Smithson's eye. The fellow seemed somewhat suspicious of Smithson, and looked with surprise at Longarm, evidently disappointed to see him appearing so healthy. "You say you want the shroud now?"

"You heard me. Bring it in here."

"Yes, Brother," the fellow said, and vanished back out through the open doorway. As Longarm looked back at Smithson, he saw that he had pulled the Walker Colt out of his belt and now rested it on the table in front of him, its muzzle pointing at Longarm's head. Longarm sat back in his chair and studied the man.

The lamp gave Longarm a much better look at Elder Smithson's features than he had been able to get either in the Boggses' library or when Longarm

168

was a prisoner in Little Zion. The man was not very tall, but his chunky figure contained not an ounce of tallow. He was in his late forties, his facial whiskers a steel gray, his eyes now hard and resolute—with little in them to indicate the soul-deep torment he had spoken of when he had visited Longarm in his cell in Little Zion. But the anguish was still there, eating at him; Longarm could feel it.

The fellow whom Smithson had addressed as Grimsby returned carrying a soogan-like tarpaulin over his shoulder. He dropped it to the floor and moved back out the door.

"Thank you, Grimsby," said Smithson.

Grimsby had seen the big Colt in the elder's hand and seemed a lot happier as he pushed the door shut. Smithson waited until he heard the key turn in the lock before he looked back at Longarm, and leaned toward him.

"Listen to me, Longarm—carefully."

"I'm listening, Elder. There ain't nothing much else I can do, seems like."

The elder held up a hand to caution Longarm and leaned still closer. "You must keep your voice down," he whispered. "What I tell you must not be overheard. Is that clear?"

With a frown, Longarm nodded.

"You were right, of course," the elder told Longarm, his voice barely audible. "This is not an execution. It is murder. But I cannot kill any more, Longarm— no matter how anxious Sarah is to see you dead." He paused to let that sink in, then continued. "That shroud on the floor is our trademark, Longarm. Wherever our night riders go, they carry one of these rolled neatly behind their saddles—a terrifying and melancholy reminder of our slide back into persecution. After I shoot you, I am to tuck you within that grisly sleeping bag and lace it up. From a nuisance and a threat you become a neat bundle slung over a rider's cantle, to be buried somewhere in our fair

169

valley. It will be good to leave such horror behind. . . ."

As Smithson talked, Longarm began to get a handle on what the man intended. It was in the soft, regretful tone of his voice. Smithson was readying himself to pass from this present torment into another. . . .

Abruptly Smithson stood up and stepped away from the table, the Colt still clutched in his right hand. "I said I cannot kill any more, Longarm. I meant that, except for one more time—an execution long overdue."

Longarm got to his feet. "No need to make that kind of sacrifice," he whispered urgently. "There's no need, I tell you. Just give me that Colt and we'll both shoot our way out of here."

The man smiled and shook his head. "No. Very gallant and brave, but foolish. This way I will be gone, but you will be alive to bring Wolverton down and destroy his nest of scorpions. Now listen carefully. When I pull this trigger, you must act swiftly. Put on my hat and jacket. Squeeze into the jacket as best you can, then place me in the shroud and lace it up. My wife and Grimsby will come for the shroud. Let Grimsby take it without a word. You and my wife, sitting at that table, must wait until he leaves with my body. After that it will be up to you. What you do with my ambitious new wife is also up to you." He smiled and his voice dropped still lower, so that Longarm could barely catch the irony in it. "I am sure she will be able to think of something."

He moved swiftly to the door and called loudly through it. "Sarah! Get Grimsby! *Now!*"

As barely audible footsteps ran down the corridor, Smithson removed his hat and jacket and threw them onto the table. Before Longarm could protest further, Smithson rested the muzzle of the Walker Colt upon his right temple. The man's hand tightened. Longarm looked quickly away as the ferocious detonation filled the tiny room.

170

Reaching out quickly, Longarm caught the falling body as the Colt clattered to the floor. Then he lowered the dead man gently but swiftly to the floor beside the shroud, picked up the Colt, and jammed it into his belt. After unrolling the bag, he lifted the dead man into it—trying not to look at the shattered skull, the colorless mask of a face. He stuffed his own hat and jacket into the shroud, then laced it up tightly. Stepping swiftly to the table, he slapped the elder's wide-brimmed hat onto his own head, pulled the brim down to obscure his face, and slipped into the jacket. It was a tight fit, but he managed and was sitting at the table with his head bowed in apparent anguish at the execution he had just performed. His back was to the door when Grimsby and Sarah Smithson hurried in.

Sarah moved to his side and placed a comforting hand on his shoulder. Longarm reached back and took her wrist firmly in his, then drew her with a steady, unrelenting force into the seat opposite him. When she caught sight of his face, she could see also the black muzzle of the Colt staring at her from out of his jacket. It froze the cry on her lips.

"You going to give me a hand, Elder?" Grimsby called. He had been tugging on the body and had only just managed to get it through the doorway.

"No," said Sarah, her voice trembling from the menace in Longarm's eyes. "Elder Smithson is too upset. You'll have to get someone else to help."

The man muttered something and then Longarm heard him call to someone else. In a few moments he was joined by another Avenging Angel. They lifted the body of Elder Smithson easily between them and were soon gone.

"I don't understand," Sarah said. "Did—did you kill him?"

"He killed his own self, ma'am. A brave and terrible thing it was, too. He said I was to take care of you as I saw fit."

She started to snatch her hand out of his grasp, but

171

Longarm just squeezed it a bit tighter and drew her across the table toward him. Then he took the Colt out with his free hand and pointed the muzzle at her right eye, holding it less than an inch away. "If you are quiet, I will not harm you, ma'am. If you raise an outcry, your husband's sacrifice will be in vain, for then both of us will be on our way in one of those real convenient sleeping bags you people carry around. Is that clear?"

"Perfectly, Mr. Longarm."

"It's Mr. Long to you, ma'am," Longarm said.

"We—we don't have to be enemies, Mr. Long. I assure you, I can be very understanding to them that needs it." She reached out and held his shoulder gently.

"Smithson said you would be able to think of something. You really are a caution, Mrs. Smithson, but I'd sooner curl up with a sidewinder than the likes of you."

She was furious, and this time she did manage to pull free. She jumped back and slammed against the wall, sending the chair crashing to the floor. Longarm stood up, his Colt trained on her. "I will not stand for your insolence!" she hissed.

"Do you know what I'll tell Wolverton if you don't help me out of here? I'll tell him this whole thing was your idea, that you and me had ourselves an affair while we were journeying back to Little Zion—and that this was why you wanted to come along with your husband. He knows, I am sure, how loyal and faithful a wife you have been to your husband."

"You're hateful!"

"I know that. Meanwhile, you go out of this place just a little bit ahead of me and tell Wolverton that I'm not up to that long ride tonight, that the two of us are going to stay the night in Salt Lake City. Do you think you can remember all that?"

"You are much taller than my husband," she said. "They'll all notice."

"Not if you go first and speak for me, then return

172

to help me to one of the carriages. I'll be stooped over quite a bit. Killing a man does not come easy to men like Elder Smithson."

She hesitated.

"Do you really think you will have a chance to supplant Emilie Boggs in the heart of Elder Wolverton? You *are* ambitious, ma'am. But it takes more than that, don't it? Remember all that talking we did about pretty ankles? Things ain't really so different on the Mormon side, are they?"

"I'll help you," she snapped. "But only because I know what a treacherous and coldblooded man you are! I am in fear of my life while in your presence!'

"That's real comforting to these ears, you have no idea. So lead the way now, and take it real careful."

Without another word, Sarah turned and preceded him out of the small room. As they started down the corridor, Longarm caught sight of two men hurrying toward them carrying lanterns.

"Is that you, Elder Smithson?" one of them called.

"It is!" replied Sarah. "Get back to your horses. We do not need your help. Elder Smithson is feeling much better now."

The two men turned and hurried ahead of them. A few moments later, Longarm paused at the door of the building while Sarah walked out into the night. He watched her approach the lead rider, who was already mounted up and waiting. His long white beard fairly glowed in the moonlight.

Elder Wolverton leaned down to catch Sarah's words. He nodded curtly when she had finished, and took up his reins, as Sarah turned about and walked back toward the building. Longarm moved out of the doorway. Wolverton waved to him and called, "Take a little holiday. You have done well! Remember! He was a gentile! No need to get nervous over that!"

Then he put his spurs to his horse and the crowd of horsemen headed out toward the desert, with the inevitable water wagon and a small remuda following

173

close behind. Stooping a bit, Longarm waved to the disappearing riders, then stepped back into the doorway. Longarm saw Boggs step down out of one of the two waiting carriages and hurry across the moonlit ground toward him. As Boggs neared him, the other carriage turned about and was driven off in a sudden clatter of hoofs, a hectic series of whipcracks sounding above them. The carriage and its occupants, Longarm sensed, were in flight from an obscene and terrifying place.

Longarm waited for Boggs with a slight, grim smile on his face. When Sarah reached his side, he pulled her to him with an iron grasp that made her cry out slightly. "Well done, woman. Now continue to behave and you might get out of this better than you deserve."

He relaxed his grip on her arm slightly and stepped out of the doorway to meet Boggs. Boggs pulled up suddenly, staring uncomprehendingly at him, his face suddenly as pale as the moonlit ground at his feet.

"My God! Is it really you, Longarm?"

"It is, thanks to a very brave man—a Saint who'd had his fill of murder and other such villainy. He has left me a charge, and I intend to fulfill it, no matter what Washington or my superiors have to say in the matter. Are you with me?"

"Of course, Longarm. You are all the hope I have now!"

"Are you alone in that carriage?"

"There are two Avenging Angels—and Molly."

"What is this place?"

"It was built to serve as a warehouse for the cotton we were supposed to produce in this land, but you know to what use it has been put—as does every Mormon in the city. It has become a charnel house, an abomination that haunts every child's nightmare—and every adult's as well."

"Are there any guards?"

"This place needs no guards. Its reputation alone is enough to keep every living soul well away from here.

174

You saw how empty our streets became when those riders escorted us to this place?"

"I noticed."

"What do you plan on doing now?" Boggs asked.

"Are Marilyn and Audrey safe?"

"For now, yes. They are at home."

"Stay here with Sarah Smithson, Boggs."

Longarm walked swiftly across the dark ground to the waiting carriage and pulled back the leather side curtains. The three waiting occupants froze into immobility when they saw the gaping muzzle of the Walker Colt in Longarm's hand.

"Out!" Longarm directed sharply.

One of the Avenging Angels acted on a foolish impulse and his hand dropped to his holster. Longarm brought the barrel of the Walker down with such force that the sound of the man's wristbone shattering under the impact filled the interior of the carriage. With a cry, the fellow grabbed at his wrist. He was the first out; the other two followed hard on his heels.

Longarm disarmed the two men, told Molly she'd better not have any weapons hidden on her, then herded them all toward the building. When they reached the doorway, Longarm gave one of the weapons to Boggs and told the man he would be needed to help cover them. Boggs agreed as Longarm directed the three ahead of him down the long dark corridor toward the cell he had just quit.

When they reached it, he told them to walk on into it. The two men did as they were told, but Molly hesitated. An unsteady hand went up to her face, as if to push away a strand of loose hair.

"She has a small pistol in her bosom!" hissed Sarah into Longarm's ear.

At once Longarm leaped forward and was in time to grab Molly's wrist as she pulled the derringer free. The small pistol went off, sending its slug into the ceiling, the detonation surprisingly powerful. Wrenching the pistol from her hand, Longarm wagged

175

the barrel of the Colt at her and the woman stepped into the small cell after the others, her eyes glancing with withering hatred at Sarah.

Longarm turned to Sarah.

"You too, Sarah. Get in there with your friends."

Sarah's face went white. "In there? With them? But I just—" She looked into the cell. The lantern on the small table still burned and the light from it showed the three watching her, it seemed, with eyes gleaming malevolently. It was she, after all, who had just prevented Molly from killing Longarm. Sarah looked back at him. "Please! Not with them! I saved your life!"

"Get in there, Sarah!"

"Please!" she screamed in terror.

"Get in there, or I'll throw you in."

Weeping softly, Sarah Smithson walked into the room. Longarm kicked the door shut. He slid the bolt and snapped the lock. He did not have the key to the lock, but he had no intention of worrying about that. Let the four of them—betrayers all—eat each other alive like scorpions in a glass.

As Longarm and Boggs hurried down the dim corridor, they heard faint screams coming from within the tiny cell.

Outside the grim building, as they walked toward the carriage, Boggs said finally, "She did save your life, Longarm. Wasn't that a very cruel thing to do?"

"I saw the bulge in Molly's bosom, Boggs, and I told her she had better not have anything on her to see if I could make her give it up voluntarily. When she didn't, I just decided to wait and let her make the first move. I knew what she was up to the moment her hand went to her face."

He shuddered. "Still, that poor woman!"

"That 'poor woman,' Boggs, put her husband into such a bind that he blew his brains out less than an hour ago in that same blamed cell."

"Blew his brains—? You mean Elder Smithson shot himself? He's dead?"

176

"That body they slung over a horse was dead, Boggs—sure as shooting. Like I said a little while ago. He was a brave man who'd just about had his fill of this dirty business."

Boggs was silent as they got into the carriage. He took up the reins and looked at Longarm. "What now, Deputy?"

"A little more of your hospitality, Boggs, if you don't mind. And then tomorrow I'll go see about retrieving a pair of army mules."

"Army mules!"

"That's right. Thieves took 'em. Larceny, I call it. Do you know what good, healthy army mules are worth today, Boggs? Three hundred dollars a span, that's what. Leastways, that's what the good captain told me, so I aim to help him get his mules back."

"I don't understand, Longarm."

"I know you don't, and that's your protection. But after I leave tomorrow, I'd be much obliged if you'd send a telegram to Denver for me."

Boggs started up the carriage. "Of course, Longarm."

"I'll give you the address. You just say I'll be reporting back to Denver as soon as I bring in some stolen army mules. And you can sign my name to it."

Longarm leaned back in the carriage while Boggs, shaking his head slightly in puzzlement, drove over the railroad tracks and turned his horses onto the broad, once again busy streets of Salt Lake City.

Chapter 8

Sergeant Dillon mopped his face with a red polkadot handkerchief, then stuffed it into his tight rear pocket. He was worried about the operation, but unwilling to speak of his misgivings openly. That's how Longarm figured it, anyway.

"What is it, Sergeant?"

"Sorry to bother you, sir, and I know the captain said you was to be in charge, but we ain't got to no wagon tracks yet, and it's pure misery trying to find our way in this here pitch dark."

"Well, you just rest easy, Sergeant. I've been over this country twice already and I'll sing out when I smell those wagon tracks."

The sergeant was riding beside him at the moment, with the rest of the ten-man contingent strung out in a double line over the rocky terrain. They had crossed the Great Salt Desert during the night, then camped during the day, and had been riding now for close to four hours. What was left of the moon hadn't been up for long. They were going in the right direction and the land held a vague familiarity that was enough for Longarm, but he could understand the sergeant's concern. All this for two Army mules?

"Pardon me, Deputy, sir, but I'm still a little uncertain about them orders the captain gave me."

"Just call me Longarm, Sergeant. You're liable to get your tongue all twisted into a knot with that

178

'Deputy, sir' handle. Now just what is it you don't understand about Captain Meriwether's orders?"

"Mules, sir. Is that what we're after? All this for two mules?"

"Stolen government property, Sergeant. Let's not forget that."

"No, sir. I understand, sir. But dynamite?"

"If you'll just let us eat this apple one bite at a time, Sergeant, you'll get all those important questions answered proper. But right now, let's not have this troop straggling any. And tell them to quiet down. This ain't Indian country, but it might as well be."

"Yes, sir!" The man started to pull away.

"Just a minute, Sergeant. Send up that Corporal Toohey, will you?"

"The dynamite man?"

"That's the man, Sergeant."

"Yes, sir."

"Call me Longarm, Sergeant."

"Yes, sir."

Longarm shook his head and peered through the gloom. They were at least five hours away from Little Zion, but already the grotesque rock forms that reared out of the darkness seemed vaguely familiar as they loomed ominously over the trail. He expected the trail to begin to rise presently, bringing them onto a ridge. When and if it did that, he would know for sure that he was on course.

Like Boggs, Longarm did not believe that Emilie had finally consented to marry Wolverton. The old fox was just making with moondust, and hoping more than thinking. But Longarm had tough going when it came to convincing Boggs not to panic. The man was all for selling his house and moving out of the territory, taking his daughters with him. The fact that Molly had been a spy all these years—for nine years, it turned out—had really shaken Boggs up and Longarm could hardly blame him. Naturally, under the circumstances, all Boggs could think of was saving his remaining

179

daughters from this arrogant band of night riders who had been so bold and so damned sure of themselves that they had ridden right into Salt Lake City, marched into his own home, and put a Deputy U.S. Marshal on trial.

Longarm had located the other members of the council as soon as he could. They, too, were equally uncertain, until Longarm pointed out to them that if they let these jaspers get away with what they had just done, they might as well do what Boggs was ready to do—hightail it like scared rabbits, or march their kin and their own daughters up to the nearest Avenging Angel and tell him to do his damnedest.

What they all had to realize was that if they didn't fight back, they left themselves no compromise. They would either have to get out or give up.

Longarm figured he'd set some bees loose in their bonnets. If he succeeded in bringing back Emilie and destroying that scorpion's nest as Smithson wanted, he hoped they'd be able to muster enough gumption to organize and encourage the other Mormons to take a hand in things and maybe take their land and their city back at the same time.

Of course it was only a hope. Nothing's as easy for most people, Longarm realized, as letting things drift without doing anything—until the bugs are out of the walls and crawling over the tables and chairs. And by then, as likely as not, it's too late. Still, he had promised Emilie he would come back for her—and there was poor little Annie Dawkins waiting for him, too.

So it didn't really matter what Boggs or his fellows told him or how many telegrams he got from the chief—he was going back to Little Zion for those two army mules. He chuckled, wondering how he could explain all this to that sergeant, or if he should even try.

A trooper pulled up beside Longarm. Longarm glanced at him and saw the corporal's stripes in the dim moonlight.

180

"You'd be Corporal Miles Toohey, I reckon."

"That's right, sir."

"Call me Longarm. Think you can do that?"

"Yes, sir—I mean, Longarm."

"Fine. What experience have you had with dynamite, Corporal?"

"Plenty, Longarm."

"How much is plenty? You talk like an Indian. Details, Corporal. You work for the railroad?"

"No, Longarm. I'm not a Chinaman."

"Didn't figure to hurt your feelings with that question, Corporal. So out with it, if you don't mind. What's your experience with that stuff?"

"I worked at the Sutro mine in Nevada in '74, when they switched from nitro. Dynamite was a hell of a lot safer, and it did a whale of a job blasting that tunnel."

Longarm had heard reports about the Nevada tunnel and how it had been blown. His question concerning the railroad, though, had been equally legitimate, no matter how pained the corporal was at his question. The Chinese were not the only ones who learned to blow tunnels for the railroad, though they seemed to like black powder, not dynamite.

"You got what you need?" Longarm asked.

"I checked it out before we left Fort Douglas, Longarm. You must have spent quite a lot for all that equipment."

Longarm smiled as he recalled the puzzlement on Boggs's face when he told him he needed the dynamite to help him recover two army mules. But Longarm was careful not to tell the man why he wanted the dynamite, just as he had told none of them what he was about, really. It was best for all concerned that they know only what he told them—and that was precious little. Maybe he wouldn't even tell Vail—not all of it, anyway.

"Yes, I did spend quite a bit, Corporal, and it wasn't even my money. So you be damn sure you take good

181

care of it. I don't want it going off too soon—or too late. Right on time. You got that clear?"

"Yes, sir."

"Call me Longarm, Corporal, and go on back to that wagon. I want you to ride alongside it until we get to where we're going."

"Yes, Longarm."

Longarm waved to him and the fellow pulled his mount around and waited for the column to move past him.

The trail, Longarm noted, was rising definitely now, heading for a high, rocky ridge that seemed to lift into the stars. He felt much better, suddenly. Though the sergeant didn't know it, they were traveling over that wagon road right now. Sometime before dawn they'd be close enough to get down off their horses and start searching the rocks surrounding Little Zion for Mormon lookouts.

The tall finger of rock that Sarah had pointed out to him the last time he had come this way still beckoned to him as it towered against the stars. Longarm led the troopers across the short rise and then along the precarious rocky ledge. In the darkness it was a nervous passage, but the weary troopers followed Longarm in good order. Longarm ignored the trail leading down into the canyon, cutting carefully up a steep slope, trashy with detritus, until they found a level stretch.

He turned in his saddle and motioned the men off their mounts as soon as he saw that the remuda and the wagon had joined them on the flat. The driver of the wagon was cursing, not very softly, as he brought his wagon to a halt. The remuda was a mite skittish, Longarm noted.

He swung off his mount and waited for Sergeant Dillon to approach. As the sergeant stopped before Longarm, he looked about nervously.

"What's this place, sir?" he asked. "We almost there?"

182

"We're getting warm, Sergeant, and that's a fact. Leave Corporal Toohey back with the wagon and the remuda. The rest of your men follow me."

The sergeant nodded and returned to the troopers. Longarm could hear the man issuing orders and called out to him softly to keep it down. From then on there was almost perfect silence as the sergeant issued his orders and the rest of the men moved up to join Longarm.

When the sergeant rejoined him, Longarm led the party due west over the rocky flat. It would be dawn in less than two hours, Longarm realized, which meant they would have to shake it. The night seemed to be getting blacker. At last Longarm noticed a great emptiness yawning at him just ahead.

He held up his hand. "Careful now!" he whispered.

They crept forward until they were on the lip of the escarpment. Below them, stretching into the night for a distance of at least five miles, was the valley—Little Zion. The men sucked in their breaths. Lying under the night sky, the valley was still breathtaking. The broad stream issuing from the canyon was visible. Coiling easily about the valley, punctuated by a series of four dams, it looked like a vast hair ribbon holding the valley together.

The fields, lush under the night sky, seemed to exhale a heady fragrance that hung in the air about them. It was an almost tangible presence. Longarm sighed. It would be a shame to bring all this to an end. And then he thought of the night riders, the fear, the furtive executions in the dark of night, the implacable dogma on which this lovely, fertile valley was built, and he felt regret no longer.

Pointing to the settlement in the distance, he said to the sergeant, "We'll circle this valley and meet above those buildings."

"Circle the valley?"

"That's right. This valley is well-guarded. There are

183

sentries up here all along this rim. When I rode in a week or so ago, I saw them."

"You want us to take them?"

"Without firing a shot. Capture them, truss them up, and leave them. Think your men can do that, Sergeant?"

The troopers crowded around them had been listening. There was a low mutter of assent. Of course they could. A few grinned, their teeth flashing in the darkness, and they elbowed one another eagerly. Action was something they had given up on, stationed in that sweltering hot box on the edge of the Great Salt Desert.

"They'll do it," said the sergeant.

"Good. We'll split up then. You take half and circle south. I'll take the rest and go north. We'll meet above the settlement."

The sergeant nodded and quickly divided the men.

The low shack was barely visible on the horizon, its slanted roof cutting a straight line across the stars, the only straight edge in a nightmare of rock forms crowding upon them out of the predawn darkness.

Trooper Billy Perkins was at Longarm's elbow. Longarm turned to Billy. "Tell the others to hold up. Looks like we've got one ahead of us."

"I don't see nothing."

"That's all right, Billy. You just go and do what I say or I'll lay this barrel across your head."

The fellow vanished quickly back into the darkness. Longarm waited patiently, heard the low mutter of voices, and a moment later was joined by two other troopers, with Billy just behind them.

Longarm pointed without a word at the shack. The men peered closely, then nodded. "Spread out," Longarm said softly. "Circle the place. And remember what I said. No gunfire. Use your rifle butts if you have to."

They nodded and melted away in the darkness. Longarm, keeping low, moved swiftly forward and found himself on a rough path that led straight to the

184

front of the shack. He left the path before he reached the shack, and circling around behind it, found a window and peered in. In the darkness he could see nothing for a while until at last he made out a sleeping form on a cot directly across from the window. There was another cot against the adjoining wall. It was empty.

With his Colt drawn but not cocked, Longarm circled around the shack, and found himself on the lip of the escarpment, staring at a thin man with a long, straggly beard, a slouch hat, and a Sharps rifle resting in the crotch of his pants as he leaned back against a smooth rock face. The man was snoring softly, his straggly whiskers moving with each exhalation.

As the three troopers scrambled silently over the rocks toward him, Longarm put up his hand to halt them, then turned back around, and leaning forward, slowly placed one hand around the long barrel. When he was certain he had a firm grip, he yanked.

"Hey! What in tar—!"

The muzzle of Longarm's Colt, held a few inches from the man's face, quieted him almost instantly.

"Get up," said Longarm softly, moving back. "And don't do anything sudden."

The fellow swallowed unhappily and did as he was told.

"Now lead the way back to the shack," Longarm directed. "And keep those hands up."

As the man started past him, Longarm spoke softly to Billy, who hurried ahead of Longarm, taking the two troopers with him. In a moment, as he followed behind the lanky Mormon, Longarm heard his men bursting into the shack. There were no shots and only a single, stifled cry.

He smiled. So far, this operation was proceeding as slick as silk.

Leaving both sentries securely bound in the shack with the door locked and barred, the three troopers, with

Longarm in the lead, continued along the rim. Longarm had only three troopers with him because he had decided to leave one man with Toohey to guard the wagon and horses in case of a surprise strike by the Mormons. Since the sergeant had a greater distance to cover, Longarm sent five men with him. All in all, a force of eleven men to take this hotbed of Avenging Angels was cutting things a mite fine, but the way Longarm had it planned, the element of surprise was the key. And so far, they still had that on their side.

The next two pairs of sentries were not as easy to take as the first two had been. One sentry almost got off a shot before Billy Perkins lifted the back of his head with a rifle butt. His companion heard the scuffle and came running just in time to throw both hands into the air. The remaining two were just stirring about in their shack, making breakfast. When they heard Longarm's men approaching, they picked up their rifles, stepped out in front of their shack, and asked loudly if that was Burt something-or-other with the salt pork and what was he doing coming up that early. When Longarm appeared out of the darkness with his Colt trained on them, they were too surprised to offer resistance and were trussed up like the others and left in their locked shack.

In less than an hour Longarm and his party had reached a position above the settlement. It was still quite dark, but he could make out the individual houses and outbuildings clearly as he peered down from the rocks.

The settlement was laid out with great precision. Most of the homes and buildings were neatly spaced inside what appeared to be an almost perfect square. The windmill tower was at the very center, and south of this were three rows containing five homes each. Broad avenues ran between the three rows. Each home was spaced the same distance from the next, like checkers on a checkerboard, with even the outhouses

186

spaced with tight precision at the right rear corner of each home. In the soft light filtering down from the stars, the privies looked just as neat and finely engineered as the homes.

Most of the sheds and barns and other outbuildings were north of the windmill tower. What had been the largest barn was now a blackened crater and next to it was another, smaller crater—the tiny hut that had served as their armory. The Avenging Angels were undoubtedly hurting for firearms as a result, Longarm realized. At the same time that he thought of this, he thought of that man he had trussed and left to burn on that cot. It was not something he would ever be able to think about without wincing slightly, he realized.

Next to the windmill were the fenced-in compounds that held Emilie and anyone else in violation of Little Zion's laws, and still farther to the west, well out of the square that made up the settlement, there was a large, almost baronial residence. This house was not built of wood, but of stone faced with stucco—and beside it there was another residence—a long, low building with curious gabled windows running down its length. At once Longarm was reminded of another such building that had been pointed out to him by the driver of the carriage who had returned him to the hotel from Wells Daniel's home—the residence of Brigham Young. There was no wooden eagle perched atop the main gate before this particular residence, but otherwise this structure was a perfect duplicate of the apartment building with its twenty gables that adjoined Brother Brigham's residence in Salt Lake City, the *seraglio* that housed his many wives.

There was no doubt in Longarm's mind who lived in this impressive residence. Or why Lorenzo Wolverton wanted so much to have Emilie Boggs move into that gabled residence.

Trooper Sim Johnson approached through the darkness. Longarm pulled back from the rocks and stood

187

up. He had sent Johnson scouting for a trail of some kind leading down to Little Zion from this point. He knew there must be one, since he had seen a roadway leading in this direction from the stables when he had been led into his prison.

"What did you find, Johnson?"

"There's a trail, all right. It leads from the settlement up past here and over that ridge. It's pretty well-traveled, too, and heads north into the mountains."

"How much traffic could it carry, you reckon?"

"Not much heavy stuff, sir. It's pretty steep and rocky and narrow. No wagons carrying supplies and such could make it. Just horses, mostly."

"Thank you, Johnson."

The fellow nodded and moved back to where the others were waiting. Longarm looked up at the sky. He was wishing Sergeant Dillon would hurry up and beginning to wonder if maybe he and his men had been stopped, when the sergeant and his four men materialized out of the gloom.

Dillon walked up to Longarm, a smile on his face. "We surprised them all. I guess they were so used to never having anything happen, they just couldn't believe it when it did. Like you told me, they're trussed up and locked away."

"Have any trouble?"

"One of them tried to run."

"You didn't shoot, did you? I didn't hear anything."

"One of the men caught up to him and tripped him with his rifle. The fellow went down so hard on the rocky ground that we had to carry him back to his lookout post."

"All right. Now listen. This is going to be the hard part. I'm going back to Corporal Toohey. While I'm gone I want your men to build the makings of a fire on top of that rock up there. I've already scouted it. There's an easy way up. After you've done that, I want you to wait for me at the head of the trail Private

188

Johnson has discovered. I should be back before dawn if I don't run into any trouble. Wait for me."

"Yes, Deputy, sir."

"It's Longarm, damn it! And that's an order, Sergeant."

The sergeant smiled. "Yes, sir, Longarm."

Longarm groaned and hurried back through the predawn darkness.

Corporal Toohey was not in sight, but Cal Brenner, the trooper Longarm had ordered to stay back with him, was asleep under the wagon. He slept with his mouth open. Longarm wished he had a scorpion handy that he could drop into the trooper's mouth. He was looking for something when he heard a twig snap behind him and whirled, his Colt appearing in his right hand in one quick, striking motion.

Corporal Toohey was standing just behind him with a stick of dynamite in his hand and a grin on his face.

"I was gonna drop this in," the corporal told Longarm. "That's a big mouth he's got."

Longarm smiled, turned back around, and nudged the trooper awake with the toe of his boot. Then he holstered his Colt and looked at Toohey.

"Did you look over that canyon wall like I told you?"

"I did that."

"And?"

"Let me get this straight, now. You want to blow the wall so that it closes off all the water coming through, and then you want to blow the other side of the canyon to block it off completely."

"You got it."

"Mr. Longarm—all this for a couple of *mules?*"

"*Army* mules, Corporal. *Army* mules."

"Yes, sir, Mr. Longarm."

"Let's get busy. Trooper Brenner can help us carry the stuff." Brenner nodded sleepily. "That's dynamite you'll be carrying, Trooper," Longarm informed him.

189

"You better wake up a little or you'll be blown up a lot!"

The fellow hopped to it and Longarm left him to the corporal, went back to his horse, and rode down into the canyon. In a moment the two followed, Toohey carrying a spool of fuse, the corporal—wide awake now—carrying a couple of boxes of dynamite. Longarm got off his horse, accompanied Toohey to the face of the canyon wall, and looked up.

The jagged hole in the canyon wall from which the thick gout of water was spurting was not more than ten or fifteen feet above the canyon floor. They were standing upstream from the spot. As they stood watching, a fine spray fell over them.

"We better move back," Toohey said. "I don't want to get this fuse wet."

"This is Bickford Safety," Longarm said.

"I know. I've worked with it before. But this here batch is old stuff and the waterproofing tape is loose."

"It will work, won't it?"

Toohey looked at Longarm. "We'll know when it blows. But that ain't all our problem. The only good crack that'll go deep enough for me to use as a blowhole is about five feet over that crack where the water is pouring out. And if you'll look close, you'll see the canyon wall leans out some at that point. I'd need to be a fly to make it up there."

"You'll have to reach it from above, then."

"That's what I been thinking," Toohey said with a sigh. "You think you can lower me down that wall?"

"Sure, but we'd better do it fast. That sun's due up in an hour. What about the other side?"

"Let me do that now while I'm down here. That won't be no problem, not with that overhang. I'll tamp in the dynamite and leave the rattails hanging till later."

Longarm looked across the canyon at the wall Toohey was planning to blow. The water had cut well in under the canyon wall, so deeply, in fact, that it

190

looked like a cave. Several great cracks in the wall were visible, despite the darkness. It would not take much to bring the whole wall crashing down. But Longarm wanted to cut off the water supply as well. It was the only way he could see to discourage more or less permanently this nest of night riders.

As Toohey and Brenner splashed across the canyon floor to the other side, Longarm went back to his horse and remounted. Before he rode out of the canyon, he took one more look at the face of the canyon wall above the spot where the water was coming from. In the darkness he could not see the overhang the corporal mentioned, nor could he see any cracks that could be used for blowholes, but the fellow seemed to know what he was doing, and he had been studying the problem since Longarm had left him here. The problem now was to find a good spot above the canyon from which to lower a man carrying dynamite and blasting caps down this face of rock.

He rode out of the canyon and back to the wagon and the waiting horses. He dismounted, took a rope with him to the canyon's edge, and looked over. It was difficult in the darkness to find reliable footing as he moved along the rim, but finally he came upon a spot that was almost directly over the break in the canyon wall. He looked around then and found a small juniper whose roots seemed pretty deeply spread, around which he could snub the rope.

In the darkness he could not make out the two men placing the dynamite charges below him in the canyon, so he moved back from the rim and began knotting the rope to make it easier for Toohey to make it down. He had almost finished the task when Toohey and a pale, shaken Trooper Brenner, hefting two boxes of dynamite, one on each shoulder, struggled toward him out of the gloom. The footing was precarious in the darkness and the private kept stumbling.

Longarm looked nervously at the fellow as the trooper neared him. "Careful, damn it! You're liable

191

to start this party before any of us gets a chance to send out the invitations."

Brenner didn't laugh; he just set the boxes down very carefully, then collapsed on a rock and began mopping his brow.

Toohey looked over the rim and nodded, satisfied, then walked back to the boxes and began stuffing sticks of dynamite down his shirtfront. Next he gathered up a handful of copper blasting caps and stuck them into his shirt pocket. As he did so, he picked up the spool of fuse, and passing by Longarm on his way to the rim, said, "Got to be careful with these blasting caps. A friend of mine, a real Cousin Jack, got some of them mixed in his pipe tobacco. Fellow was awful careless."

Toohey tugged on the rope, checking to see how well Longarm had snubbed it, then, with his arm through the spool and a small hammer for tamping and a knife to cut the fuse stuck in his belt, he started down the rope.

"What happened to Cousin Jack?" the private wanted to know.

As Corporal Toohey's head disappeared below the rim of the canyon, he called back, "Oh, Cousin Jack ruined a perfectly good meerschaum and the end of his nose."

Then there was silence as Toohey climbed down the rope. Leaning over the edge, Longarm watched the man until he disappeared in the gloom of the canyon. After a short while the rope stopped tugging on the lip of the canyon and remained relatively still.

Longarm turned to Brenner. "Put them two boxes back in the wagon and hobble all the horses. Then get back here."

The fellow struggled off with the dynamite and Longarm turned back to the straining rope. It was still quiet as Toohey worked. Longarm glanced at the eastern sky. There was still no sign of the dawn, but he knew he had less than an hour to put this all together.

192

Then the rope began to smoke some as Toohey began his climb back up. Calling to Brenner to give him a hand, Longarm reached over the rim and began hauling Toohey up out of the canyon.

In a few moments Toohey was standing on the lip of the canyon, a broad grin on his face. "Mr. Longarm, sir, I found myself the biggest damn blowhole in the world. Then I stuffed in every stick I had with me and tamped it in real solid. When that blows, this whole damn mountain's gonna cave in."

"All right, Toohey. Now I got just one more question for you. How much time do I have after you light both them fuses?"

The man considered for a second or two. "About fifteen, twenty minutes. Give me less'n a half-hour on the outside, if—like you explained to me—you want this side of the canyon to go first."

"I do." Longarm turned to Brenner. "Take the hobbles off one of the horses," he told the trooper. As Brenner hurried away, Longarm turned back to Toohey. "After it blows, stay here with Brenner to guard the horses and the wagon."

"From who?"

"Mule-stealing Mormons."

Longarm's horse had a difficult time in the darkness. The terrain along the rim of the escarpment was no help, either. But Longarm made it back to Dillon and the rest of the troopers in half the time it had taken him to return on foot. Some of the troopers were asleep on the bare ground. Dillon himself looked worn, his red face still sweating, his eyes weary and filled with uncertainty. Like Toohey, he was probably asking himself how they could be going through something like this just to retrieve a couple of army mules.

"We've got a few minutes by my reckoning, so relax," Longarm told the Sergeant.

The man nodded unhappily and shivered in the

193

cool night air. "Toohey get all that dynamite set to blow, Longarm?"

Longarm was pleased that the trooper had finally managed to call him as he preferred to be called. He smiled at the man. "Not all that dynamite, Dillon. Just enough to do the trick, I hope."

The fellow nodded.

Longarm looked at the eastern sky and decided he had better get things rolling. He cleared his throat. "Sergeant, take your men down this trail now. Break them up into pairs and spread them out in the shadows of them buildings on this side of the windmill tower."

"And then what? Go looking for them danged mules?"

"We'll get the mules later, Dillon. When that canyon blows, there's going to be one hell of a lot of confusion down there. Men'll be running from their houses, the women right after them. And while everyone's rushing around like chickens with their heads lopped off and the others are mounting up to go see what happened, I'll be freeing a young Miss from her prison. Now if I have any trouble doing that, I'll be looking for you fellows to give me a hand. You got that clear, Sergeant?"

The fellow took out his handkerchief, his eyes bugging slightly, and nodded.

"Okay, go on down there." Longarm looked at the other men waiting farther down the trail. "You men remember! Keep your asses down and your mouths shut until you hear that canyon blow."

Sergeant Dillon turned and motioned the men ahead of him down the trail. Longarm watched them go for a moment, then turned and hurried up the slope toward the bonfire makings waiting for him. He found the spot. There was plenty of tinder, and he wondered as he struck a sulphur match where they found it in this barren country.

In a matter of seconds the bleached wood had caught

194

and the flames were as high as his waist. Longarm let the fire build still higher for a few more minutes, then kicked aside the burning wood and heaped dirt and sand on the flaming embers that remained. The fire was out almost as quickly as it had been ignited, but he had no doubt Toohey had seen the signal. He now had a little less than half an hour before the canyon went.

Longarm moved back down the slope, hoping he could make it to the settlement before it grew much lighter. Glancing to his left, he saw the eastern sky beginning to light up. From far below him came the crowing of a rooster, his clarion call echoing and re-echoing about the rocks.

Good, thought Longarm. In such a natural amphitheater those two blasts would not go unnoticed.

As Longarm crouched down in the shadow of the settlement's small blacksmith shop, his broad shoulders still heaving from the exertion that had brought him down that trail so swiftly, he remembered Captain Meriwether's first reaction to Longarm's request for ten troopers to go with him after two army mules.

Meriwether shared completely Longarm's concern for Emilie Boggs and his contempt for the Avenging Angels. Since his recent transfer to the Utah Territory, he had been anxious to find out the truth about this rumored band of night riders. But how could he bring an arm of the U.S. military down on an apparently peaceful settlement of Mormons, especially considering the touchy relations between the U.S. War Department and the Mormons since the so-called Mormon War?

Longarm had agreed that this was a dilemma, then pointed out that the captain now had a perfect excuse to do something. As Longarm explained, if horse stealing was a major crime, then stealing U.S. Army mules —far more durable and valuable in this country—was a crime against the Union that no self-respecting com-

195

manding officer could allow to go unchallenged—not when there was a Deputy U.S. Marshal handy who was perfectly willing to take full responsibility.

Meriwether had thought of it a bit longer and then, with a smile, he had agreed to let Longarm lead ten of his troopers into the badlands. . . .

Trooper Billy Perkins ducked around the blacksmith shop and dropped to one knee beside Longarm. "It's daylight, Mr. Longarm, sir. Sergeant Dillon wants to know what happened to that diversion you was expecting."

"Tell him to—"

A deep, ground-shuddering growl filled the air, followed by a heavy *whump*. Immediately after that, another, even more violent shaking of the earth occurred, and this time the explosion rattled among the rocks that surrounded the settlement like a series of stupendous cannon shots. The detonations rolled and surged about the escarpment, appearing for a while to get louder with each echo. By the time the roar of the two explosions had faded away, the sound of men's and women's voices began filling the air with cries of alarm. Longarm heard doors slamming, the sound of running boots. A hastily constructed corral alongside the burnt-out barn was crowded with horses. All of them were milling nervously.

With Billy Perkins staying close beside him, Longarm rose to his feet and moved to the corner of the building to peer out at the settlement. The morning sun had not yet risen above the cliffs crowding Little Zion, but enough light from the sky was filtering down to give Longarm a good picture of the situation. In the distance, a dark plume of dust and smoke was rising into the rapidly lightening sky. As Longarm watched, the column, after reaching a great height, began to spread out, the dust and debris filling a larger and larger portion of the sky—while beneath it more smoke and dust continued to pump skyward.

Women and children were pointing to this towering

196

pillar of smoke as they ran from their houses, and Longarm saw not a few of them falling to their knees in supplication. Men were crowding into the corral, lugging their saddles and rifles. Other men, already on horseback, were galloping down the road toward the site of the explosions, and at the same time Longarm could hear men calling out to others to get their weapons—that this must be some kind of an attack.

A very tall, bearded fellow in his twenties appeared suddenly around the other corner of the shop. He halted in the act of strapping on his gunbelt. As Longarm turned to face him and swing up his rifle, the fellow vanished back around the corner. Longarm could hear the man running to warn the others. Peering around the building, Longarm saw him covering the distance to the corral at a steady run. But as Longarm had hoped, no one in all this confusion was paying much attention to him. They were too busy cutting out their horses.

Longarm leaned his rifle against the building and took out his Colt. "Where are the others?" he asked Trooper Perkins.

Perkins pointed to a thick clump of junipers at the base of the cliff far over to Longarm's right, near the boundary of the settlement, and then to a small wagon shed close to the road. "Sergeant Dillon's in the shed with his men. Perkins and Sim and the rest of the men are behind them pines."

Longarm nodded. The men behind the junipers were closer to where Emilie was being kept. "Go on over to the pines," he told the private, "and tell the men to cover me. I'm heading for that small building over there, the one with the high wire fence around it. As soon as you see me coming back toward this shop, fall in with me."

Billy nodded and darted across the open space toward the pines, his uniform bright and shiny in the morning sun that was now breaking through the dissipating cloud of smoke. Longarm held his breath, wait-

197

ing for someone to spot him. But not a cry was raised and in a moment he disappeared from sight.

Longarm moved out from behind the shed, then, and walked swiftly toward the small, fenced-in prison where he hoped Emilie was still being held. There was a padlock on the gate. He shot it off. Someone running by looked at him curiously, but Longarm paid no attention. Pushing the gate open, he walked rapidly to the door and leaned his head against the panel.

"Emilie! You in there?"

"Yes! Who is it?" It sounded as if she were standing just on the other side of the door.

"Longarm! Step back. I'm going to shoot off the lock."

He fired at the lock. It flew apart, and Longarm pulled the door open.

Emilie was standing before him, a look of terror on her face. "But you are dead! Elder Wolverton brought your body back from Salt Lake City."

"Am I buried?"

"Yes!"

"Well, I wouldn't put much stock in what Elder Wolverton told you. Or ain't you got wise to that yet?"

She ran to him. He took her hand, pulled her from the house, and was almost to the fence when he heard shots coming from the road. Longarm looked in that direction and saw two Mormons staggering back away from a fusillade of bullets, trying to return fire from the wagon shed.

Sergeant Dillon and his men had been discovered.

At once those men who were not already far down the road on their horses began to run toward the shed. There were perhaps seven or eight of them and most of them carried rifles.

Longarm pulled Emilie through the gate and together they ran toward the blacksmith shop. But as they neared it, the young fellow who had discovered Longarm earlier stepped out of the doorway with two companions, rifles in their hands. Longarm flung

198

Emilie to the ground. Moving sideways and crouching low, he began firing at the young man standing in the doorway. Longarm's first shot caught him high in the chest and sent him crashing back against the fellow behind him. The other had his rifle already up and firing as Longarm continued to crab sideways. The ground exploded at his feet as he carefully returned the man's fire. His first shot at the Mormon took a portion of the doorjamb, the second one caught the man in the shoulder and spun him back into the shop.

By this time, Trooper Perkins, Johnson, and three others had raced up to join Longarm; their combined fire cut down the third man crouching in the doorway. But the fire had alerted the other Mormons, and as Longarm dragged Emilie to her feet and dashed with her the remaining distance to the blacksmith shop, he saw at least five men peeling back from the wagon shed and coming after them on the double.

And then they were inside the shop.

"Billy," Longarm said, "you wait until me and the others are clear of this shop, then take Miss Emilie up the trail to wait for us. You got that?"

"Yes, sir, Mr. Longarm."

"Remember," Longarm repeated. "Wait until we are well clear."

As Billy nodded, Longarm told the other troopers to follow him and darted out of the shop. Retrieving his rifle from the rear of the shop, he levered a fresh cartridge into the chamber, then led a charge across the compound toward the five oncoming Mormons. He stayed low, and levering rapidly, pumped out a rapid, murderous fire that destroyed the enthusiasm of the Mormons. Two dropped almost at once, another staggered.

Dragging their wounded, they ducked behind what was left of the barn. Longarm and his troopers crowded down beside the charred remains of the arsenal. The firing immediately diminished. Then Longarm saw Ser-

199

geant Dillon and his men coming at the Mormons from behind.

"Let's go," cried Longarm, as he led his men toward the beleaguered Mormons. A bullet cut down the trooper beside Longarm. Longarm ducked to one side, and then he was in among the barn's blackened timbers.

A crazed Mormon raised himself up out of one of the damaged stalls, a large revolver in his hand. Longarm fired in one quick reflex, driving the fellow back through a railing. But he was not dead. As Longarm tried to duck past him, he twisted, raised his gun, and pointed it at Longarm. Longarm crabbed sideways, his shoulder crashing through loose, charred slats, and fired point-blank into the man's chest. The Mormon was flung back, lifeless, and disappeared in a shower of ashes and soot.

It was every man for himself now. As Longarm looked quickly around him, he caught sight of filthy, sooty creatures wrestling or shooting it out point-blank in a nightmare of hanging beams and blackened walls. He heard a cry of rage behind him and felt a hand come down like a sledgehammer on his right shoulder. As Longarm went down, he twisted and turned away, shielding his head. A beam struck his forearm and glanced off. Longarm leaped to his feet and met the ferocious charge of a man at least two feet taller and a foot broader than he was.

The fellow drove him back into a stall, through the partition, and then onto his back inside another. The fellow managed to get two blood-slicked hands around his throat, but Longarm twisted over, knocked the fellow's grip loose, and rolled over onto him in turn. He was slugging away at the man's head and shoulders when he realized that the battle was over. The man was lying there silently beneath Longarm, both eyes wide open.

Longarm scrambled to his feet. Only then did he notice the fire-blackened steel tines—two of them—poking up almost an inch out of the man's chest. He had also been shot twice, Longarm noted, shaking his head in disbelief.

The fighting around him had subsided. Picking up his rifle and the Colt he had dropped when he was surprised, he called out to Sergeant Dillon.

"Out here!" the man called back.

Longarm stumbled out of the wreckage and found that all but one of the troopers were unscathed. This one—Win Truit—had a calf wound and was in great pain. Longarm didn't see any Mormons around.

"No prisoners, I see," said Longarm.

The sergeant shook his head. "None. But we ain't out of the woods yet!" The man pointed down the road. "Look!"

A crowd of riders was racing back from the canyon with more than fire in their eyes, Longarm had no doubt.

"We better get ourselves into position," said the sergeant. "I figure behind that wagon shed, up the slope amongst those rocks, and behind that there windmill tower."

Longarm nodded. "Let's move it!"

As the troopers moved out with the sergeant to take up their positions, Longarm looked back at the blacksmith shop. He could not see Perkins nor Emilie, and he assumed that they had long since cleared out and were up the slope somewhere, waiting. Then he looked more closely and caught sight of an arm hanging out of the doorway—a uniformed arm.

He ran back across the compound and found Perkins lying on his back, his eyes open, his face gray with pain. "I got hit," he whispered, "Mr. Longarm, sir. In the back. I can't move. I can't feel nothing at all!"

Perkins was frightened, terribly frightened, his slightly freckled face pale, his light green eyes filled with mute terror at his condition. Longarm wanted to comfort him, but all he could think of at the moment was Emilie.

"You'll be all right, Perkins. What happened?"

201

"Riders. Three of them. They came from that big house out there. One of them had a beard—a long, white snowy one!"

"Go on, Perkins. What happened to the girl?"

"They charged the shop. I swear, they musta knowed we was holed up in here. I never got the chance to pull out like you told me. I shot one of them out of his saddle, but they kept coming. Then one of them sneaked up behind the shop and cut me down. They took the girl, Mr. Longarm, sir."

"Where?"

"Up the trail."

"The two of them?"

"That's right, but one was wounded bad. I winged him as he started up the trail."

"Which one did you hit? The one with the beard?"

"No. The other one. I didn't want to chance a shot at the other fellow with the beard. The girl was riding up front of him on the horse." Perkins closed his eyes for a moment. "I wanted to go after them," he continued a moment later, his voice growing fainter, "but that was when I lost the feeling in my legs. Now . . . it's just traveling all the way up my body, Mr. Longarm. Right up to my chest . . . !"

Longarm brushed the young man's hair back off his forehead. "You'll be all right, Perkins. Just you lie still."

The fellow nodded. "Leastways," he said, "it don't hurt no more." He closed his eyes.

Longarm glanced out of the doorway and was astounded at what he saw. Three houses were in flames. As he watched, one of a trio of women ran from each house, a firebrand in her hand. Two of the women had guns and were shooting at the windows of houses not aflame. A crowd of screaming, panicked women and children were fleeing the burning homes; and though Longarm could not be sure at this distance, he thought he recognized one of the women carrying a firebrand. Annie Dawkins.

202

Each woman carrying a torch disappeared into another home. Shots and screams came from these homes, and almost at once, smoke began pumping from the shattered windows. As the three left the now burning homes, Longarm saw that they had been joined by two other women. And soon others were joining them.

The women were burning their homes!

The sound of firing from the direction of the road caused Longarm to spin around. He saw Mormons falling from horses as they ran into Sergeant Dillon's ambush. His men were firing from well-concealed emplacements and they were making each shot count. Longarm looked back at Perkins.

"Perkins, I'm going now. But we'll be back for you."

Perkins's eyes remained closed. Longarm shook the trooper and felt the heavy immobility—the softness of the still body. Perkins was dead.

Longarm ducked out through the doorway and raced across the compound to join three troopers positioned at the base of the windmill tower. Sergeant Dillon had waited until the Mormons had ridden past the shed and were well into the compound before opening fire. By this time many of the Mormons had lost their mounts in the withering crossfire and were lying, some dead, others severely wounded, behind their downed horses. Those Mormons still capable of returning fire were doing it in a desultory, halfhearted fashion.

These were the Mormons, Longarm realized, who had ridden to inspect the rubble-filled canyon. Now they were being treated to the piercing lamentations of their wives and children as they watched their homes and all their possessions go up in flames. Surely they must now be ready, Longarm concluded, to admit the hopelessness of their cause.

Longarm called out to the troopers, "Hold your fire, men! Let's see if these jaspers want to stop this thing right here!"

The firing ceased. Longarm waited. Slowly, obviously with great reluctance, a mean-looking fellow, his

203

scowl directed at Longarm, got to his feet from behind a downed horse. He kept his hands in the air and he was not wearing a sidearm. As soon as he was upright, two others got to their feet also. From behind a shed two more stepped out; their hands were in the air as well.

All that were left were five men. Longarm recognized the first man to surrender. It was Karl Barker, the brother of the sheriff Longarm had shot in the Utah House.

As the troopers left their emplacements and hurried over to frisk the men and pick up what weapons were lying about, Longarm left the cover of the windmill tower and walked up to Karl Barker.

The elder bristled as Longarm approached. He was half a foot taller than Longarm; his face was lean, with sharp, prominent cheekbones, his chin jutting, his eyes smoky and filled with a merciless fire. He was still vibrant with indignation and threw his shoulders back, like a skittish horse about to bolt, as Longarm came to a halt in front of him.

"You'd be Elder Barker, I take it," said Longarm.

"Damn you," the man growled. "Elder Wolverton said you were dead. We buried you last night."

"Alongside your other victims," commented Longarm. "That must be some graveyard, Barker—with not a marker in sight."

Barker's gaze did not waver, but the fellow seemed to lose a little of his iron defiance. "I don't care, Longarm. I am only sorry you were not buried there."

"Do you know who you *did* bury, Barker?"

"No."

"Elder Smithson."

Barker's eyebrows shot up in surprise.

"He was a true martyr, Barker. A martyr to his conscience—not like your brother or the other Avenging Angels lying around us now. I'll leave you to see to your wounded, and then you may do as you please. But I suggest you leave off riding at night and intimi-

204

dating innocent Mormons, who have as much right to what they believe as you do. Or maybe that's too much for you to chew on at one time."

The man started to make a retort, but the ramrod posture he had been maintaining sagged slightly as he looked about him at the dead and wounded and heard the faint cries for help. The other men who had surrendered with him were looking to him for guidance. He started to turn to them, to issue orders—then paused and looked back at Longarm.

"What was it you used on the canyon?" he asked. "Nitroglycerin?"

"Dynamite. Forty percent straight dynamite—supplied by Job Welling, a Mormon you couldn't intimidate, Barker."

Barker shook his head sadly. "There's no canyon there anymore. The water has been cut to a trickle. I told Wolverton he was going too far, intimidating Boggs, Welling . . . the others."

"You didn't tell him loud enough."

"Where is he?" Barker's eyes lit slightly, as if he were hoping to hear that Elder Wolverton had been killed in the attack.

"He lit out with Emilie Boggs. He took the trail north."

The man seemed confused by this. "He . . . ran away? Left us?"

"That's right, Barker. But he won't get far, I promise you."

Barker's smoldering eyes fastened implacably on Longarm's face. "Get him," Barker said softly. "Kill the son of a bitch!"

Then Barker left Longarm, and with his remaining men began seeing to the dead and wounded. Women ran up to him to help, while others, sobbing and wailing, dropped beside sons or husbands still prostrate on the ground.

The sergeant stepped over to Longarm. "Two

205

wounded," Dillon said, with some satisfaction. Then he frowned. "Where's Perkins?"

"He's dead, Sergeant. You'll find him over there in the blacksmith shop, with four dead Avenging Angels nearby."

The sergeant swallowed, his face suddenly sober. "I'll get a detail over there right away."

"Before you do, Sergeant, there's one thing you should see to at once."

"What's that?"

"The *mules*, Sergeant. The army mules! What in tarnation did you think we came this far for, anyway? Don't you remember?"

"Oh! Yes, sir, Mr. Longarm. At once! Right away! I'll get men on it at once!" The sergeant looked around at the desolate, body-strewn compound, and then beyond, at the still burning houses. Not one of them had escaped the flames. The air was dim with smoke. Obviously, the sergeant didn't know where to begin. This much confusion and desolation was a new experience for him.

"Try the stables near that large stone house outside the compound, Sergeant. Try everywhere," Longarm told him. "I don't care how long it takes, Sergeant. Find those two army mules and bring them to me."

The sergeant nodded and hurried off toward his men, who were busy building a huge cache of weapons near what had become their headquarters, the wagon shed. Longarm turned about and started across the compound toward the small, single-story buildings that had been used for the detention of those the Avenging Angels considered their enemies—or their future brides.

Before he could get there, he saw about six women running from the burning houses with guns and the remnants of firebrands in their hands—toward the same buildings. They wasted no time in shooting off the locks and as Longarm approached, three very happy women poured out of the shabby, unpainted buildings.

206

Longarm caught sight of Annie, then. He was right. She had been one of the leaders. She had a huge revolver in her hand, and she was hugging a fragile young thing who was weeping with relief to find herself free.

"Annie!" Longarm called.

Annie turned swiftly, and jumping to see over the heads of the other women, squealed with delight when she saw him. The huge revolver still clutched in one hand, her other hand pulling the young girl after her, Annie burst through the crowd and flung her arms around Longarm's neck.

"I knew when I heard those explosions that you'd come back!" Annie cried. "I knew it! They said you were dead and buried, but I knew you weren't!"

She hugged him more tightly about the neck, causing the butt of the Colt to dig into his back. Grinning, Longarm gently disengaged her arms from around his neck and then carefully took the revolver from her.

"Oh, don't worry about that, Longarm," she assured him. "It's empty."

"We'll see," he said, pointing it at the sky and squeezing the trigger.

A thunderous report erupted in their midst, freezing every laugh, stilling every cry of delight. Longarm was a little awed at the power the old Colt packed still. He examined it. It was a Colt Navy .36, still in fine shape. He checked the chambers. Now it was empty.

He handed it back to Annie. "Never say a gun is empty until you check it."

Annie took the gun back, shivering slightly.

"Who's this young lady with you, Annie?"

"She hasn't been here long," Annie said. "Her name is Marylou."

Longarm frowned and looked more closely at the girl. "Marylou Wellings?" he asked.

"Yes," she said, nodding eagerly. "You know my father! Did he send you?"

"In a way," Longarm replied. "At least he supplied

207

me with what I needed to wake this place up this morning."

"They told me if I didn't come with them, they would harm Daddy. I told him not to send anyone after me. But I'm so glad you came!"

Longarm admitted that he was glad, too. He told them, then, that those women who wanted to could go back with Sergeant Dillon and his men. Many of them would have to saddle what horses were left in the corral and ride astride. It would be a long trip, but there was a wagon for water, and there would be plenty of fresh horses. "And when you get back to Salt Lake City," Longarm said, finishing up, "I hope you'll tell whoever has a mind to listen that the Avenging Angels have just had their wings scorched—so that means you people ought to stand up a little straighter now, the next time they come sneaking around. You think you two can remember that?"

"I certainly can," said Marylou stoutly, her tears gone completely now. "I'm going to tell everyone!"

"And I will too," said Annie.

"We both will," said Marylou, "because Annie is coming to live with me!"

"Marylou!" Annie exclaimed. "You *know* what I told you . . . I mean . . ."

"Never *mind* that. I don't care." She smiled. "And if *you* don't tell anyone, I am sure *I* won't."

Annie looked at Longarm and smiled. "Well, maybe I'll give it a try."

Sergeant Dillon was approaching. There were two troopers behind him leading the two army mules. The troopers seemed enormously relieved and the sergeant just a bit troubled.

"This here what you wanted, Mr. Longarm?" Sergeant Dillon asked.

"Where did you find them?" Longarm asked, as he approached the mules.

"In a stable in back of that big stone house."

"Did you notice anything a bit special about the

208

long, low building next to the stone house, the one with the gabled windows?"

"The one that looked like a chicken house?"

"It looked a mite more substantial than that, Sergeant."

Dillon nodded. "It was. And I did notice. Seemed like there were some women in there. Some of them were pounding on the windows. But we got enough women about, so I left them in there—for their own safety."

"I see. Well, first chance you get, Sergeant, let them out. Then tell them I'll be bringing back their husband as soon as I can."

"Their *husband,* sir?"

"That's right, their husband. Will you do that?"

"Of course, Mr. Longarm."

Longarm had been inspecting the mules carefully all this while. The examination made him feel much better. "These are the mules I wanted, Sergeant. And they are in fine condition, just fine."

The sergeant cleared his throat, his face growing red. He reached for his polkadot handkerchief.

"Something bothering you, Sergeant?"

"It's just . . . hard to believe, Mr. Longarm, sir. All this—" He mopped his brow, then waved his arm graphically about him. "All this destruction, these wounded men—just for a few mules. Even if they *are* army mules."

"You're right, Sergeant. There is a deal more to it than that. And in an hour or so, soon's I get myself organized proper, I'll be riding off with these mules to finish what we started here. Meanwhile, I suggest you confiscate every weapon you can find." As he spoke, he took Annie's Colt from her and tossed it at the sergeant. "Add them to that pile your men started and burn it. Make a nice snappy bonfire, Sergeant."

"Are you sure we can do that, Mr. Longarm?" the man asked weakly.

209

"Of course, Sergeant. Those weapons are stolen army ordnance. No doubt about it."

The sergeant sighed and nodded.

"And Sergeant, you'll also have to see to it that these women get safely back to Salt Lake City. You are responsible for them now."

The sergeant looked around with astonishment at the circle of women that had slowly been forming around Annie and Longarm. There were at least nine women. Many of them wore skirts that were singed, while their faces were smudged with soot as a result of their recent fiery revolt. These were the women who had never really wanted to become a part of this hidden settlement, and who, like Annie, had only given in to the custom of multiple marriage out of desperation after being brought here under duress. Once they had seen their chance to strike back at their masters, they had taken it—with a vengeance.

The sergeant looked back at Longarm. He didn't seem unhappy at what Longarm had told him. "Well, if they'll help me with some of my wounded troopers."

"I'm sure they will, Sergeant. Just ask them."

As Longarm led the mules away, he saw an eager circle of women closing tightly about a very flustered —but not at all displeased—Sergeant Dillon.

Longarm smiled.

An hour or so later, as Longarm rode past the blacksmith shop and thought of Trooper Billy Perkins and of the two-hour start Lorenzo Wolverton had on him, he wasn't smiling at all.

The ride up the steep trail was a difficult one, but the mule he was riding handled the climb with a fine, steady nimbleness. Lorenzo Wolverton and the other rider with him were forking horses, he reminded himself with some satisfaction; the elder and Emily were riding double and Perkins had wounded the other rider. He would catch them.

As Longarm reached the crest finally, he looked

210

down at the ruin of Little Zion. A heavy pall of smoke still hung over the valley. In front of the wagon shed a tall bonfire was burning, pumping a fresh column of black smoke into the air. Longarm nodded in satisfaction. He wasn't worried any longer about Annie and the rest of the girls getting back all right. Sergeant Dillon could be counted on to follow orders.

Now all Longarm had to do was concentrate on overtaking Emilie Boggs and her two captors.

Chapter 9

Four hours or so later the trail leading from the settlement petered out as the badlands gave way finally to foothills and gentler, less wild terrain. Longarm still had no difficulty tracking the two horses, and he was a little relieved to be leaving the arid basin behind him for the higher plateau country. The air was already cooler, brighter.

Following Wolverton's tracks, he came to a small and narrow meadow. He pulled up and saw nothing moving on it and ran his mule across it into the timber. The tracks kept steadily on through a sparse stand of pine. It looked like first-growth stuff, massive at the butt and rising in a flawless line toward a canopy of top covering that made a solid umbrella against sunlight. It was cool as he rode, the pines sawing high above him, and very little underbrush to hide any tracks. At some angles he was able to look a hundred or two hundred yards in a single direction.

Wolverton and his companion's tracks were sharply etched in the spongy humus. It was almost as if Wolverton were beckoning him on, daring him to come and take Emilie away from him.

The land grew rougher again and the pines turned smaller and ravines began to come down toward him, but these were almost gentle ravines—a far cry from the rugged, wild draws he had left behind. Longarm found the tracks taking him onto the crest of first one ridge and then another. He dropped at last into a

212

broad ravine clothed in good, thick ground cover that for a while gave him some difficulty in tracking. He crossed over it and rode to the next ridge.

The land was no longer tame, he noted. Rolling dunes of sand lifted across the trail and clay gulches cut sharp barriers before him that he could not jump. Here and there a pine tree stood as sentinel over the bleak hills before him, black and bulky and high. For an uncomfortable period Longarm lost sign and was relieved to find it again as he trailed up a shallow creek.

Dismounting, he found the tracks close to the water's edge. No moisture had yet crept into the prints. He stood and peered ahead of him in the direction the tracks were taking and saw they were heading into still higher, more rugged country. He let both mules drink for a few moments in the swift creek, filled his canteen, and mounted up.

The tracks now seemed to trace a line as straight as a telegraph wire to the mountain range he had noted earlier. Soon the tracks were cutting through a rocky defile, one side of it a cliff reaching straight up, gray and weathered and cracked. Longarm rode cautiously along, alert now to the possibility of ambush. Wolverton and his companion had simply done too little to cover their tracks.

Once through the defile, Longarm found himself approaching a rising wilderness of huge boulders that seemed to have been piled there by some furious giant long ago. Beyond the broken world in front of him the dark bulk of the mountains rose high into cold, clear sky: formidable ramparts that seemed flung up before him as a warning.

The sign was getting clearer, fresher. He was gaining on them. Longarm rode more cautiously as great, shouldering masses of rock and timber lifted on both sides of the trail. Then he caught the glint of a rifle barrel in the rocks to his right, high above him.

Swiftly he untied his lead from his trailing mule

213

and at once the mule made no effort to keep up. Longarm suddenly spurred his mule, pushing it to a gallop. He held his breath, waiting for the shot to come, gambling that when it did it would prove the owner of that rifle a poor marksman. The shot came when Longarm had almost concluded that whoever it was had about given up the idea of ambush. It was a flat report that sent a flurry of echoes chasing after it.

Longarm grabbed his Winchester from his saddle boot and flung himself from the saddle. There was another shot. This time the bullet whined uncomfortably close and ricocheted off a boulder just behind him. It had not been a poor shot for that distance, Longarm realized. He slapped the rump of his mule and sent him trotting up the trail into some rocks, then dove to cover himself in a small stand of pine. Quickly, he unstrapped his spurs, pocketed them, then levered a cartridge into the chamber of his Winchester.

Another shot from above showered him with tiny shards of pine cones, and this time the *thunk* of the round as it buried itself in one of the pines was just too damned close. Wolverton or his wounded ally had a pretty good bead on him. But Longarm was remembering the vantage point where that glint had come from, and he knew that from his present position he could outflank it.

Keeping down, he ducked back across the trail and lost himself in a very thick growth of young timber, then angled quickly up the rockstrewn slope. From somewhere above there came another shot, but there was no sound of a bullet coming to rest anywhere around him. The rifleman was just shooting to keep up his courage. As Longarm approached the crest, there was another shot, followed by the sound of a slug whining off rocks far below. The fellow was still firing blind, hoping.

Racing along the crest of the ridge, Longarm leaped down to the flat surface of a huge boulder, then clambered swiftly up its slope until he was well above the

214

narrow perch where he had first sighted the gleam of that rifle barrel. Dropping to his belly, he inched his way along the stone ledge until his head was just peering over the lip. Below him at a distance of perhaps a hundred feet, a single Mormon was crouched, his rifle resting on a shelf of rock in front of him. The man had an unobstructed view of the trail far below, yet the man—seemingly without aiming—was methodically squeezing off shots at nothing.

Longarm watched the fellow send two more rounds onto the trail, then decided to look around for Wolverton and Emilie. He slipped back down the rock, then followed a narrow ridge of a trail until he was still higher, high enough to see well beyond the trail below and the meadowland beyond it. But there was no sign of Wolverton and no horses—not even one for this fellow still peppering the trail like a mechanical toy someone had wound up and left.

Returning to the boulder, Longarm took careful aim—and fired. The rifle jumped from the Mormon's hands with a suddenness and violence that profoundly satisfied Longarm, who watched the shattered rifle clatter down the slope, then stood up.

"Stay where you are, mister," he called.

The fellow turned slowly toward him. He made no effort to draw the sixgun at his waist. He waved a feeble right arm and Longarm saw the long dark stain that extended from just under the arm all the way down past his waist. Even as Longarm watched, the fellow collapsed forward onto the rocks.

Longarm pushed himself back down the rock, got to his feet, and raced along the ridge until he was able to drop to a trail that wound onto that small overlook where the Mormon had positioned himself.

He found the man still slumped among the rocks. Longarm pulled him upright and examined his wound. The slug had entered his back just below his left shoulder blade and apparently ranged through the man's lungs to come to rest somewhere in the chest

215

cavity. His face was pale, his breathing labored, a thin trickle of blood coming from one corner of his mouth. Tiny beads of perspiration stood out on his forehead and his straggly beard was damp. Private Billy Perkins had more than winged this man.

His eyes remained closed as Longarm examined him. They flickered open when Longarm let him down gently, his back resting against a rock. Coughing slightly, he looked up at Longarm, his eyes showing a kind of grudging respect.

"I told the elder it was you come back," he said softly. "I told him, but he insisted, said you was dead—said it was someone else leading that attack . . . wouldn't believe it was you . . . !"

"They left you?"

"The girl didn't want to—but *he* did. Had another one of his revelations, he did . . . son of a bitch! They were going to the northwest . . . then into Canada, set up another Little Zion, the girl at his side." He smiled bitterly. "The martyrdom of his followers would bring flocks of true Saints to his banner! He's mad—all of us were mad . . ." He began to cough then and each hack sent a shudder through Longarm. It sounded as if pieces of the Mormon's lungs were coming loose with each paroxysm.

"How far ahead of me are they?"

The man left off coughing with an exercise of iron will. "They each got a horse now, so they'll be making good time. But the man is riding his horses too hard. He thinks they are as mad as he is. . . ." The man started to cough, then forced himself to quit. He looked back up at Longarm through watering eyes. "He left me for dead . . . but I crawled up here, Longarm, to wait for you—"

"That loyal, are you, still?"

"No . . . not loyal . . . wanted to warn you, tell you which way he went. . . ! Those shots to get you up here—" He smiled weakly. "Took you long enough."

216

"Tell me, then."

"Snake Creek Pass, northwest of here . . . got a cabin there . . ." He smiled bitterly. "Used it for supplies on our . . . missions to keep the faithful . . . faithful . . ."

He resumed coughing, the sound more harrowing now than before. Longarm knew then that all he could do was watch. This loyal lieutenant of Elder Wolverton had goaded himself into living just long enough to betray his former master and was now making his agonizing way through a very narrow passage into whatever heaven or hell awaited him. The man's coughing grew weaker with each paroxysm, his hands bracing him feebly as they clutched at a slab of a rock before him. He began to lean over the rock now as blood came in fresh clots from his gasping mouth.

"Jesus," the man whispered in wonder. "Oh, my Jesus!"

He tried to push himself away from the rock and the sight of his blood, but succeeded only in falling away from the rock and collapsing to the ground beside it. Longarm reached down and tried to pull the man upright. The fellow's head swiveled toward him, his eyes wild with fear.

He started to cry out something—then went slack in Longarm's arms. It was almost as if the man's tormented spirit had flung itself past him at that moment as it quit this dying carcass of a sinner. Longarm let him fall back onto the narrow, rocky ground and stepped back.

He did not have time to bury the man. He glanced skyward and thought he saw a single buzzard coasting high up, well to the north. He looked back at the quiet body. He did not even know the man's name, he realized, and hadn't thought to ask him. Well then, he would leave him for the buzzards as so many other Saints had been left before him when the Avenging Angels had collected their tithes and settled their scores.

217

Longarm turned his back on the dead man and made his way carefully down the mountainside. The mule he had been riding had found a home in among the rocks where he had sent him. When he approached, the mule cleverly managed to present to Longarm only his hind end, his rear legs poised and ready. Realizing that the worst place from which to consider a mule is directly from behind anywhere within a radius of ten feet, Longarm pulled back and contemplated the back of the mule's head. His ears were pricked, alert for any comment Longarm might care to deliver. Longarm thought for a moment that the mule was smiling.

"All right, you four-footed son of Satan! I'll leave you for the Indians. Not a one would lower himself to ride you, but they'll sure as hell find time to boil you in their pots! The damn fools just love mule meat!"

He turned, then, and hunted for the other mule. He was leading it behind him on his way through the canyon when he looked back and saw the other mule standing well out of the rocks, looking rather anxiously after him. Longarm pretended not to notice, and when he heard the animal cantering after him, he did not look back. The mule reached his side in a few moments and slowed to a walk.

"What's the matter?" said Longarm. "Don't you cotton to feeding the Indians hereabouts?"

The mule jerked his head up angrily, his cheeks quivering indignantly. Longarm reached over, grabbed the trailing reins and mounted up. Dropping his rifle into the boot, he leaned over the neck of the mule and said, "I was just riling you a mite. No Indian in his right mind would eat anything as tough and ornery as you!"

The mule bucked slightly, then went back to his walk and Longarm snubbed the lead from the other mule about the saddle horn and pointed the animal toward the high country and Snake Creek Pass.

Longarm knew this country in northwestern Utah Territory just well enough to realize that if Lorenzo

218

Wolverton was allowed to go on through Snake Creek Pass and into Oregon, Longarm would have a long, long chase ahead of him. He clapped spurs to the mule and was pleased at its response as it began a smooth, ground-devouring lope.

Longarm came upon Snake Creek before sundown. He had decided against following the trail left by Wolverton and Emilie and had cut across very rough country, counting on the surefootedness and stamina of his mules, in an effort to arrive at the pass before or not long after Wolverton. He had changed mounts twice in the process and was well pleased with the mules' performance. The mountains he had glimpsed earlier, that had seemed so ominous and dark, he now perceived as pine-clad and gently rolling, enormous hills. The creek was a wild, shallow torrent with great handsome boulders in its midst that rushed out of these hills, heading for a dusk-shrouded V in the distance—Snake Creek Pass.

Longarm followed the creek until he was within five miles of the pass; then he cut south to a higher benchland that roughly paralleled the creek, keeping in the timber as much as possible. It was dark when he reached the pass. Moving well up onto the benchland through the pines, he found the hills scarred with great white outcroppings of rock, some of them extending straight up and disappearing into the gloom of the young night, an effective barrier that forced him to ride farther into the pass.

He kept the wall of rock to his left as he rode, using it as a guide in the darkness under the pines that crowded close to the mountain wall. The rich pine humus underfoot effectively muffled the sound of his passage, but soon the encroaching shoulder of the mountain began to force him back down through the timber toward Snake Creek. It was not long before he came upon a well-worn game trail overlooking the stream. He followed the trail until the moon crept out from behind the shouldering hills and hung directly overhead.

He pulled off the trail, then, and kept in the timber for a while longer until he was through the pass. At once the character of the land changed as he broke out onto a vast meadow that dropped by imperceptible degrees to a dark timberland far below, stretching like a vast carpet into the night.

Where was the cabin?

Feeling too exposed out on the meadow, Longarm cut back into the timber he had just left, and then dismounted. He was weary, having ridden most of the day and now well into the night. He hunkered down, his back to a pine, considering whether or not he should camp for the night. He didn't want to do that. He needed to corner the elder in this pass before Wolverton went on through, or he might never find the man, or Emilie. One look at that carpet of forest extending westward to the Sierras and the Pacific beyond had shown him that.

He was taking out a cheroot when he came alert. He stood up and put away the cheroot. Raising his head like something wild, he sniffed at the night air that swept down from the north. It carried with it the strong scent of pine and cedar—and woodsmoke. It was not a campfire. The concentration was too great for that. In his mind's eye, Longarm could almost see the freshly cut wood being fed into a Franklin stove, the sheet iron stovepipe shuddering as it belched the heavy, pungent woodsmoke into the night.

The cabin was across the creek on the north slope of the pass, more than likely.

Longarm mounted up and rode toward the creek, keeping in the timber all the way. It was not easy finding a ford in the moonlight, but at last he cut across the creek and up a steep embankment that gave way to a high meadow. At the far end, against a background of towering pines, he caught a glint of lamp-

220

light. As he rode toward it, the light winked out periodically. The cabin was set among trees.

If he had ridden by during daylight, he considered ironically, he might well have missed the cabin. From the game trail on the other side of the creek he would not have seen the meadow.

He rode east across the high meadow; the damp night air was pungent with the scent of sage and bearberry. Finally he reached the timber. He dismounted and followed the timber line on foot until he was close enough to see clearly the cabin window he had glimpsed from a mile below. He tied the mules to a sapling and moved closer to the cabin until he was almost within the window's bright rectangle of light that flooded the woodland crowding close upon the cabin. The building was set well back in the trees, in keeping with its purpose, Longarm realized.

Circling the cabin, Longarm found his progress blocked by the beams of a large corral leading from a low pole barn. There were only two horses in the corral, both trembling with exhaustion in the moonlight and with streaks of lather still drying on their flanks, their noses buried in a grain trough. They were too exhausted and too hungry to spook at his appearance and he kept moving, circling the barn and returning to the cabin. It was built of rough pine logs, the chinks filled with clay. The roof was shingled and the north end of the building consisted mostly of a fireplace and chimney. Longarm had been mistaken. The woodsmoke had been pumping out of a fireplace, not a Franklin stove.

From all the signs, Wolverton and Emilie had recently arrived at the cabin. The fire was probably the result of Emilie's demand that Wolverton rid the cabin of its chill. It was just a guess, of course, but Longarm could imagine Emilie doing everything she could to forestall the eager Wolverton.

By this time Emilie must have concluded that all hope of deliverance was futile.

Once he had circled the cabin, he pulled up, con-

221

sidering. There were only two entrances, front and rear. He went back around to the woodpile and selected three hefty pieces, then returned to the front of the cabin.

Facing the door, he placed two of the pieces of wood on the ground beside him, kept one in his left hand, drew his Colt, shifted the Colt to his left hand and the wood to his right, then heaved the wood up onto the shingled surface of the roof. It struck with a loud thump, then rolled end over end down the roof, slid sideways, and then dropped off the roof into the high grass.

At once the lantern inside the cabin was turned low and blown out.

Longarm waited. He thought he heard the sound of a table being overturned, or a chair, and the sound of heavy-booted footsteps approaching the door. He waited, but the door was not flung open. Of course. That would be too foolish a move for a man like Wolverton. Longarm bent, picked up another piece of neatly split cordwood, and flung it at the door. It hit with a resounding thump.

He could imagine Wolverton standing by the door, his hand on the latch, trying to fathom what it was for sure. Perhaps it was a bear. This was not the usual way one man called another out. Longarm reached down for the last piece of wood and hurled it onto the far end of the roof. It struck smartly, rolled up a few feet, then tumbled backwards until it dropped off the roof.

That was too much for Wolverton. He flung open the door and rushed out, turning at once to the roof. There was a rifle in his hand and he raised it to his shoulder as he faced that end of the roof where the last piece of wood had landed.

"Emilie!" Longarm called. "Get out the back door! Hurry!"

Wolverton flung himself around, firing as he did so. The slug sang past Longarm's cheek. Wolverton levered

222

and fired a second time as Longarm crabbed sideways, returning the elder's fire. As a pine came between him and Wolverton, Longarm heard the rear door slamming, and realized that Emilie was out of the cabin and hightailing it into the woods.

There was no chance now that Wolverton would be able to use Emilie as a shield, or force Longarm to deal by threatening her. It was just between Lorenzo Wolverton and Longarm now.

From behind the pine, Longarm called out to Wolverton. "Put down that rifle, Elder! You ain't going nowhere with that! The girl's gone! And your latest revelation ain't worth a bucket of warm spit."

"You are dead, Longarm! I do not need to listen to a dead man!"

Wolverton fired. The slug buried itself in the pine. Longarm fired back; it was his third shot. The round whined off one of the cabin's logs. Wolverton had been crouching. Now he stood up, and levering rapidly, loosed a deadly fusillade at the crouching Longarm.

"You can't kill me, Longarm! Just as I can't kill you! Perhaps we are both immortal!" The man's voice cracked in near-hysteria.

As the bullets whined past Longarm, he managed to get off another shot. Abruptly Wolverton turned and darted around the corner of the cabin. Swearing, Longarm scrambled to his feet and raced after the man. He stayed low as he rounded the corner of the cabin and it was a good thing he did. Wolverton was waiting in the darkness. Wielding his rifle like a club, he swung on Longarm. The rifle butt knocked off Longarm's hat, but that was the only damage as Longarm's shoulder rammed the elder amidships. Both men went down. Longarm's head struck the cabin wall, momentarily stunning him.

He managed to hang on to his Colt, however, and fired at Wolverton as he rolled away from the cabin. Wolverton pulled back as he scrambled to his feet and pumped a round at Longarm. The bullet buried itself

223

in the ground at Longarm's right temple as he squeezed off another shot at the figure towering over him in the darkness.

The slug must have caught him. Wolverton appeared to stagger back against the cabin. Still upright, however, Wolverton chambered another round and managed to get off another shot at Longarm. But this one went wild. Longarm aimed carefully and squeezed the trigger.

The hammer came down on an empty chamber.

Leaning against the cabin, Wolverton laughed—a low, sinister laugh that told Longarm his quarry had slipped over the edge into madness—if, indeed, the man had ever really been sane.

"Now we'll see who's mortal," whispered Wolverton as he pumped another cartridge into his Winchester's chamber.

"How many times have you tried to kill me, Wolverton?" Longarm asked, hoping for time now to gather himself so that he could charge the elder before he fired. "Twice? Three times? You even buried me once, didn't you!"

Wolverton gasped. Longarm saw the rifle barrel, gleaming dully in the darkness, begin to waver.

"You said the Angel Moroni sent me. He *did*, Elder! To punish you! To bring you to perdition! Look about you now in this darkness, Elder. See those faces! They are the faces of those children you slaughtered long ago. Do you really think the Angel Moroni will forgive you that deed? Have you repented that crime? Have you gone to your knees before him?"

"Stop!" cried the elder. "Stop! For the love of God, Longarm! You cannot know these things!"

Longarm flung himself upward at Wolverton. Knocking the rifle from the man's hands, he grabbed him by his shirtfront and flung him to one side, sending him crashing into a tree. The fellow slumped to the ground without a word. Longarm snatched up the rifle and walked over to the elder.

224

The man's head was hanging loosely forward. Longarm looked down at him. "Can you get up, Elder?"

The man was weeping softly.

Longarm went down on one knee beside the elder, using the man's rifle for support. He looked into the man's face. The fellow looked at him. "The faces . . . the faces . . . " Wolverton whispered, his eyes wide with horror. "The young faces—all around me in the darkness . . . " He looked closely at Longarm. "You . . . see them, too!"

"Can you get up, Elder?"

From the darkness beside Longarm, Emilie, looking wan and ghostly in a long, torn dress, stepped closer. "Is he dead, Longarm? Did you kill him?"

"I don't know, Emilie. Help me to get him inside."

The old man offered no resistance at all as they pulled him to his feet and gently led him into the cabin. Emilie lit the lantern and turned it up as Longarm guided Wolverton to a small cot against the wall. The wood in the fireplace was still burning, but the fire needed more fuel. Emilie went after it as the elder, his eyes closed, lay on his back on the cot and let Longarm examine him.

The single round that had struck Wolverton had caught him just below the right shoulder; it must have done considerable internal damage before coming out just below his shoulder blade, but it was by no means a fatal wound. Had the man possessed the will, he could easily have fired upon Longarm when he came up with an empty gun.

The elder opened his eyes as Emilie reentered the room, her arms piled high with firewood. As she knelt in front of the fireplace to feed the wood to the fire, Wolverton said, "But she was in my revelation." He grabbed Longarm's vest with long, powerful fingers and pulled Longarm closer. "Does she know of them, too?"

"Them?"

"The children . . . ! And the others . . . ! All

225

around. In every dark place, they wait. And now they wait for me—*there,* too!"

He released Longarm's vest, closed his eyes, and turned his head to the wall. Longarm waited to see if he would speak again, then got to his feet and went over to Emilie. She was standing before the fireplace, her still fearful eyes on the elder.

"How is he?" she asked. "Will he—?"

"Die? I don't think so. His wound is not fatal. But we'll have to get him some help or it might be—back to what's left of Little Zion. I did promise his wives I would bring him back to them."

She left Longarm's side, walked over to the cot, and looked down at the old man. "He looks so . . . shrunken now," she said. "And just a little while ago . . . " She shuddered, as if she still expected the elder to rise in a fury before her, his wild eyes fixed upon her.

Suddenly Emilie bent closer. "Longarm . . . !"

He knew from the tone of her voice what she had discovered. He was at her side in an instant. She turned and bowed her head on his shoulder. He held her gently and looked past her at the elder. Yes. Longarm had seen enough of it lately to recognize death when he came upon it. The curiously shrunken, alabaster features of the old man spoke only of mortality now.

Weeping softly, Emilie looked up into his face. "But you said he wasn't wounded that bad."

"I was thinking only of bullets, Emilie. He had other wounds."

She looked at him. "Those things you said to him out there. I heard you. What did you mean?"

"It's a long story, Emilie. It had to do with that Mountain Meadows Massacre. He was there—a part of it."

"Oh?" She frowned and pulled away. "I've heard about that."

"Elder Smithson told me about it. Wolverton's real

226

name was Mordecai Lee. Like Smithson, he had been running from that business ever since."

"Running? Elder Wolverton?"

Longarm nodded. "We all got different ways of running from things, I reckon."

She turned slowly then and looked down at the sunken face, the long, shriveled figure. "He was such a terrifying man. He had these visions. He told me about them. He frightened me, Longarm."

"I guess maybe they frightened him more."

Longarm led her away from the cot.

"Why don't you take that lantern into the next room and wait while I go to the barn for his bedroll," Longarm suggested. "Did he leave it with his saddle?"

She nodded, picked up the lantern, and took it with her into the other room. The only light left in the room came from the flames flickering in the fireplace. The dancing light gave a rosy hue to the dead man's features and imparted a hectic life to his quiet limbs.

Longarm turned quickly and left the cabin to get the bedroll for Elder Wolverton's last sleep.

227

Chapter 10

It was well on toward dusk of the following day when Longarm and Emilie reached Little Zion. The body of Elder Wolverton was slung over one of the mules; Longarm and Emilie were riding the horses. As they reached the bottom of the steep trail that led down from the rocks to the valley, Emilie looked at Longarm, her eyes wide with astonishment.

"You told me what had happened, Longarm," she said. "But it's even worse than you said!"

Longarm could only agree with her. All but one of the houses had been razed to the ground, which— added to the destruction Longarm himself had caused when he set fire to the barn—gave the entire settlement the look of a place that has just lost a war. Sherman's March to the Sea could not have appeared more devastating than this.

A small knot of somber men was standing in front of the wagon shed. Sergeant Dillon and his men were nowhere in sight. As the knot of men broke up and started toward them, Longarm saw that what he had thought at first were rifle barrels, were instead long-handled spades. He saw then the neat mounds of raw earth spaced evenly about the compound and realized how busy these men must have been this day.

Elder Barker was in the lead as the men approached. His face hardened when he saw Longarm, but there was a question in his eyes. Then he caught sight of the

228

soogan slung over the back of the lead mule, and a grim, barely noticeable smile lit his features.

Longarm pulled his horse to a halt as Barker walked up to him. With a brisk nod of his head, he indicated the soogan. "You got him?"

"Guess you could say that."

Barker looked at Emilie then. "You all right, woman?"

"Yes," she said. "I am. Now."

That seemed to satisfy him. He looked back to Longarm. "We still got some digging to do and as long as there's light, we'll tend to it. If I were you, I wouldn't stay here past dark. We ain't got any firearms left us— but we'll find something."

Longarm nodded. "Obliged for the warning."

"Just didn't want you tempting us." His grim smile lit his face for a moment. "Old habits die hard."

Longarm urged his horse on, leaving the elder leaning wearily on the handle of his shovel.

The yard between the stone house and the wives' quarters was crowded with women all busy cleaning and cooking with four very large kettles hanging over open fires. The women were coming and going from the impressive mansion with a familiarity that told Longarm it no longer served as the citadel of a tyrant. As he and Emilie rode into their midst, they all turned to face him silently, their work ceasing on the instant.

"I said I'd bring back Elder Wolverton," Longarm announced. He indicated the body slung over the mule. "There he is. His wives and the rest of his kin can have him now."

"Why?" a woman called sharply, angrily.

"To bury him," Longarm told her. "I reckon you'd be wanting to give him a decent burial. You his wife?"

"One of them," she snapped.

Longarm looked quickly around. He could sense the antagonism, but it did not seem to be directed at him or Emilie.

One of the women stepped closer to Emilie's horse

229

and looked up at her. "You got away from him, did you?"

"Yes," Emilie said, her face coloring.

"You were lucky," the woman replied. She looked up at Longarm, approvingly. "Very lucky."

Longarm took a deep breath. "If you don't want his body," he said, "I'll bring him over there to those men to bury."

"No," a woman said, walking slowly toward the mule over which Wolverton's body was slung. "We want him."

Longarm watched as the women—acting in concert now—approached the mule. Suddenly one of the women broke from the tightening circle, rushed at the body, and began beating on it. Her sisters pulled her back, as others—their fingers flying—untied the burden and pulled it off the mule's back. The excited crowd of women caused the mule to buck some, but Longarm paid no heed as he turned his face away so that he would not see the vicious abandon with which the women vented their fury on what was left of the man who had been their lord and master.

"Let's get out of here," Longarm said to Emilie.

"Yes, please!"

As they approached the trail a moment later, Emilie called to him, "You knew that would happen, didn't you?"

"I had a notion."

"Why? Why did you bring his body back to them?"

Longarm shrugged. "I just thought they might like to get that off their chest. Maybe they'll feel better now. He had ridden off with you and left them, you know—locked in those quarters he'd built to keep them."

She shuddered. "It was awful!"

"Yes it was." He looked at her. "Remember what Barker told us. If we're as wise as we should be, we'll take that warning of his to heart, I'm thinking."

"Can we get far before dark?"

230

"Far enough. And this time we've plenty of transportation. Two army mules, and no one on our tails."

She brightened considerably as Longarm led the way back up the trail. It was dark when they both took their last look at the valley and headed for the badlands and the Great Salt Desert beyond.

Longarm chuckled again as he puffed on his cheroot and read the telegram a second time.

WASHINGTON RAISING HELL FORGET MULES STAY ON THE CASE FORGET MULES

VAIL

Longarm folded the telegram and put it into his vest pocket alongside his new derringer. A bright new gold chain connected it with the recently purchased Ingersoll, courtesy of a very grateful Quincy Boggs.

"As I was saying," said Boggs, looking around him happily at his three daughters, "we've got back our backbones, thanks to you. Never again will any of us allow a band of night riders to tell us what we believe. We are Mormons and proud of it. But we can differ among ourselves without intimidating those who believe differently than we do. That's in the United States Constitution, Longarm, and as soon as we join the Union, there will be no more doubt about it."

"Oh, Daddy," said Audrey. "All you've been doing lately is making speeches."

"I know," the man said, glowing. "As a leader of the reform movement which brought in U.S. Deputy Custis Long, I find that I am asked to speak everywhere—with devastating effect, I am sure."

Longarm laughed. "I am sure."

"But as I was saying, I was very improper and read that telegram. As soon as I did, I decided to act. Together with the rest of the council, we took direct

231

action on that infamous detention center in our midst. You remember the place, I am sure, Longarm."

"Took action?"

"We freed those you had imprisoned, Longarm. One of the women was in very bad condition, the widow of that man who shot himself. We let them go, Longarm, with the provision that they leave Utah. Two of our council members paid for their tickets and sent them on their way. I need not tell you how glad I was to see Molly go."

"And then?"

"We gave the Salt Lake City fire department a chance to show how they can control a fire once it gets under way. It was quite a successful demonstration. I am sure we can find something more constructive to erect on that abandoned site."

"Daddy," Marilyn said, "we'll be late!"

The man grabbed at his pocket watch and noted the time. "Oh, dear! So we will be, if we don't hurry—and I don't want to miss Eddie Foy. He came through before, and I was unable to see him." He stood up. "Are you sure you won't join us, Longarm? The Salt Lake Theater is the finest theater west of St. Louis!"

"Oh, Father," said Emilie, shaking her head. "You're an incorrigible booster, really. I am sure there are theaters just as large in Denver." She smiled at Longarm. "Isn't that true, Longarm?"

"I won't get no prizes contradicting your father. Fact is, I'm never in Denver long enough to go to any of them places. But I hear Eddie Foy is a very funny man."

Boggs looked at Emilie. "Are you sure you won't come with us, Emilie?"

"Oh, Father!" said Marilyn. "You can't have us all go off and leave poor Mr. Longarm all alone in this big house!"

"And besides," said Emilie with a laugh, "I'm exhausted. Longarm and I have ridden over half of Utah

232

in the past weeks. A quiet evening at home is something I have been dreaming of for a long, long time."

"Of course, of course," said Boggs. "Forgive me. Come, girls!"

With Marilyn on one arm and Audrey on the other, the man fairly flew out of the living room. Longarm heard the girls' laughter on the front steps, then listened as they hurried down the long walk. After a few moments all was silent, and Emilie looked quizzically at Longarm.

"Would you like another grape, Longarm? You seemed to favor them at the dinner table."

"They are a luxury after such a long, hot ride."

There was a bowl on the table. Emilie took a bunch from the bowl, got to her feet, and approached Longarm's armchair. Perching on one of the arms, she smiled and held up a grape for him. Longarm obliged by leaning his head back.

"Open up," she said.

"Make me."

She did by tickling the corners of his mouth with a finger. As he smiled, she dropped the grape in. He chewed on it.

"Delicious," he admitted. "I sure could have used a bunch of them when I was fixin' that wind wagon, or whatever you call it."

"I'm sure. Longarm?"

"Yes?" He opened his mouth for another grape. She dropped it in.

"Do you know what I've been doing for the past two weeks—even longer, in fact?"

He smiled at her. "Keeping out of Wolverton's clutches."

"Yes, Longarm." She dropped another grape into his mouth, and then took one herself. "That's exactly what I was doing. And do you know what I felt when I saw them leave you in the middle of the desert like that?"

"No, Emilie, I don't."

233

"Well, you can imagine," she told him, suddenly serious. "Despair. I was certain I would never see you again. But you had promised to come for me, and I clung to that through all that followed."

"I'm glad I didn't disappoint you, Emilie."

She smiled and dropped another grape into his mouth. "And you won't disappoint me now, will you, Longarm?"

She took another grape for herself. She had been leaning closer all during this conversation, and Longarm was aware of tiny beads of sweat standing out on his forehead—and of other side effects, as well.

"In short, Longarm," she said, dropping a very large, juicy grape into his mouth, "I have been saying no for the longest time and dreaming of you. I don't want to say no any longer and I don't want just to *dream* about you, either." She swallowed a grape and smiled with delight. "Do you understand what I am telling you, Longarm?"

"I've been concentrating real careful, Emilie," he told her, smiling. "But it seems to me I heard you tell your father you was hoping for a quiet evening at home."

She dropped an especially succulent grape into his mouth. "Afterwards, Longarm," she told him, leaning forward and lightly brushing his forehead with her lips. "Afterwards."

She slipped off the arm of his chair. "I have a hundred little things to tend to, Longarm. Why don't you finish that cheroot you just lit. Then, if you want the rest of these grapes, well . . ." She smiled, and left him smoldering in the chair.

He was astonished at how long it took him to finish the cheroot, but at last he dropped its remains into the cuspidor by the door, left the room, and hurried up the stairs.

Her bedroom was dark, and as he entered, he found her by the maddening smell of her. They embraced, and he felt her cloud of hair fall about his neck and

234

shoulders. She was wearing nothing, he realized, under the long silk nightgown. Her fingers found his lips and she dropped into his mouth a large, most succulent grape. He laughed delightedly as its sweet moisture filled his mouth.

"This," she whispered huskily, "is my thank you, Longarm—for keeping your promise, for not disappointing me."

He kissed her on the lips, then on her sweet, graceful neck and told her that she was more than welcome, and that she should now consider the debt paid and let him concentrate on this more delightful mission, because he sure as hell did not want to disappoint her this time, either.

She laughed and drew him to her bed, determined, he could tell, that neither one should be disappointed this evening.

SPECIAL PREVIEW
Here are the opening scenes
from
LONGARM AND THE WENDIGO
fourth novel in the bold new
LONGARM series from Jove

It was a glorious morning in Denver and Longarm felt like hell. The tall deputy squinted as he left the musty brown darkness of the Union Station to get punched in the eye by a bright morning sun in a cloudless sky of cobalt blue. A sharp breeze blew from the snow-topped Front Range, behind him to the west, as he walked stiffly east toward the Civic Center. The mile-high air was clear and scented with summer snow and green mountain meadows. Longarm wondered if he was going to make it to Larimer Street before he threw up.

At the corner of Seventeenth and Larimer he found the all-night greasy spoon he'd aimed for and went in to settle his guts. He wasn't hungry, but ordered chili and beer as medication.

The beanery was nearly empty at this hour, but Longarm recognized a uniformed member of the Denver Police Department seated at another stool down the counter and nodded. He'd only nodded to be neighborly, but the copper slid his own stein and bowl over next to Longarm's and said, " 'Morning, Uncle Sam. You look like somebody drug you through the keyhole backwards! You spend the night drinking, whoring, or both?"

"Worse. I just came up out of Santa Fe on a night train that had square wheels and no seats worth mention. Rode shotgun on a gold shipment bound for the mint, here in Denver. Spent the night hunkered on a box in the mail car, drinking the worst coffee I've tasted since I was in the army. I suspicion they use the same glue in Post Office coffee as they put on the back of their stamps."

He took a huge gob of chili, washed it down with a gulp of beer, and added, "Jesus, you can't hardly get real chili this far north of Texas. Pass me some of that red pepper to the lee of your elbow, will you?"

The copper handed him the pepper shaker and opined, "Oh, I dunno, the cook here makes a fair bowl of chili, for a white man."

Then he watched with a worried frown, as Longarm

239

proceeded to cover his beans with powdered fire. To the policeman, Longarm was sort of interesting to study on. The Denver P.D. was sincerely glad the deputy marshal was a lawman rather than on the other side; arresting anything that big and mean was an awesome thought to contemplate.

The Deputy U.S. Marshal was civilly dressed in a threadbare business suit of tobacco tweed, but a bit wild and woolly around the edges. His brown flattopped Stetson had a couple of large-caliber holes in it and the craggy face under the brim was weathered as brown as an Indian's. The big jaw masticating chili under the John L. Sullivan mustache needed a shave, and though he wore a shoestring under the collar of his townsman's shirt, he somehow managed to wear it like a cowhand's bandanna. They said he packed a derringer in addition to the double-action .44 in that cross-draw rig he wore under the frock coat. They said he had a Bowie in one of the low-heeled army boots he stood taller than most men in. But the big deputy was one of those rare men who didn't look like he *needed* weapons. When he was in one of his morose moods, like this morning, Longarm looked able to knock a lesser man down with a hard stare from his gunmetal eyes.

The copper asked, "You aim to *eat* that shit with all that pepper in it, or are you aiming to blow yourself up?"

Longarm chewed thoughtfully and decided, "That's better. Chili's no good unless it makes a man's forehead break out in a little sweat. I can still taste that damned Post Office coffee, but I reckon I'll live, after all."

"You must have a cast iron stomach. You, ah, wouldn't want to let your friendly neighborhood police in on it, would you, Longarm?"

"In on what? You want me to fix your chili right for you?"

"Come on. They never detailed a deputy with your

240

seniority to ride with the Post Office dicks. Somebody important robbing the mails these days?"

Longarm took a heroic gulp of beer and swallowed before he belched, with a relieved sigh, and replied, "Jesus, that felt good. As to who's been robbing the midnight trains between here and Santa Fe, I don't know anymore than yourself about it. I just do what the pissants up at the Federal Building tell me."

"I hear since the Lincoln County War's run down there's about eighty out-of-work gunslicks searching for gainful employment. You reckon any might be headed for my beat?"

Longarm studied for a moment before he shook his head and said, "Doubt it. Denver's getting too civilized for old-fashioned owlhoots like we used to see over at the stockyards. Your new gun regulations sort of cramp their style. To tell you the truth, I sort of dozed off once we were north of Pueblo. Colorado's getting downright overcivilized of late, what with street lamps, gun laws, and such."

"By gum, I run a cowboy in for a shooting just two nights ago, over on Thirteenth and Walnut!"

"There you go. That's over on the other side of Cherry Creek where the poor folks live. 'Fess up. You ain't had a real Saturday night in the main part of town this year, have you?"

"The hell we hasn't! I'll bet Denver's still as tough a town as any! I disremember you saying you heard any shooting in Santa Fe! I'll bet the hands riding into Denver of a Saturday night are just as mean as any you met down New Mexico way!"

"No bet. Santa Fe's got sissy as hell since the new governor said folks can't shoot each other any more in Lincoln County. Hell, I was in Dodge last month and you know what they got? They got uniformed police and honest-to-God street lamps in Dodge now! Things keep up this way and we'll likely both be out of a job!"

Leaving the policeman nursing his injured civic pride, Longarm paid the silent, surly Greek behind the counter for his breakfast and resumed his walk to work,

241

feeling almost human. He knew he rated the day off for having spent the night on duty, but these new regulations about paperwork meant he had to report in before he could go home to his furnished digs for some shuteye.

The Federal Building sat at the foot of Capitol Hill. Longarm went in and climbed to the second floor, where he found a door marked, *UNITED STATES MARSHAL, FIRST DISTRICT COURT OF COLORADO.*

He entered, nodded to the pallid clerk pecking at his newfangled typewriting machine, and made his way to an inner door, where he let himself in without knocking.

His superior, U.S. Marshal Vail, glared up with a start from behind his big mahogany desk and snapped, "Damn it, Longarm! I've told you I expect folks to *knock* before they come busting in on me!"

Longarm grinned and was about to sass the plump, pink man behind the desk. Then he saw Vail's visitor, seated in an overstuffed leather armchair near the banjo clock on the wall and tipped the brim of his hat instead, saying, "Your servant, ma'am!"

The woman in the visitor's chair was dressed severely in black, with a sort of silly little hat perched atop her coal-black hair. She was about twenty-five and pretty. She wasn't quite a white woman. Maybe a Mexican lady, dressed American.

Marshal Vail said, "I'm glad to see you on time for a change, Longarm. Allow me to present you to Princess Gloria Two-Women of the Blackfoot Nation."

Longarm managed another smiling nod before the girl cut in with a severe but no less pretty frown to say, "I am no such thing, Marshal Vail. Forgive me for correcting you, but John Smith and Pocahontas notwithstanding, there is no such thing as an Indian Princess."

Vail shrugged and asked, "Aren't you the daughter of Real Bear, the Chief of the Blackfoot, ma'am?"

"My father was war chief of the Turtle clan. My

242

mother was Gloria Witherspoon, a captive white woman. There are no hereditary titles among my father's people, and even if there were, no woman could inherit the rank of war chief."

Vail looked annoyed but managed a wan smile as he nodded and asked, "Just what is your title, then, ma'am?"

"I'm a half-breed. On rare occasions, I'm called *Miss.*"

Longarm ignored the bitterness in her almond eyes as he leaned against the back of another chair and suggested, "I don't reckon your family tree is what you've come to Uncle Sam about, is it, Miss Two-Women?"

Vail cut in before she could answer, saying, "I've got the lady's complaint down, Longarm. It's your next job."

Longarm didn't think it was the time to point out that he rated the day off. He knew it wouldn't do any good and the odd little bitter-eyed woman interested him. So he nodded and waited for Vail to fill him in.

The marshal said, "This lady's daddy sent her to see us, Longarm. A bad Indian's gone back to the blanket. I've got his wanted papers here somewhere . . . anyway, I want you to run up to the Blackfoot reservation in Montana Territory and—"

"Ain't you assigning me to a job for the B.I.A., Chief?"

The girl said, "The man my father is worried about isn't a problem for the Bureau of Indian Affairs, sir. They don't know he's alive. My father reported him to the Indian agent at Fort Banyon. They told him they'd file a report on the matter, but of course we know they won't. Like myself, Johnny Hunts Alone is nonexistent."

Longarm asked, "You mean he's . . . "

"A half-breed. You don't have to be so delicate. Half-breed's one of the nicer things I'm used to being called."

Vail found the "wanted" flyer he'd been rummaging

243

for and said, "He may not exist to the B.I.A., but Justice wants him bad. Matter of fact, we don't have him down as an Indian, half or whatever. We've got him as one John Hunter, age thirty-six, no description save white, male, medium height and build. When he ain't hiding out on reservations he robs trains, banks, and such. We got four counts of first degree on him in addition to the state and federal wants for armed robbery."

Longarm pursed his lips and mused, "I remember seeing the wanted flyers, now. Funny, I had him pictured in my head as just another old, uh . . . "

"White man," Gloria Two-Women cut in, stonefaced. Both men waited as she continued, "Like myself, Johnny Hunts Alone is a Blackfoot breed. In his case, his *mother* was the Indian. They say his father was a Mountain Man who, uh, married a squaw for a trapping season. She gave him his half-name of Johnny, hoping, one would presume, his father might come back some day."

Longarm asked, "Was he raised Indian, then?"

"To the extent that I was, I suppose. I've never met him. They say he ran away to look for his white father years ago."

Vail explained, "The way I understand it, this Johnny Hunts Alone, John Hunter, or whatever, can pass himself off as white or Indian. He sort of raised himself in trail towns, hobo jungles, and such till he took to robbing folks instead of punching cows. The reason he's been getting away with it for years is that we could never find his hideout. According to this little lady's daddy, the jasper's up at the Blackfoot reservation right now. Miss Gloria, here, will introduce you to her daddy and the chief'll point the owlhoot out to you. Seems like a simple enough mission to me."

Longarm sighed and said, "Yeah, it always does. You mind if I ask a few questions? Just the result of my suspicious nature."

Without waiting for permission, he stared soberly at the girl and asked, "How come your Blackfoot relations

244

are so suddenly helpful to Uncle Sam, Miss Two-Women? Meaning no disrespect, the Blackfoot have a reputation for truculence. Wasn't your tribe sort of cheering from the sidelines when Custer took that wrong turn on the Little Big Horn a few summers back?"

"Like the Cheyenne and Arapahoe, the Blackfoot were allied with the Dakota Confederacy, if that's what you mean. Since you're so interested in the history of my father's people, you probably know the survivors have been penned like sheep in one small corner of Montana."

"I read about it. Did this Johnny Hunts Alone take part in the Great Sioux Uprising of '76?"

"Of course not. Do you think my father would inform on a fellow warrior?"

"There you go. So why *is* your daddy so anxious for us to arrest one of his people?"

"Honestly, don't you know anything about Indians? The renegade is *not* a Blackfoot to my father and others like him. Johnny Hunts Alone ran away before he was ever initiated into any of the warrior lodges. When our people were fighting for their lives against the Seventh Cavalry he was off someplace robbing banks."

"So your dad and the other chiefs don't owe him much, huh?"

"Not only that, but the man's a known thief and a troublemaker. Thanks partly to my mother, Real Bear speaks English and can read and write, so perhaps he's more aware than the others of what a wanted fugitive on our reservation could mean to us."

"What's that, ma'am?"

"Trouble, of course. Our tribe is . . . well, frankly, licked. Most of us are resigned to making the best of a bad situation. But there are hotheads among my father's people who'd like another try at the old ways. Some of the Dream Singers have been having visions, and meetings have been held in the warrior lodges of which I don't feel free to tell you the details. My father is one of the more progressive chiefs. He's trying to cooperate

245

with the B.I.A. He's trying to lead his people into the future; he's man enough to face it. An outlaw hiding among the young men, boasting of how many whites he's killed—"

"That makes sense, ma'am. As you were talking just now, it came to me I'd heard your daddy's name before. Real Bear was one of them who voted with Red Cloud against the big uprising. Though, the way I hear tell, he did his share of fighting once his folks declared war. You mind if I ask you some personal questions, ma'am?"

Vail cut in to point at the clock above Gloria's head as he snapped, "She might not mind, but I do, dang it! You folks have a train to catch, Longarm! You can jaw about the details along the way. Right now I want you to get cracking. I'll expect you back here about this time next week, with Johnny Hunts Alone, or John Hunter, or whomsoever, dead or alive!"

It wasn't until he'd escorted Gloria Two-Women aboard the northbound Burlington that Longarm gave serious consideration to her race. Under most circumstances, he wouldn't have given it much thought, for she was a pretty little thing and his mind was on the job ahead.

As the conductor nodded down at the railroad pass they were traveling on, Longarm asked, "What time are we due in Billings? I make it about twelve hours before we have to change trains, don't you?"

"We'll be getting into Billings around ten this evening, Marshal. Uh . . . you mind if I have a word with you in private?"

Longarm glanced at the girl seated across from him, gazing stone-faced out the window at the passing confusion of the Denver yards, and got to his feet to follow the conductor with a puzzled frown. The older man led him a few seats down, out of the girl's earshot, before he asked in a low whisper, "Is that a lady of color you're traveling with, Marshal?"

"You're wrong on both counts. I'm only a deputy

246

marshal and she's half white. What's your problem, friend?"

"Look, it ain't *my* problem. Some of the other passengers has, uh, sort of been talking about the two of you."

"Do tell? Well, I'm a peaceable man. Long as they don't talk about us where we can *hear* it, it don't mean all that much, does it?"

"Look, I was wondering if the gal might not be more comfortable up front in the baggage car."

Longarm smiled wolfishly, and took the front of the trainman's coat in one big fist as he purred, "She ain't a *gal*, friend. Anything in skirts traveling with me as her escort is a *lady*, till *I* say she's something else. You got that?"

"Loud and clear, Marshal. This ain't *my* notion!"

"All right. Whose notion might it be, then?"

"Look, I don't want no trouble, mister!"

"Old son, you've already got your trouble. You just point out who the big mouth belongs to and then maybe *you'd* best go up and ride in that baggage car!"

"I'm just doing my job. Forget I mentioned it."

"I'd like to, but I got a twelve-hour ride ahead of me and I don't aim to spend it fretting about my future. I'm going to ask you one more time, polite. Then I'm likely to start by busting your arm."

"Hey, take it easy! I don't care who rides this durned old train. It's them two cowhands up near the front of the car. I heard 'em say some things 'bout niggers and such and thought I'd best head things off."

Longarm didn't turn his head to look at the two young men he'd already marked down as possible annoyances. He'd spotted them boarding the train. They looked to be drovers and one was packing a Patterson .44 and a bellyful of something stronger than beer.

Longarm let go the conductor's lapel and said, "You go up to the next car. I'll take care of it."

"I got tickets to punch."

"All right. Go on *back* to the next car."

The conductor started to protest further. Then he

247

saw the look in Longarm's cold, blue-gray eyes, gulped, and did as he was told.

As Longarm sauntered back the way he'd come, Gloria looked up at him with a bemused expression. He nodded and said, "We'll be picking up speed in a mile or so. You want a drink of water?"

"No thanks. What was that all about?"

"We were talking about the timetable. Excuse me, ma'am. I'll be back directly."

He walked toward the front of the car, shifting on the balls of his feet as the car swayed under his boots. One of the two men in trail clothing looked up and whispered something to the heavier man at his side. The tougher-looking of the two narrowed his eyes thoughtfully but didn't say anything until Longarm stopped right above them, letting the tail of his coat swing open to expose the polished walnut grips of his own Colt, and said, "You boys had best be getting off before we leave the yards. Might hurt a man to jump off a train doing more'n fifteen miles an hour or so."

The one who had whispered asked, "What are you talking about? We're on our way to Billings, mister."

"No you ain't. Not on this train. You see, I don't want you to be upset about riding with colored folks, and since I aim to stay aboard all the way to Billings, we'd best make some adjustments to your delicate natures."

The heavyset one with the gun looked thoughtfully at the weapon hanging above Longarm's left hip and licked his lips before he said, "Look, nobody said *you* was colored, mister."

"Is that a fact? Well, it's likely the poor light in here; I'm pure Ethiopian. You want to make something out of it?"

"Hey, come on, you're as white as we'uns. *You* wasn't the one we was jawing 'bout to that fool conductor!"

His companion added, "You just wait till we gits that troublemaker alone, mister. He had no call to repeat a gent's observings."

248

"Boys, this train's gathering speed while we're discussing your departure. You two aim to jump like sensible gents or do I have to throw you off unfriendly-like?"

"Come on, you can't put us off no train! We got us tickets to Billings!"

"Use 'em on the next train north, then. I'll tell you what I'm fixing to do. I'm fixing to count to ten. Then I'm going to draw."

"Mister, you must be loco, drunk, or both!"

"One!"

"Look here, we don't want to hurt nobody, but—"

"Two!"

"Now you're getting us *riled,* mister!"

"Three!"

"Well, damn it, Fats, *you* got the durned old gun!"

"Four!"

The heavyset one went for his Patterson.

He didn't make it. Longarm's five-inch muzzle, its front sight filed off for such events, was out and covering him before Fats had a serious hold on his own grips. The drover snatched his hand from his sidearm as if it had stung his palm as he gasped, "I give! I give! Don't do it, mister!"

"You did say something about disembarking, didn't you, gents?"

"Look, you've made us crawfish. Can't we leave it at that?"

"Nope. You made me draw, so now you're getting off, one way or the other. Let's go, boys."

After a moment's hesitation, Fats shrugged and said, "Let's go, Curley. No sense arguing with a crazy man when he's got the drop on us."

His younger sidekick protested, "I can't believe this! I thought you was tough, Fats!"

But he, too, slid out of the seat and followed as Longarm frogmarched the two of them out to the vestibule between the cars. Fats looked down at the blurring road ballast and protested, "Hey, it's goin' too fast!"

"All the more reason to jump while there's still time. It'll be going faster, directly."

"You got a name, mister?"

"Yep. My handle's Custis Long. You aim to look me up sometime, Fats?"

"Just don't be in Billings when we gits there, mister. We got us *friends* in Billings!"

Then he jumped, rolling ass-over-teakettle as he hit the dirt at twenty-odd miles an hour. Longarm saw that he wasn't hurt, and as the younger one tried to protest some more, he ended the discussion by shoving him, screaming, from the platform.

Longarm holstered his gun with a dry smile and went back to where he'd left Gloria. The petite breed's face was blank but her eyes glistened as she said, "You didn't have to do that to impress me. You've already called me 'ma'am.' "

Longarm sat down on the seat across from her, placed his battered Stetson on the green plush beside him, and said, "Didn't do it for you. Did it for myself."

"You mean they offended your sense of gallantry?"

"Nope. Just made common sense. They got on drunk and ugly and we have a good twelve hours' ride ahead. Had I given 'em time to work themselves up all afternoon, I'd likely have had a killing matter on my hands by sundown. This way, nobody got hurt."

"One of them might dispute you on that point. I was watching out the window. The fall tore his shirt half off and left him sort of bloody."

"Any man who don't know how to fall has no call wearing cowboy boots."

"What am I supposed to do now, call you my Prince Charming and swoon at your feet?"

"Nope. I'd rather talk about the lay of the land where we're headed. You said your daddy, Real Bear, is the only one who can point out this Johnny Hunts Alone to me. How come? I mean, don't the other Indians know a stranger when they see one?"

"Of course, but you see, it's a new reservation, just set up since our tribes were rounded up by the army in

250

'78. Stray bands are still being herded in. Aside from Blackfoot, we have Blood and Piegan and even a few Arapahoe gathered from all over the north plains. My father doesn't know many of the people living with his people now, but he did recognize Johnny Hunts Alone when the man passed him near the trading post last week."

"The owlhoot recognize your dad?"

"Real Bear didn't think so. My father knew him over fifteen years ago and they've both changed a lot since, of course. It wasn't until my father got to my house that he remembered just who that familiar face belonged to!"

"In other words, we're traveling a far piece on the quick glance and maybe's of one old Indian who might just be wrong!"

"When you meet Real Bear, you'll know better. He doesn't forget much. Aren't you going to ask about our house?"

"Your house? Is there something interesting about it, ma'am?"

"Most white people, when they hear me mention my house, seem a bit surprised. I'm supposed to wear buckskins, too."

"Well, I ain't most people. I've been on a few reservations in my time. What have you got up there, one of them government-built villages of frame lumber that could use a coat of paint and a bigger stove?"

"I see you *have* seen a few reservations. Ours is a shambles. The young white couple the B.I.A. sent out from the east doubtless mean well, but . . . you'd have to be an Indian to understand."

Longarm fished a cheroot from his vest and when she nodded her silent permission, thumbnailed a match and lit up, pondering her words. He knew the miserable fix most tribes were in these days, caught between conflicting policies of the army, the Indian agency, and loudmouthed Washington politicos who'd never been west of the Big Muddy. He took a drag of smoke, let it trickle out through his nostrils, and asked, "What's

251

this other trouble you mentioned about the young men wanting another go at the Seventh Cav?"

"The boys too young to have fought in '76 aren't the real problem. Left to themselves they'd just talk a lot, like white boys planning to run off and be pirates. But some of the older men are finding civilization more than they can adjust to. You know about the Ghost Dancers?"

"Heard rumors. Paiute medicine man called Wovoka has been preachin' a new religion over on the other side of the Rockies, hasn't he?"

"Yes. Wovoka's notions seem crazy to our Dream Singers, but the movement's gaining ground and even some of our people are starting to make offerings to the Wendigo. You'd have to be a Blackfoot to know how crazy *that* is!"

"No I wouldn't. The Wendigo is your dad's folks' name for the devil, ain't it?"

"My, you *have* been on some reservations! What else do you know about our religion?"

"Not much. Never even got the Good Book that *I* was brought up on all that straight in my head. Blackfoot, Arapahoe, Cheyenne, and other Algonquin-speaking tribes pray to a Great Spirit called Manitou and call the devil 'Wendigo,' right? I remember somethin' about owls being bad luck and turtles being good luck, but like I said, I've never studied all that much on anyone's notions about the spirit world."

"Owl is the totem of death. Turtle is the creator of new life from the Waters of Yesteryear. I suppose you regard it all as silly superstition."

"Can't say one way or another. I wasn't there. It might have took seven days or Turtle might have done it. Doubtless sometime we'll know more about it. Right now I've got enough on my plate just keeping track of the here-and-now of it all."

"Does that make you an atheist or an agnostic?"

Longarm bristled slightly. The last person to call him an atheist had been a renegade Mormon who had left him to die in the Great Salt Desert. He had had plenty

252

of time to ponder on the godless behavior of those who accused others of godlessness. "Makes me a Deputy U.S. Marshal with a job to do. You were saying something about devil worship up where we're headed, Miss Gloria."

She shrugged and replied, "I don't think you could put it that way. People making offerings to the Wendigo aren't Satanists; they're simply frightened Indians. You see, it's all too obvious that Manitou, the Great Spirit, has turned his back on them. The Wendigo, or Evil One, seems to rule the earth these days, and so—"

"Is he supposed to be like *our* devil, with horns and such, or is he a big, mean Indian cuss?"

"Like Manitou, the Wendigo's invisible. You might say he's a great evil force who makes bad things happen."

"I see. And some of your folks are praying to him while others are taking up Wovoka's notions about the ghosts of dead Indians coming back from the Happy Hunting Ground for another go-round with our side. I don't hold much with missionaries, since those I've seen ain't been all that good at it, but right now it seems you could use some up on the Blackfoot reservation."

"We have a posse of divers missionaries on or near the reservation. My father would like to run all Dream Singers off, Indian as well as white. I hope your arrest of Johnny Hunts Alone will calm things down enough for him to cope with."

Longarm nodded and consulted his Ingersoll pocket watch, noting that they had a long way to ride yet. The girl watched him silently for a time before she murmured, "You're not as dumb as you pretend to be."

Longarm smiled. "Pretending such things sometimes gives a man an advantage. Speaking of which, you've got a pretty good head on your own shoulders. I can see you've been educated."

"I graduated from Wellesley. Does that surprise you?"

"Why should it? You had to go to school someplace to talk so uppity. I know those big Eastern colleges

253

give scholarships to bright reservation kids. It'd surprise me more if you'd said you'd learned to read from watching smoke signals."

"You are unusual, for a white man. By now, most of your kind I've met would have demanded my whole history."

"Likely. Most folks are more curious than polite."

"You really don't care one way or the other, do you?"

"I likely know as much about you as I need to."

"You don't know anything about me! Nobody knows anything about me!"

Longarm took a drag on his cheroot and said, "Let's see, now. You're wearing widow's weeds, but you're likely not a widow. You're wearing a wedding band, but you ain't married. You were born in an Indian camp, but you've been raised white and only lately come back to your daddy's side of the family. You've got a big old chip on your pretty shoulder, too, but I ain't about to knock it off, so why don't you quit fencing with me?"

Gloria Two-Women stared openmouthed at him for a time before she blurted, "Somebody gave you a full report on me and you've been the one doing the fencing. Who was it, that damned agent's wife?"

"Nobody's told me one word about you since we met, save yourself. You knew I was a lawman. Don't you reckon folks in my line are supposed to work things out for themselves, ma'am?"

Before she could answer, the candy butcher came through with his tray of sweets, fruits, sandwiches, and bottled beer. Longarm stopped the boy and asked the girl what she'd like, adding, "We won't stop for a proper meal this side of Cheyenne, ma'am."

Gloria ordered a ham on rye sandwich, a beer, and an orange for later and the deputy ordered the same, except for the fruit. When the candy butcher had left them to wait on another passenger, she insisted, "All right, how did you do that?"

254

"Do what? Size you up? I'm paid to size folks up, Miss Gloria. You said your mama was a white lady, and since you're about twenty-odd, I could see she must have been taken captive during that Blackfoot rising near South Pass in the 'fifties. When the army put 'em down that time, most white captives were released, so I figured you likely went back East with your ma when you were, oh, about seven or eight. You may talk some Blackfoot and you've got Indian features, but you wear that dress like a white woman. You *walk* white, too. Those high-buttoned shoes don't fret your toes like they would a lady's who grew up in moccasins. You sure weren't riding with the Blackfoot when they come out against Terry in '76, so I'd say you looked your daddy up after he and the others settled down civilized on the reservation just a while back. Here, I'll open that beer for you with my jackknife. It's got a bottle opener and all sorts of notions."

He opened their drinks carefully, aiming the warm beer bottles at the aisle as he uncapped them. Then he handed her one and sat back to say, "I was born in West-by-God-Virginia and came West after the War. I fought at Shiloh. . . ." Longarm's voice trailed off.

"You were doing fine. What made you stop?" Gloria asked.

"Reckon both our tales get a mite hurtful, later on. We're both full-grown, now, and some of the getting here might best be forgot."

"You know about my mother deserting me once she was among her own people, then? How could you know that? How could anyone know so much from mere appearances? Is that orphanage written on my breast in scarlet letters, after all?"

"No. I never met your mama, but I know the world, and how it treats a white gal who's ridden out of an Indian camp with a half-breed child. You ought to try to forgive her, Miss Gloria. She was likely not much older than you are right now, and her own kin likely pressured her some."

255

"My mother had a white husband waiting for her. I wonder if she ever told him about me. Oh, well, they treated us all right at the foundling home and I did win a college scholarship on my own." She sipped her beer and added in a bitter voice, "Not that it did much good, once I tried to make my way in the white man's world. I was nearly nine when the soldiers recaptured us, so I remembered my father's language and could identify with that side of my family. You were right about my reading about the new reservation and running back to the blanket, but how did you figure out my widow's weeds?"

"Generally, when folks are wearing mourning, they mention someone who's dead. On the other hand, one of the first things I noticed was that chip on your shoulder and your hankering to be treated with respect. I'll allow some folks who should know better can talk ugly to any lady with your sort of features, but widow's weeds and a wedding band give a gal a certain edge in being treated like a lady."

"It didn't stop those two cowboys you put off the train."

"They were drovers, not cowhands, ma'am. And neither had much sense. Most old boys think twice before they start up with a lady wearing a wedding band, widow's weeds or no. They were likely drunker than most you've met. So 'fess up, that's the reason for the mournful getup, ain't it?"

She laughed, spilling some of her beer, and answered, "You should run away with a circus! You'd make more as a mind reader than a lawman!" Then she sobered and added, "You're wrong about the ring, though. I am married, sort of."

He didn't rise to the bait. She'd tell him in her own good time what she meant by "sort of" married. From the smoke signals he'd been reading in her eyes, she couldn't be married all that much.

256